Pirate

The Unkindly Gentlemen

Stephanie Lauren

iUniverse, Inc.
New York Bloomington

Pirate
The Unkindly Gentlemen

iUniverse books may be ordered through booksellers or by contacting:

iUniverse
1663 Liberty Drive
Bloomington, IN 47403
www.iuniverse.com
1-800-Authors (1-800-288-4677)

ISBN: 978-1-4401-8920-3 (sc)
ISBN: 978-1-4401-8921-0 (ebk)

Printed in the United States of America

iUniverse rev. date: 1/30/2010

In memory of Zack Gallaway,
"Big Z"

And to my granddaddy, who has been so supportive of my
writings, I love you

And special thanks to Greg Smith for the map

Kirkston

Akito Berry Island

Danger
Shallow Waters

E

Caldara

Caldara City

BEWARE
Annihilators make
bay here

N

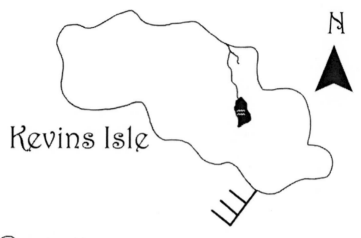

Kevins Isle

🕱 Skull Island

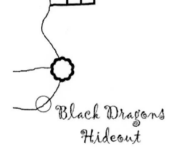

Black Dragons
Hideout

*Property of Captain
Smith*

PART ONE
Peter "Smith" Barons

Prologue

"Open mine first, Peter!" Elizabeth demanded, placing the gift in his hands. Peter's little eyes glistened at the carefully wrapped box. After smiling at her, he tore into the wrapping. In his hands, he held a small brown journal.

"Elizabeth, I love it!" Peter stood up in his chair to kiss his sister's cheek and then sat back down to revere his new journal. While opening it, he noticed she had written *Happy twelfth birthday, Peter! We love you! Elizabeth and Anna.* Peter stood back up and went over to his five-year-old sister, Anna, who was half-asleep in their mother's lap, and kissed her nose. "Thank you too, Anna."

"Don't wake her up, Peter," his father said.

Peter nodded and returned to his seat between his friends Ron and Theresa, who were there in celebration of his birthday. His mother passed her gift to him from across the table. It was a beautiful blue quilt that she had knitted herself. His mother had knit an image of their home in the center of it. "Mama, it's so pretty!" he cried, wrapping the quilt around him. Peter allowed Theresa to take the quilt and examine the fine knitting of Mrs. Barons's tedious work. He then moved on to the gift his father had brought home from work that night. It was not wrapped; it was merely trapped inside a large brown sack and tied with ropes.

3

With furious excitement, Peter's little fingers struggled with the thick rope tying the sack. He could see the smile on his father's face as he undid the ropes. When finally he saw the gleam of the blade sliding out of its sheath, he pulled out the gift and cried out from pure amazement

Almost immediately, his parents began arguing about the sword, while Peter and Ron admired the fine craftsmanship. Peter swooshed the sword out of its sheath and swung it around a bit. It was too big for him to handle, but he was exhilarated to hold it in his hands. The handle was carved in the shape of a dragon; the blade came from the dragon's mouth as though it were breathing fire. Peter could tell his father had made the sword, and he had clearly spent a lot of time on it.

"William, you can't give a twelve-year-old a sword!" he heard his mother exclaim, thereby awakening Anna.

"Hush up, Ellen! I'm not going to let him run around with that until he's older. You don't need to worry. Besides, he won't be allowed to show that sword to just anyone."

"And why not?" she asked, putting Anna down on her feet.

Peter's father lowered his voice in an attempt to lure them all in. "I made it look like the swords used by the Black Dragons." Peter's mother crossed her arms in frustration; she could surely sense a ridiculous story coming up.

"Peter, who are the Black Dragons?" Anna asked in the heat of the argument that had begun between their parents. Peter had heard the stories several times, but before he could answer, his mother spoke for him.

"They're bandits!" she cried.

"They're good people, Ellen; most of them are Peter's age. They're just children. They steal from King Harold's ships at night while they're still in port, easily outsmarting the few guards who underestimate the children," their father explained. "I guarantee that when they are older, they'll be attacking ships in broad daylight. Won't that be fascinating to hear about? They take the money and give it back to the poorer people in Kirkston. Well, most of it anyways."

"Like Robin Hood?" Theresa asked.

"Like a whole fleet of Robin Hoods!" Mr. Barons was clearly exuberated, ready to tell the story and excite the young group of children. "They sail a huge red ship with black sails—can't miss it. It has a painting of a black dragon on each side. All of them dress in red and black; all their families were killed because of Kirkston laws ... or so I've heard. Their days are spent learning about ships and sailing. They're planning something. I just know it. Those poor children have lost so much."

"They're still criminals, either way you look at them. Stealing is stealing, no matter what you do with the money." It was evident that their mother was trying to end the conversation quickly, before her husband got too far into the story.

"They bought the ship earlier this year; a while back they stole from carts bringing supplies to the ships rather than the ships themselves." As if sensing that his wife was becoming annoyed, William ended the conversation. He pointed at the blade of the sword. "Here, Peter, look at this."

Carefully engraved on one side of the blade were the words *Happy Birthday, Peter! Love you, Dad.* Before Will had a chance to brag about how much the sword looked like that of a sword belonging to a Black Dragon, there was a knock on the door.

"Hide the sword," his father said, visibly afraid of who might be at the door so late at night.

Peter hid the sword in a cabinet and ran back to the table while his father went to answer the door. "General Stevenson?" he heard his father say.

"Are you just going to stand there, or are you going to invite us in?" The general didn't bother to wait for an invite. The general pushed him into the wall and stormed inside. Two men followed him, all three of them carrying large muskets.

"We're here to collect the rest of your taxes," the general said.

"I already paid, General," Peter's father said politely.

"What are we celebrating here?" the general asked.

"My birthday, sir." Peter attempted to smile at him.

The general looked disgustedly at Peter's gifts. He seemed to have to force himself to smile at Peter so as not to appear too rude. "Well, the tax," the general said, turning back to Will, "has been increased by fifteen silver shillings."

"What?" William raised his voice. "We can barely survive off the shillings we have now! We don't have any more money!"

The general tapped his foot for a moment. "All right, then … you can sell me something." The general acted as though this were an incredibly kind gesture. "Something worth fifteen silver shillings. I don't have all day. What about the wedding ring? It's worth more than the tax; you wouldn't have to worry about the tax for some time." General John Stevenson pointed at Ellen's ring. Ellen covered her hand.

"No! I'm going to visit King Harold about this! This is wrong! Our people are dying, and he doesn't even realize it!" Will pointed at the door. "Get out of my house!"

General Stevenson shoved past Will and snatched Ellen by her wrist, trying to take her ring. This infuriated William. He shoved the general away from his wife, inadvertently causing the general to tumble back. Without even standing, the general shot his musket up at Will, hitting him in the chest. As Will fell over, John stood.

Peter took Theresa's hand in a panic. Ron ran behind Elizabeth, and Anna shielded her eyes against her older sister. When the general cocked his musket to shoot Will again, Peter felt Theresa squeeze his hand. Thankfully Mrs. Barons stopped him; she yanked off her hat and shoved it into the general's hands. "It's worth five gold pieces and ten silver shillings; you could sell it if you want. Please just leave us be!"

John held the hat in his hands. Peter could, for a moment, see *some* shame in the general's eyes as he looked at Peter's father, but the notion quickly faded. John looked at the hat. "This hat looks more expensive than this entire house." He chuckled. "I'll excuse you from the next month's pay as well. Good day, Mrs. Barons." General Stevenson and the other two men left, none of them showing any concern for Peter's father.

As soon as the door closed, Ellen bent down next to Will, tears filling her eyes. Ron and Theresa had no idea what to say or do. Elizabeth hurried to help her mother bring Will back to her parents' bedroom. Anna was scared and confused, and she held on to Peter desperately. Their mother wouldn't allow them into the bedroom. Eventually, Elizabeth came out of the room after the younger children had waited impatiently in the small family room.

"Is Daddy okay?" Anna asked.

"He's fine," Elizabeth said, and Peter knew that she was lying. He sat on their little couch, not saying much to anyone. Elizabeth came over to them. She helped Ron and Theresa down from the couch and suggested that Anna sit with Peter. "Ron, you and Theresa come with me. I'm going to take you two home."

Peter and Anna sat together on the little couch for almost a half hour before Elizabeth arrived back home. With her was Ron's father, Nick Katch, and Theresa's father, Wilson Stern. They had been friends with Will as far back as Peter could possibly remember.

Peter was in a daze for the rest of the night. He paced for hours; his mother, Mr. Katch, Mr. Stern, and Elizabeth were constantly coming in and out of the bedroom. He was told to stay with his little sister, but he wanted to check on his father. Once that night, Peter snuck back to the bedroom. His father's ghostly face frightened him, and Peter felt a tear roll down his cheek. Mr. Katch was the first to see him standing in the doorway. Mr. Katch picked up Peter and took him out of the bedroom. Peter leaned against Mr. Katch, who sat rocking him. Anna came over and sat with them. Even Elizabeth sat on the floor in front of him, her head on his knee, crying.

***

The night had been such a blur that the next morning it took Peter a moment to recall everything. He blinked his eyes open; his stomach ached. Desperately, he tried to convince himself that the night before was nothing more than a nightmare. He sat up and saw Mr. Katch sitting at the foot of his bed.

"Morning," he said quietly. "You sure did sleep in late. I didn't bother waking you up. Elizabeth and Anna are in the kitchen with your mother making lunch if you're hungry."

"Papa …?"

"Asleep. Wilson's with him. He and your mother stayed with him all night. I stayed in here with you and your sisters."

Peter could vaguely remember waking up in the middle of the night and someone cradling him. Apparently, it had been Mr. Katch. Peter smiled a little at him. He hadn't really known Ron's father that well before then. "Thank you, sir." Peter would not look him in the eye at first. He sat there, fiddling with his fingers. Finally, he asked, "Is he going to be okay?"

"That's hard to say, Peter. He won't be able to work, you know?"

"Maybe I could … I could help out around the shop. I probably can't do all the things Papa could, but I can sweep and do other things for Mr. Anderson. Do you think he would let me?" Peter asked, and Mr. Katch nodded.

"He's a good man. I'm sure he would allow that." He stood. "Peter, don't be scared, okay?" Peter nodded and followed Mr. Katch out of the room. "Dr. Conal came by after you fell asleep last night," Mr. Katch said. "He looked at your father's wounds."

Peter noticed that Mr. Katch didn't mention what Dr. Conal had said about his father's condition … and it worried him.

Peter spent as much time with his father as possible, for his mother feared the worst was to come, but Peter refused to believe something like that could happen.

***

Peter's little fingers trembled as he made the first entry in his journal. His quill moved quickly in the dark.

> *Papa died last night. Mr. Katch and Mr. Stern dug a grave under the big oak tree by the river. I will start working for Mr. Anderson, the blacksmith. He'll train me like he did Papa. Elizabeth will have to clean houses every day now. I miss my papa very much. I'm afraid of what will happen to us now. I wish my papa was here.*

Ch 1

With his blistered fingers, aching back, and his entire body covered in soot, it was clear that Peter Barons had had a long day at Mr. Anderson's shop. It had been two weeks since his father's death, and Peter had to learn more than sweeping and cleaning from Mr. Anderson in order to make enough money for his family to live on. His fifteen-year-old-sister, Elizabeth, cleaned houses since Peter made very little money in the shop. Their mother did every chore in the house, including working in the garden, which was once one of Peter's old chores.

After work that day, Peter went to town since Anderson had let him off early. He loved to see what other people in Caldara, the capital city of Kirkston, were up to. He walked down the dirt streets, passing house after house, shop after shop.

The farther north he traveled, the richer the town seemed to be—because he was getting closer to the palace. After a while, he was the only one walking around in rags. Soon he spotted the fence that wrapped around the school. Peter ran up to the fence and gazed into the schoolyard. Children were laughing and playing and learning. It had always been Peter's dream to go to school. "Be gone with you, peasant!" a boy from the other side of the fence shouted.

"Sorry." He began to back away. The boy picked up a rock and threw it over the fence at Peter.

He felt a stinging sensation on his head, and he screamed. Warm blood dripped into his hand. Laughter from the kids on the other side of the fence mocked him. Peter did not want them to see him cry. A loud and threatening voice shouted at Peter, "Get away from that fence, you little peasant!" A large man came running toward him with a stick in his hands.

Peter took off running. The man stopped chasing him, but Peter didn't stop, for he could still hear the laughter of the children in the schoolyard. He didn't stop until he heard another voice shouting, "Everyone out of the way! Hurry up!"

A man on horseback was shouting at the crowd. Three other men, also on horseback, were with him. They were surrounding a young boy on a white stallion; it was Prince Richard. As the man shouted, the people in the streets hurried out of the way to avoid the oncoming horses. Bored and curious, Peter could not help but follow them. He had never been to the palace, at least not that he could remember. He wanted to see the young prince close up; he rarely was out in public. Soon they were out of town and on the path to the palace. There was nothing but grassy hills, the river to the left of them, and trees scattered here and there.

They must have seen me, Peter thought when they stopped. A man rode his horse out of the group and over to Peter. "Turn back, beggar. Do not follow us." The horse reared back, and Peter, in his surprise, fell down. The man laughed at him. Peter tried to hide his face, for he had been humiliated enough that day.

"Leave him alone," Richard ordered him. He trotted over near them and tossed Peter a small sack. "Take this and be gone."

Inside were silver shillings. "Oh! Thank you ... Your Majesty." They all rode off toward the palace, and Peter managed to get a glimpse inside the wall that surrounded the palace before the gates closed. He was reminded of the intense throbbing on his head from the rock that had been thrown at him earlier. He hurried over to the river that flowed through the small country. The river ran from the mountains in the northwest, turning south at the palace, and later turning east until it reached the waterfall that led to the ocean. It was the only river in Kirkston that Peter knew of.

When he splashed water on his face, he could see soot mixing with the river water. Figuring that his mother would make him bathe as soon as he got home, he decided to go ahead and wash himself clean now so that when he got home, he could just relax before dinner rather than bathing. He removed his shirt and cleaned his face and arms first. Once most of the soot was gone, he took his shirt and laid it against a large rock on the riverside. He scrubbed it against the rock in the water in hopes of getting a large stain out.

A voice from behind, obviously belonging to a young girl, asked him, "Why are you washing that rag? You should throw it out." Peter did not turn around to face her; he figured she wanted to pick at him as everyone else had that day. "You don't actually wear that, do you?" she asked him.

"I'd be able to afford better clothes if the taxes weren't so high."

She was quick to argue with him. "The taxes go to good use. They're for the schools and the military—"

"A military? Does it look like we're in a war to you? Harold is going to kill off his own kingdom." Peter kept his back to her.

The girl sounded angry, and Peter tried to appear busy in hopes she would leave him alone, but she wasn't backing down. "King Harold is a great king," she said.

Peter still did not turn around; he didn't want to face the little brute. He kept on cleaning his shirt. "He doesn't even care how people like me are treated."

The girl took a moment to reply. "How *are* you treated?"

Immediately, Peter began to complain about King Harold and John Stevenson, and he did so rather harshly. The angrier Peter got, the harder he scrubbed his shirt in the water. "Kathleen will be a better ruler than her father," he said in order to calm himself. The king's daughter gave him hope for the country. "I'm not saying she will lower the taxes, but maybe she will be a little more aware about how the poor are treated—hopefully, she'll do something about it."

After putting a tear in his shirt from scrubbing, he decided to stop. He stood to face the girl. She wore a long red dress and little red shoes. Her black hair was pulled up on her head, she was covered in jewelry, and a little tiara rested on her head. "Princess Kathleen?" He felt his legs shaking, and he dropped to his knees. He knew it was her, not by her crown but by her face. She looked like Richard—the same three small but noticeable freckles were on her right cheek. Her hair was the same as Richard's, as were her bright blue eyes. Peter struggled to get his apology out; it was hard to believe that he had insulted both her father and the general so harshly in front of her. He looked at her feet, afraid to meet her eyes.

"At ease. Who are you?" she asked him.

"Peter," he said.

Kathleen smiled down at him. "I won't say anything to my father." Kathleen encouraged him to stand, but he was too frightened to move. "Peter, I have a favor to ask of you."

"Anything, Lady Kathleen."

"Call me … Kathy. You and I are friends. Do not call me 'Your Highnesses,' 'Lady,' 'Your Majesty,' or 'Princess.'"

Peter nodded. "Yes, ma'am."

"Not 'ma'am' either." She laughed. "Just Kathy. And get off the ground—stand up." This girl was nothing like Peter had imagined her; she was just a child. "Peter, will you take me to town?"

"No!" He backed away from her. "I would get in trouble if I took you into town. Are you even supposed to be outside the gate with no guards?"

"Please, Peter? I've only been to town a few times, and I was surrounded by guards. No one's looking. It would be fun."

Peter shook his head. "You go alone, then."

"I don't know my way around town. I'm not allowed to go anywhere by myself, not after my older brother was killed. Papa's too protective."

"Then go with your guards. I would be beaten if I went with you." Peter wrung out his shirt and held it down at his side. "I'm sorry about your brother," he added.

"It's okay. I didn't really know him. He died when I was young." She sighed. "Won't you *please* take me to town?"

"Have Stevenson take you."

The young heiress crossed her arms and stuck out her tongue. "He's so boring. You're funny … I like you."

Peter smiled. "You don't like the general?"

"He's okay. He's nice to me because we are going to get married once I reach marriage age." Kathleen sighed again. "It's a tradition, you know?"

"What is?" he asked her.

"For the general to marry the king's firstborn daughter," Kathleen explained.

"But you're even younger than me," Peter said with surprise.

"I know, but since Papa is giving me the crown, the general wanted to keep the tradition," Kathleen said. "Papa is giving me the crown instead of Richard to influence the way men treat women in Kirkston. He says it will help the way women are treated if women inherit things from their fathers like their sons do."

Peter apologized again. "I'm sorry for what I said."

"There's no need to apologize," Kathleen said. "Hold on. Stay here for a moment. I'll be right back." She ran into the palace. Peter waited for a few minutes. Eventually, she returned with a basketful of fruits, breads, and eggs. "You would like this, yes?" she asked.

"I …" Peter looked at all the food in the large basket. *We would be full for weeks with all that. I'm so hungry …*

"If you come up here every once in a while, I'll give you breads and other foods." She shook the basket. "You want this, don't you?"

"Why, just to talk?" Peter asked.

"I get bored here alone, Peter. The only friends I have are General Stevenson or the maids, and they're always too busy …" She let out a long, overexaggerated sigh. "I'll give you and your family any food I can sneak out. Just bring the basket once it's empty. I just want someone to talk to other than that General John Stevenson." She laughed softly. "He's a real brute, you know?" She put the basket out for Peter to take. He hesitated. "You don't have to come visit me if you don't want to, Peter. I won't make you." She looked sad.

"I know I don't have to, but I promise I'll be here." Peter willingly took the basket. "Thank you, Kathy. I am lucky to have run into you." Peter looked down the road, realizing how late for supper he would be. "I can't stay. I was supposed to come home after work today."

"You work? But you can't be that much older than I, can you?" She sounded appalled.

"My papa was killed, and I had to get work."

"I'm sorry." She smiled at him. "Go on, before your mother gets anxious." The young heiress kissed his cheek and said good-bye before heading inside the gate. Peter's cheeks were red. He lifted up the basket, eager to get home.

He headed back into town. He walked quickly by the school and moved straight in the direction of home. Halfway there, he started smelling smoke. Looking up, he could see gray skies. *Something's burning,* he thought. As Peter headed farther into town, he could hear shouting. Then he saw the blacksmith shop; it was ablaze. He could see Mr. Anderson outside the shop, flailing his arms around while soldiers rode around on their horses, throwing torches at the small shop. "Stop! Enough!" Anderson was screaming. Peter saw John Stevenson ride his horse around to the front of the building and kick Anderson over as he passed by him.

"See what happens next time, peasant!" John shouted as he began riding off with his soldiers. "You've been warned, Anderson! Pay your tax by Friday or next time it will be your house!"

Before Peter even saw her coming, his mother had wrapped her arms around him. She was in tears.

"Mama? What are you doing here?" Peter tried to pull away, but she wouldn't let go of him. "What's wrong?"

Mr. Anderson came running over; he too was crying. "Ellen, I'm sorry! I'm sorry!" he cried.

Peter sensed that there was something worse going on than Mr. Anderson's shop burning down. *Why is Mama here?* he wondered. Peter felt himself getting worked up, and he began to cry. "Mama, Mr. Anderson, why are you crying?"

***

When the general burned down Mr. Anderson's shop, my mama started to cry. She thought I was still inside. Mama had sent Elizabeth to walk me home. Our little sister, Anna, went with her. I should have gone home after work like I was supposed to. Elizabeth and Anna were inside the shop when it burned down. Yesterday Mr. Stern and Mr. Katch buried them underneath the big oak tree next to Papa. It's the general's fault. I hate the general!

Peter heard voices outside his room. He put down the quill and the journal. As he was coming out of his room, he could hear his mother say, "No, we cannot accept this, Nick." Peter could see his mother in their kitchen with Mr. Katch.

"Please, Ellen. It's not much," Mr. Katch said. "Consider it a gift from Wilson and me." Mr. Katch offered her a small bag of coins.

His mother refused the money. "Your wife and son need this money just as much as Peter and I do."

"Peter is just a boy. He can't keep working for Anderson. He can't support you." Mr. Katch laid the money down on their table. "Just let us help, Ellen. William was my friend ever since we were lads. I won't stand by and watch his family die off! Just take the money."

"All right," she said. "Thank you, Nick."

"If you need anything, Ellen, you tell me." Mr. Katch kissed her forehead. "I have to go." He smiled at her.

Peter watched Mr. Katch leave and then started to go to his mother, but he hesitated when his mother broke down in tears. Peter's heart ached, and after a moment, he hurried over to her and wrapped his arms around her. "Don't cry no more," he begged.

"I'm okay, Peter," she said, and ran her fingers through his messy brown hair. "Sit down and I'll get you something to eat." Peter did as he was told, sitting down at the little table. His mother reached for the basket he had brought home the day his sisters were killed in the fire. She cut up some fruit and sliced the bread. As she was bringing it over to the table she said, "You never did tell me who gave all this to you." She laid the plate down on the table and sat beside him.

"A girl who lives in Caldara gave it to me," Peter said.

She smiled. "A girl? Does she have a name?"

"Kathy," Peter replied.

His mother was smiling, and she began to swarm him with questions. He answered his mother quickly with little depth on any of the subject matter.

"Are you hiding something, Peter?" she asked when he began to struggle to answer her questions in his attempt to keep his meetings with the princess a secret, but his mother had little intentions of backing down and, Peter was not the type of child to lie to his mother.

"It's Kathleen, Mama," Peter continued. "King Harold's daughter. I met her outside the palace."

His mother laughed. "You have such a wild imagination." His expression did not change. His mother asked, "You do jest with me, don't you, my son?"

"No, Mama," Peter said. "Kathleen gave me the food."

"Harold's daughter? She gave you this? Well, that's awfully kind of her ..." She smiled. "Perhaps there's hope for Kirkston after all."

***

It was about three days before Peter had a chance to visit Kathleen again. While there, she demanded he come visit her more often. Only after agreeing to this did she announce that she had a gift for him. "Really? What is it?" he asked.

"I'll go fetch it." She hurried inside the palace walls and returned shortly with a large box in her hands. She handed it to him, and he opened it up excitedly.

"Mama's hat." He was shocked.

"The general gave it to me. When you told me the story about how your papa died and about how your mama gave up her hat, I figured this was the one. Isn't it?" Kathleen asked.

"It *is* her hat! Mama will be so happy. Thank you!"

Kathleen laughed at him. "I won't keep you here all day. Go home; I know you want to give this to your mama."

"Thank you, Kathy, really."

Peter rushed home, eager to return his mother's hat to her.

Ch 2

Ellen danced around the kitchen, making a fool of herself in order to make her son laugh. It was always a rare moment now when the two of them had time to laugh and enjoy themselves. She had been pleased to get her blue hat back, and they were making lunch together in the kitchen. She was making Peter laugh hysterically, while he sat on the countertop, by purposely singing off-key and dancing from side to side. There was a knock on the door in the middle of the song Ellen had begun to sing. She glanced out the window to see men in uniform. She quickly tossed her hat in a cupboard, afraid that Stevenson would be with them. "Peter, don't worry. It's probably nothing." Ellen hurried to answer the door.

"Hello, Mrs. Barons." It was the general. "It seems we have a problem, ma'am, with your son."

"What do you mean, sir?" Ellen did not open the door all the way, and she used her body to block the doorway so John would know he was not welcome inside.

"Harold knows about your visits with Kathleen, son." He forced the door open, backing Ellen into her house. John was looking down at Peter. "He's not too happy about that. He wants you and your family to come to the palace at once. He's going to put a stop to this nonsense immediately. Not to mention all that food you've been running off with, which we expect you to pay back."

"General, we cannot pay that money back," Ellen began to explain. "I've already lost my husband and my daughters this year. Please do not take more from us. My son has to work, and he's just a child. He cannot make us enough money to pay you back for the fruit."

"Then your son can live in the prison cells for a while until you repay Harold for all that food he stole."

"It was given to him," Ellen argued.

"Other than her brother, Kathleen is not supposed to mingle with any young boys," John said.

"Is that what this is about?" Ellen asked. "You're afraid my little Peter will win Kathleen's heart and she will refuse to marry you?"

The general stiffened, and it was evident that he knew his true intentions had been discovered. "Unless you have the money, I'm taking that boy with me." He reached down for Peter, but she stood between them, shoving John back.

"Get out of my house; I'll report this!" she shouted in his face. "Harold didn't give you consent to come down here, did he?"

"No, he did not. But I don't want your child near my sweet little Kathleen. I'll have the two of you arrested for disturbing the peace. Harold won't question me, now will he?" He took her wrist, and she slapped him. The general backed away for a moment, giving Ellen a surprised look. When Peter spotted at least six other men outside, he held on to his mother's dress and hid his face behind her.

"I'll have you arrested for assault," the general said.

"You're a madman! Do you honestly envy a twelve-year-old boy?" When she shouted in his face again, he clutched his hand around her wrist and yanked her outside. Peter ran out after them.

"Stop it! Let her go!" Peter ran to her side after John threw her to the ground. John was shouting orders, and before Peter realized what was going on, their wrists were cuffed and they were being marched down the trail by the river.

Ellen bent over a bit as they walked, whispering to Peter, "You have to run."

"They'll shoot me if I run."

Ellen touched his shoulder. "They're going to kill you if you don't. Run into the woods; don't run straight."

"They'll shoot me, Mama," Peter whispered.

"I don't care if you end up with a bullet in your leg—just keep running. Go to Ron's home. They'll keep you hidden. All right? Don't you worry about me; I'll be fine." She gave him a gentle nudge. He yanked away so suddenly that the man holding on to him lost his grasp. Peter was able to break off into a run.

"Grab that boy!" John shouted, and one of his men hurried after Peter. He caught up with him, but Peter managed to struggle out of the man's grasp. They got too close to the river, whose bank was muddy, and Peter and the man fell in.

"He can't swim. Do something!" Ellen shook John's arm; she was in tears. The man who fell in with Peter could swim no better than he could. Peter managed to hold on to the man, who had hold of what seemed to be a large stone in the river. The water was clearly deep there.

John quickly kicked off his boots and abandoned his heavy weapons before diving into the river. "John!" the man cried out when the current started to pick up.

This man's going to kill me, Peter thought, once John reached them. The general reached out for him, and Peter yanked away. He allowed the currents to take him.

Peter struggled to keep his head above the water, but he could not. The last thing he saw was his mother running angrily at the general as he climbed out of the river. The men snatched her. Before Peter could see what was happening, he felt the strange sensation of falling. *The waterfall!* he thought.

He felt a dreadful pain in his stomach when he hit the bottom. Miraculously, Peter managed to survive the fall, but somehow he couldn't manage to get his head above the water again. He felt himself growing dizzy; he needed air. He saw a shadow over him and two small hands reaching for him just before he blacked out.

He opened his eyes a moment later to see a young girl about his age. She wore a sleeveless red shirt that was ripped just below her little breasts. A black skull was painted on the shirt. She was wearing big red hoop earrings. Her hair was short and black; it was extremely messy and dirty and was pulled back by a black bandana. She smiled at him and touched the side of his face. He could see a tattoo of a black dragon on her right forearm. She stroked his hair to calm him down; Peter was breathing quickly and gasping.

"Easy. You're all right. You're safe now," she kept whispering to him. She rested her hand on his chest, and he smiled at her, but soon he was out cold again.

***

Peter heard someone singing, a young boy. The boy was about sixteen or so, and he wore black pants, black boots, a black shirt, and black gloves. A red bandana was wrapped around his neck, giving him some color. Peter soon realized he was in a tent, wrapped in warm blankets. The boy was fixing a plate of food for Peter while he sang quietly to himself. Peter smiled when the boy turned around. The boy's cheeks turned red. Instead of laughing at the fact that he was caught singing, he became angry. "You think that's funny?" he snarled, reaching across the tent and striking Peter. The boy had a tattoo of a black dragon on his right forearm as well. The cuffs on his wrists were gone; the boy must have picked the lock so Peter would not have to sleep in chains. "Here, put these on before you come out." He tossed Peter some black pants and left the tent. Blood dripped down onto Peter's hand; his lip was bleeding.

He crawled out from under the blankets only to see that he was naked. *They must have taken off my wet clothes while I was sleeping.* He put on the clothes and ate the food the boy had left for him before exiting the tent.

Awe passed over Peter when he saw where he was. The waterfall was to his left and the ocean to his right, and in front of him was ocean as well. It was just a small bit of land, which he later learned no one knew about, south of the waterfall. Once the waterfall hit bottom, the river continued for several more yards before emptying out into the ocean. Behind him was a steep cliff where the waterfall fell, and a hidden path led up the cliff into the woods. "Wow." Peter was in shock at the natural beauty. Even more amazing was the ship that sat in the ocean. It was red with black sails, and on the side of the ship was a painting of a black dragon. *It's them. They're the Black Dragons! These are the people Papa told me about!*

While he stood there, taking everything in, three boys hurried over to him. "Look who's up," the redhead said, in what sounded like an Irish accent, and jumped him, pulling his arms behind his back while the other two spit in his face. The two who spit on him were twins, and both of them had shaved their heads completely and covered their bald heads with tattoos. All three of them had the same tattoo as the boy in the tent on their right forearm. They shoved him on the ground, and while he was down, they kicked dirt in his face.

Before they could do anything worse to him, the girl Peter had seen earlier rushed over. "Cannonball, Yin, Yang, leave him be!" She helped Peter up. "You all right?" she asked, and the three boys hurried off before she could yell at them again.

"Those aren't their real names, are they?" Peter asked her.

"No." She laughed. "It's kind of silly, but we all have nicknames."

"Why?"

"Well, it started with just me, and then another one of us got one … and then suddenly it was like you just weren't one of us without a nickname. What's your name?"

"Peter Barons."

She smiled. "You stick with me while you're here, all right, Peter? None of them will mess with you as long as you're with me." She led him over to one of the campfires they had going. "My name's Courtney, but everyone calls me Sea." She sat down on a log beside the fire. Another boy was by the fire, and he had a baby in his arms. "That's Mouth and his little brother, Jacob."

"Why do they call you Mouth?" Peter asked.

The boy ignored Peter. "Why's he still here? I thought you were going to send him away once he got up. We don't need anyone snooping around here. If the general finds out about this place, we won't have anywhere to hide."

"I'm not going to tell anyone," Peter said as a young woman approached them.

"Ruddy bastard," Mouth said, and the woman popped him in the back of the head.

"Watch your mouth!" the woman said, sitting down beside him and taking the baby out of his arms. Peter could see Mouth's hesitation to hand over his little brother. The woman started to nurse the baby, and Peter tried not to stare. He was surprised that she would nurse the child in front of everyone. The woman smiled up at Peter. "You all right, lad? You had quite a fall."

"I'm all right, ma'am," Peter said.

"Peter, this is Mrs. Keg. Her and her husband live nearby," Sea said. "They take care of us."

"Well, I wouldn't say that." Mrs. Keg smiled. She had a beautiful smile, Peter noticed. "They're pretty much on their own out here. We watch over them, but Sea and the boys honestly take care of us."

"What do you mean?" he asked.

"We give Mr. and Mrs. Keg some of the money we take from Harold's carriages," Sea explained. "Mr. Keg is teaching us about shipping, so we pay him for his troubles. He's also a swordsman." Sea pointed to the other side of the small camp. Peter looked at where she was pointing, and he could see a man who must be Mr. Keg. He was with some of the other young boys. Each of the boys carried a stick in his hands, while Mr. Keg was demonstrating different movements and techniques used by a swordsman. The boys would mimic him, and he would then correct anything wrong with their form or compliment their technique.

They're training for something. But for what? Peter glanced at the ship. *Papa was right; they are training to be pirates.* He suddenly felt nervous around them. *Criminals,* he thought. *They're criminals.* Sea smiled at him, and it calmed him down.

"Thank you all very much," Peter said. "You have been too kind. I hate to be rude, but I hope to go home soon."

"It's getting dark," Mrs. Keg said. "You stay here for tonight. There's no sense in getting yourself lost in the woods. We'll walk you home tomorrow."

"I really shouldn't. My mama … she'll worry. I need to see if she's okay."

"Let him go," Mouth said. "He doesn't want to be here any more than we want him here."

"Tommy, don't be so rude," Mrs. Keg scorned him. She turned back to Peter, saying, "Stay here tonight. We'll help you find your way home first thing in the morning."

They are so kind; it's hard to believe that they are thieves, he thought. He smiled at them and said, "Thank you, Mrs. Keg."

Ch 3

To Peter's surprise, he became attached to the strange group of children … or at least to Sea. His first night with the Black Dragons, he had slept in a tent like the rest of the crew. He had started worrying about his mother and had begun to cry; he had wakened several of the young boys, and they had shooed him away toward the beach. Thankfully, Sea had found him and brought him back to her own tent. He remembered that Mr. Keg had told him that Sea would probably be the one to captain the Black Dragons someday; it's what they were training for. It was bad luck to have a woman aboard a ship, even a little one like her, so it was odd to Peter that these young boys would follow her lead.

The two of them stayed up all night, just talking. She told him about all her crewmates, and he talked about his family. They sat on the floor in her tent playing cards. Peter had never gambled before, so Sea taught him several games he had never heard of. "I'm sorry about your family, Peter," she said, revealing her cards.

"I just hope my mama's all right. John was after me, not her. So wouldn't he let her go? If I was no longer in the way, he wouldn't hurt her, would he?"

"I hope not. John didn't hurt me." She looked away for a moment. There was a long silence, so she continued. "My parents and my older brothers were criminals. John killed them in front of me when I was little, long before he was general." She shuffled the deck of cards again. "It's where Mr. and Mrs. Keg got the idea for the Black Dragons. My parents and my brothers used to do it. They robbed the king's carriages and used the money to help people. Anyway, after they died, Mr. and Mrs. Keg took me in. I always talked about doing what they did, but the Kegs helped it happen. We help a lot of people, so that's good." She dealt the cards.

Peter looked at the cards he was given. "I'm sorry about your parents."

"All of us have been hurt, Peter. Snake was hurt pretty bad too," she said.

"Which one is he again?" he asked.

"He's the one who tripped you and made you drop your food today." She laughed. "Sorry about him; he has a bit of a temper. His father was General Robbie Lee."

"Really?'

"Yup. John Stevenson worked under him for a long time; they were friends. John treated Snake like a son. Snake looked up to him. He told me John was more of a father to him than his real father ever was. Snake loved John a lot, and they were close. Snake told me he could talk to John about anything, but one day John killed both of his parents. John told him that one day he'd understand—that his parents had gotten what they deserved. Snake ran away, and John became general." Sea sighed heavily. "Snake lived on the streets for a long time before he met up with me. I took him in. He wouldn't admit it to the others, but he cries about it a lot. He's not the only one, though. All of them are like that. They all cry a lot. You won't tell them I told you that, will you?"

"No, of course not." Peter laid down his cards. She'd beaten him again. "What about Mouth? What happened with him?"

"His friends turned his parents in for theft, just for a couple of extra silver shillings. He doesn't trust anyone anymore. It took him forever to trust me. It takes time for him to trust anyone. He doesn't even like it when Mrs. Keg is left alone with his baby brother. Mrs. Keg lost her baby to the measles not long ago, so she'll be able to nurse Jacob until he's weaned," Sea explained.

"And David, the Irish boy we call Cannonball, his father and his older brother Thomas died in a shipwreck. They were smuggling some poorer friends out of the country, and John sunk the ship. Yin and Yang's parents were falsely accused of a crime; John drowned them in the river. Knot and Blade were friends before they met up with me. John set Knot's home on fire, and his parents were killed when the roof fell in. Blade's parents took him in. But they didn't have much money, and they had little to eat. Eventually, Blade's parents passed away too. A few weeks later, Blade's uncle killed himself, and they were on their own."

"Who was the one in my tent this morning?" he asked. "The older one?"

"That's Ace," she said.

"What's with him?"

"I don't know. He doesn't talk much. When we first met him, he didn't talk at all. He was completely mute. I guess he just didn't trust us. He didn't talk, so we didn't know his name. I called him Ace, and he seemed to like it."

They continued the game in silence for a little while. Finally, he asked, "Why do you all go by nicknames … like Snake? Why do you call him Snake?"

"He's not scared of snakes, so he used to fetch them out of people's yards for money. When I found him, he had been bitten. He almost died from the snakebite, but he lived. As for the others, we mostly just came up with nicknames because we didn't know each other very well when the Black Dragons first started. The Kegs had been teaching us about ships, and everyone took interest in different things. We call David Cannonball because he was really interested in learning about the weapons on the ship. His papa owned a lot of ships when he was little, and they always interested him. He was the only one of us who was loaded with money before the Black Dragons. Terrance got the nickname 'Blade' because he already knew about swords and fighting with them. He's gotten even better since Mr. Keg has been working with us. We call Garret Knot because he knows a lot about riggings on a ship. Mrs. Keg studies with him every day about ships and their riggings. We all have learned a lot about rigging, but Knot knows a lot more than us. "

"What about the twins?" Peter asked.

"Mathew and Michael? Well, we call them Yin and Yang, mostly because it annoys them."

"What about you?" Peter asked, "Why do they call you Sea?"

She smiled. "My older brothers used to call me that because I loved the ocean. When I was little, I made them take me to the beach almost every day. Everyone's always called me Sea. My mama and papa even called me Sea." She put down the cards, evidently losing all interest in them. Her eyes welled up, and she began to cry.

Peter scooted over next to her. "Oh no, I didn't mean to upset you! I'm sorry …"

She quickly wiped her face. "I'm sorry. Don't worry about me. I'm okay, really." Sea seemed extremely upset.

"Is there something you want to talk to me about?" he asked her, and she nodded her little head.

"I miss my brothers and my parents," she said. "I really miss them. I don't like to talk to the others about it, though."

"Why not?" Peter asked. "It sounds like you know a lot about all of them. Don't they listen to you?"

"I don't want to talk to them about what happened to me," Sea said. "I don't want them to worry. They've all been through so much. They have so much more to worry about." She started sobbing heavily. "John Stevenson killed my parents; he tortured them. I hid under a chair in our den, and he *knew* I was there. John beat them and whipped them; he even burned my papa with wood from our fireplace. Christopher and Mark were so scared. There was blood all over the floor. I kept crying and crying, but John still hurt them. He finally just shot them all, and he and his men left. I know they broke the law, but he didn't have to hurt them like that! I was little, and I didn't know what to do, so I just stayed there. I lay next to them all night. The next morning, our neighbors found me. I went to live with the Keg's ... sort of. I came and went. I didn't want to be a burden, so sometimes I would go off on my own."

"I'm sorry," he said. "Sea, you don't have to be so brave. If you want to talk to someone, you can talk to me."

She smiled. "Thank you, Peter."

It grew late, and eventually they decided it was best to get some sleep. Sea kissed Peter good night. He blushed and headed back to his tent.

***

It had been three days since Peter first arrived at the Black Dragons' hideout, but he'd found it hard to leave. He now felt he had overstayed his welcome, and the Black Dragons were taking him home.

Peter had learned that they were all determined to become experienced seamen. They all learned from one another, and everyone had something to contribute to the group. Ace had his strength, Cannonball his experience with weaponry, and Snake knew how to fight.

Ace and Snake went with Peter ahead of the others, who said they would meet up with them soon. They were going on their weekly "route," which meant they were doing the one thing that made the Black Dragons so famous: giving away money. Ace led Peter and Snake upriver and stopped where the river was shallow and the current was slow. Snake swam across on his own, and

Ace jumped in. It only went up to his chest, so he didn't need to swim. "You coming?" he asked Peter.

"I can't swim," Peter said. Ace looked frustrated. He had Peter get on his back. Ace trudged across the river and threw him off his back once they reached the other side. They headed north toward the main town. It was still a little dark outside, so they remained unnoticed, for the most part.. They were passing by a poorer area. Doors opened, and a bunch of children came running over to Ace and Snake, excited. The two of them handed small sacks to each child; the children thanked them and then hurried back to their homes; Snake even got a kiss from one of the girls, who he embarrassingly nudged away.

"What's in the sack?" Peter asked.

"Money," Ace said, leading them away from the town. "All right, Peter, let's go." Ace followed Peter south into the woods.

After about twenty minutes of walking, Snake began complaining. "Where do you live? No one lives out here."

"The taxes aren't as high out here because no one wants the land." Peter didn't look at Snake when he answered. Ace walked ahead of them, uninterested in hearing any of Snake's complaints.

"That's stupid; whose idea was that?"

"It was my father's idea," Peter said, wishing that Snake hadn't come with them.

"Stevenson could kill you out here, and no one would know. I bet your pop didn't think that one through, did he?" Snake laughed.

"John killed my pa," Peter said, in hopes that Snake would stop insulting his father.

"Your pa must have been pretty dim to get himself killed by John."

"*Your* parents were killed by John too."

"Who told you that?" Snake asked him.

"Sea did."

Snake tried to defend his father. "At least my parents did something with their lives and didn't live in the middle of nowhere struggling to make a shilling an hour."

Peter was becoming irritated. He clenched his fists. "Your father was the general of his time. At least my father died with some honor. He was protecting his family from a man *just like your father.*"

"You didn't know my father." Snake shoved Peter.

Peter stood his ground, for he was tired of being insulted by Snake. "He was just another John Stevenson," Peter mocked him.

Snake punched Peter, and Peter punched back. Ace turned around and shouted at the two of them, but they didn't stop. Peter was on the ground, curled up in a ball, and Snake was kicking at him. Somehow, Peter managed to yank Snake to the ground with him and hit him once or twice before Ace jumped in. He pulled Peter up by the hair and threw him off of Snake. Peter's eyes watered, and Snake laughed at him. Ace looked at Snake and clasped his wrist, pulling him up. "Do you think that's funny, Johnny?" Ace rammed Snake into a tree and punched him. "What? You going to cry now?"

"No," Snake said sternly, and Ace hit him again. "Stop!" Snake shouted, and Ace hit him yet again. Ace appeared to be waiting for him to cry, and when he didn't, Ace punched him even harder, and in the face. A few tears fell down his cheeks. "Stop," he mumbled.

Ace squeezed Snake's wrist tight. "You're not so tough, Snake. Quit picking on the kid because he's smaller than you, all right?" Ace knocked Snake to the ground and turned to face Peter. "No more fighting, all right?"

Peter nodded. Ace stood up straight and marched on as though nothing had happened. Snake was leaning up against the tree, cleaning off his bloody lip with the back of his hand. Peter looked at his own hand to see Snake's blood on his knuckles; he was surprised at himself. He walked over to Snake and was even more surprised at how he acted. Snake wouldn't look at him, almost as if he was afraid of Peter. *No, he's not afraid of me; he's embarrassed,* Peter thought. *He's afraid of Ace.* Peter offered Snake his hand and helped him stand. "No one's ever slugged me like that before."

Peter left Snake behind and caught up with Ace. "We going the right way?" Ace asked.

Peter smiled. "I can see my house from here." And he hurried off ahead of them. He ran inside his home, shouting, "Mom, Mama, I'm home! I'm home!" Ace headed inside after him, Snake following close behind.

Peter ran throughout the house, searching desperately for any sign of life. Finally, after realizing no one else was in the house but the two pirates who had brought him there, he sat down in the middle of the floor between their kitchen and den. His heart sank. *She's not here. John got to her. I know it! He's killed her ...* He felt pain in his chest and started sobbing. He tried to stop crying before Snake saw, but he couldn't.

"Your mama isn't here, is she, kid?" Ace asked.

Following Ace's lead, Snake came and sat down by Peter. Ace put a hand on Peter's shoulder but said nothing. Peter heard a noise behind them, and he turned his head to see that the others had finished their route and had met up with them.

"Now what?" he heard Yin whisper to Sea.

"Peter, I'm sorry," Sea told him from the doorway. "If you want to stay with us, you're welcome to. Pack your things; we're leaving."

Peter stood and got the few things he wanted, putting everything in a brown knapsack. He got the blanket his mother had knitted for him, as well as the journal his sisters had given him. Then he got their family "portrait," which was actually just a small drawing that Theresa's father had done of them back when he was a thriving artist. Then, finally, he got his sword his father had given him. When he came out of his bedroom, there were many amazed faces looking at the sword. "Where did you get that?" Mouth asked. "Did you swipe that off our ship?"

"My papa made it for me." Peter had to prove it to Mouth by showing him the blade where it read *Happy Birthday, Peter! Love you, Dad.*

"Do you know how to smith?" Sea asked him.

"I had to take over as apprentice blacksmith after my papa died," Peter explained, wiping away tears that were still present on his face.

"It looks like we have an official blacksmith for the Black Dragons," Mouth said, heading out, carrying his little brother, Jacob, in his arms.

"Come on, Smith," Sea said, turning to leave.

Smith, is that my name now? He followed them out. He took one last look at his house and the graves before following Sea to his new home with the Black Dragons.

Ch 4

Five years later ...

"Lower the anchors!" Captain Smith of the Black Dragons shouted to his crew one foggy evening in Kirkston.

Captain Smith was one of the most wanted men in Kirkston. If he was captured and brought to Kirkston's king, he would be hanged with no question. Whoever captured him would earn thousands in gold pieces. At the time he was seventeen, he was already a master swordsman and criminal.

Sea, the captain's first mate and present girl, was barking out orders to the crew. She herself had once been the captain of the Black Dragon, but she had stepped down when Smith proved himself a more valuable captain during pillages. Today Smith wore the traditional Black Dragon uniform: black pants, red shirt, boots, and gloves. Now he too, like the others, had a tattoo of a black dragon on his right forearm.

"We're all set, Captain! The fog is hiding us well!" Knot shouted from the lookout tower. He slid quickly down the rope ladder to the main deck.

"Good job, Knot." Smith met him on the main deck. Knot was a year younger than all of them, and at sixteen, he was short for his age as well.

Sea approached the two of them; the others were all coming over as well. "Ready, Captain?" Sea asked him.

"Aye," Smith replied.

Sea took out a knife and ripped holes in his clothes, also removing his red bandana.

"Stay out of sight," he reminded them. "Keep to the fog long enough for me to get hold of a hostage." Then, in a joking manner, he stood aside and asked, "How do I look?"

"Like an idiot," Mouth jested.

Smith laughed. He kissed Sea's cheek and headed to the side of the ship.

"Fair winds, Smith," Sea said, and Smith jumped over the side of the ship, diving down into the salty water. He swam in the water a good ways, and the ship disappeared in the fog behind him. The water was gentle. The only waves were those created by the Black Dragon and the occasional gust of wind. A second ship appeared in the fog. Smith heard voices coming from the ship.

***

"Kathleen, Your Majesty, don't lean over the side of the ship."

"Hush up, John. I was just looking at the fish." Kathleen was now of marriage age, fifteen, and she would be marrying General John Stevenson soon. John had invited Kathleen on a fishing trip across Kirkston's eastern shores. Today Kathleen was fashioning a huge amber-colored dress, and she had her hair pulled up in a bun, her favorite style. She still had the three freckles on her cheeks that she had had when she was younger. She gazed over the side of the ship, looking at the water. "John!" she screamed. "There's a boy in the water! Get him before he drowns!"

John ordered his men to fetch him. A man lowered himself into the water inside the little cockboat and pulled Smith inside. Smith lay on the deck, motionless. Men surrounded him.

"It's Captain Smith of the *Black Dragon*," one of the men said.

Kathleen knelt down beside him. "Kathleen, step away from him," John ordered. "He's dangerous!"

"You're not going to let him die, are you?" Kathleen did not recognize Smith as the boy she once knew. When she bent down next to his head to check his breathing, Smith held his breath. "John, he's not breathing," she said. She was so concerned that she did not notice the young man reaching for his sword. Before any of the men had time to react, he yanked the sword from its sheath, pulled Kathleen to her feet, and held the blade to her throat. He stood behind her with one arm wrapped around her waist and the other clenching his sword at her neck. "Let go of me!" she cried, attempting to yank herself away. Smith held the sword closer to her throat.

"Drop your weapons," Peter ordered, and no one reacted. "Do you think I'm joking? Drop them now." Peter pressed the sword against the side of her neck. She cried out for John, and he ordered his men to listen to Smith. All of them dropped their weapons.

Kathleen elbowed Smith in his side.

He whispered in her ear, "Kathy, I don't think someone in your position—"

"Princess Kathleen to you, Pirate."

Smith snickered.

"What do you want?" John Stevenson shouted.

"Take a look, John." Smith nodded out at the water; they could see the *Black Dragon* appearing from the fog. "Have your men help my crew carry over every last gold piece and silver shilling on this ship, got it?"

"Very well." The general clenched his fists. The *Black Dragon* dropped anchor only a couple of yards away from the general's ship. They placed long boards from their ship to the general's so the general's men could bring over the gold and silver. The Black Dragons remained armed, their guns pointed at the men crossing between the two ships.

Smith held on to Kathleen the entire time. He was holding her close to him, and he felt her squirm with discomfort. He kissed her cheek and her neck to aggravate John more than anything else.

"Don't worry, Kathleen," John said. "You'll be fine."

"Shut it, John," Smith said.

"You're a filthy man, Captain Smith," Kathleen whispered to him. She stomped her foot in anger, and he wrapped his hand around her arm and clasped it tight.

"Don't hurt her!" John shouted at him.

"What? Hurt a cute face like this?" Smith laughed at them. "Come along, Princess." He walked backward toward the planks to cross over onto their ship, bringing Kathleen so none of the crewmates would dare shoot at him.

Once Smith was on the other side, John shouted at them to release her. Snake took it upon himself to kick her over the side of the ship. Although it created enough distraction for the *Black Dragon* to get out of range, it did not please his captain. Smith watched John dive in after Kathleen, who was struggling in her large dress to stay afloat. John and Kathleen climbed into the cockboat that John's crew had rushed to lower. John wrapped Kathleen in blankets and hugged her, asking, "Are you all right? Did he hurt you? Do you want to go home, sweetheart?"

"Yes, John. Just take me home, please."

The *Black Dragon* had drifted deep into the fog. The crew cheered over their victory; Smith, however, did not. He marched right up to Snake and pulled him by the hair on the back of his head. "Why'd you push her in? She could have drowned!"

Snake struggled with his words; Smith just shoved him over. "Don't let it happen again."

"Aye, sir."

***

Kathleen sat in her chair as her servant combed her wet hair. Her father was in the room, expressing his fury about the stunt the Black Dragons had pulled earlier that day. He had been angry enough about Smith's crew robbing his ship, but when John told him how Smith had treated his daughter, he became enraged.

"Papa, calm yourself," Kathleen said. She gazed at herself in the mirror, anything to avoid looking at her father during his tantrum. Kathleen had chills now. She was angry that the man had touched her the way he had. She knew that it was just to annoy John, but it still angered her. Now John was sitting beside her, holding her hand. "John, is it just me ... or did that Smith character seem familiar somehow?" Kathleen asked him.

John wasn't even paying attention to Kathleen, so she sat still while her servant girl finished with her hair.

Harold looked at his daughter and touched her shoulder. "We don't mean to worry you about this, Kathleen. John, come with me. We need to see what we can find out about these Black Dragons."

"Yes, sir." John kissed Kathleen and followed Harold out.

Kathleen let the servant finish her hair before she sent her away. It wasn't long before her brother, Richard, and his fiancée popped in for a visit. "Sister, are you all right? I heard about what happened today."

Abigail, Richard's fiancée, sat quietly by Kathleen and smiled at her. *Oh, Abigail,* Kathleen thought, *you're in love, but not with my brother. I know you loved that stable boy Papa sent away to school. You don't love Richard any more than he loves you.* Kathleen touched Abigail's hand.

Richard sat down with Abigail, with his arms around her. *I can see right through those looks. They don't love each other.* Kathleen squeezed Abigail's hand softly, and their eyes met for a moment.

Abigail, as if sensing what Kathleen was thinking, yanked away from the two of them and stood. "Excuse me," she said. "I don't feel well." Abigail hurried out of the room before too many questions were asked.

Richard would not look at Kathleen after that.

"I'm sorry, Richard," Kathleen said quietly.

"For what?" he asked, pretending nothing was wrong. Then he gave her a dirty look. "You hush about what you've been saying about me and Abigail, all right? You don't know anything about the way we feel."

"I'm no fool, Richard. A year ago, you two were very close, but then Papa told you two about the arrangement. Abigail and her parents spent five months in their summer home trying to get her to stop crying after she found out she was going to be forced to marry you. You wouldn't even come out of your room."

Richard took her arm and threatened to strike her. He quickly let go and laughed quietly at himself. "Sometimes I forget that we are no longer children and that I can't get away with striking you."

He stood and walked to the head of her bed, where her wedding gown hung on a hook. He took it in his hands, and Kathleen came over. "A beautiful dress for a beautiful bride." Richard held it in front of her, and the two of them looked at her in the mirror. "You should wear your hair in a bun on the wedding day."

"Papa does not want me to wear my hair up. He says it makes me look foolish." She was admiring the dress in the mirror.

"It's not his wedding day—it's yours. Do what pleases you, Kathleen. You're only going to have one wedding day; make it special for you, not Papa." He looked at her in the mirror. "You still have those little freckles on your cheek."

"Aye, so do you," Kathleen said, and both of them touched their right cheeks. "These freckles make us look like fools, far more than a bun ever would."

Richard laughed, kissed her cheek, and put her dress back. "I'll see you at dinner tonight, Kathleen."

∗∗∗

It was dark when the Black Dragons dropped anchor by the waterfall. They were on a mission tonight. They made their way to poorer homes in Kirkston to give them enough money to make it through for a bit longer. They snuck through the towns quietly, not wanting anyone to hear them, going door-to-door. Tonight, the captain had three homes he said he had wanted to visit in particular. The others did not question why, or at least most of them didn't. "We never come out this far," Mouth whispered to Ace. "Do you think the captain's lost it? No one lives this far out in the woods."

"He did," Ace reminded him. Mouth was carrying his younger brother on his back; they called him Squirt now, and he was about five or six. Squirt had been raised on the ship, and he had good sea legs for a child, but when they made the transition to land, he would tumble over, needing his brother's support for the first half hour he was on land.

They saw a house in the distance, and Smith hurried to knock on the door. A large hairy man answered the door. He was covered in soot and smelled like tar. "Do I know you?" He gazed at all of them and then smiled, taking a step back in surprise. "Black Dragons, am I right?"

Smith laughed. "It's good to see you again, Mr. Anderson." And he handed the man a bag of money.

"How do you know my name, son? You haven't ever been out here before. You Black Dragons don't ever come out this far."

Smith smiled. "You'll figure it out. I have to go, sir."

They left, leaving a confused man at the door. "Come back!" he shouted. "Who are you?"

Not too long afterward, they spotted two smaller houses right next to each other in the distance. A young couple was sitting on the steps of one of the houses, holding hands and looking into each other's eyes. Smith watched the boy ease in closer for a kiss. "All of you stay here," Smith said, and he went up to the couple. When the couple saw him, they stood and let go of each other's hands.

The boy asked, "You're Captain Smith, aren't you?"

"I am." Smith handed each of them a sack of money. "Happy birthday, Theresa." He met her eyes for a moment.

"Peter?" Theresa almost fell over, and the boy, Ron, had to hold on to her.

Ron stared at him. "You're alive? You died five years ago. You can't be alive!"

"Somehow I always knew you two would wind up together." Smith looked at Theresa. "You seem speechless. Last I remember, you had quite a mouth on you."

"You have to tell everyone you're alive, Peter." Theresa hugged him and buried her face in Smith's chest.

"I'm sorry, but no." Smith kissed her cheek and hugged Ron. "I have to go. I'm sure you've noticed that I'm in a lot of trouble, but it was so good seeing you two again. And I'd appreciate it if no one knew about our little meeting here."

"You can't just leave, not now. We thought you were dead, Peter. You have to tell everyone you're alive. Everyone thinks that Peter and Captain Smith are two different people." Ron wouldn't let go of Smith's arm. "You can stay here with us. Please, Peter. We'll keep you safe."

"I'm a Black Dragon now, Ron." He hugged them both before leaving. They watched him disappear with the others into the woods.

Suddenly, Ron broke out into a run. "Peter! Peter, wait, please! Not again. Come back. Please come back, Peter!" But Smith was already gone.

Smith and his crew were sneaking back to their ship. "Who were they?" Sea asked him.

"Just some old friends, no one important. We need to go before we're spotted." Smith led the way, and he came up with the perfect excuse to keep anyone from asking about his special visits that night. "Who's up for Skull Island tonight?"

They all cheered. Mouth was ahead of the others, with his little brother on his back, and he screamed out, "Let's go before Benny runs out of drinks!"

Ch 5

Skull Island was a small island off the east coast of Kirkston. It was a retreat for criminals; no one would turn them in. Benny, the man who owned much of the island, including the most decent bar and inn, offered them a good deal on rum and rooms because he'd known them since they were young. There were inns for lodging and docks for ships. It was a great place to stay.

They normally only stayed at Benny's when it was too stormy to sleep on the ship or at the base of the waterfall, or just to celebrate a victory. Smith called them all over to the booth that Benny always had open for them at the bar. Smith wanted to talk to his crew.

"John needs to be kicked out of office; he's getting worse. The country will die out, and we're the only ones who realize it. He and Kathleen will marry soon, and there's no stopping him after that."

"We'll kill him then," Snake suggested. "We break into the palace and hang him in King Harold's bedroom. I bet that will send the big guy a message."

"Please, Snake, you've never killed anyone in your entire life." Sea laughed at him. She was sitting by Smith, leaning up against him. "Where's Ace?"

Ace came up behind them, surprising Knot and Yin. Knot and Yin were quiet compared to the others, and they frightened easily at times. Ace put a bottle of grog on the table.

"Are you going to drink that?" Mouth asked. Ace shook his head, and Mouth took the bottle.

Ace sat down; he had a serious look on his face. "There's only one thing keeping John interested in his job." As he spoke, the others listened carefully. Ace only talked when he had something important to say. "And that's Kathleen. Without her, he won't get the throne. Kidnap her; hold a ransom. John leaves the country or Harold never sees his little girl again. Even if Harold doesn't agree to that, we'll still have Kathleen, and John will have no way of becoming king." Ace stood and left them there to ponder.

"Kidnap Kathleen?" Mouth watched as Ace walked away, heading for his room upstairs. "We've never done anything like that before. We've robbed ships, sure, but we've never hurt anyone."

"That' not a bad idea," Yang said. "We'll demand John be banished. Harold wouldn't risk his heiress's life."

"I don't know about this," Smith started to protest, but he was unheard.

"Smith can take care of getting Kathleen."

"It's perfect."

"Agreed."

Smith sank down in his seat. This would be dangerous, but when he was asked if he was up to it, he sat up straight and said, "Of course. Where do we start?"

***

It had almost been two weeks since Kathleen's last run-in with the Black Dragons. Tonight she sat in her little chair, looking into the mirror and brushing her short hair. Her father had hired a new tutor, who was just as rude as the last one. Kathleen was just thankful the woman had finally left.

After knocking, her brother entered the room. "How was the new tutor, Kathleen?" he asked her.

"Bleck!" was all she said.

He laughed. "That bad?"

"Would you want her as your tutor?"

"No, not really," Richard said. "John's a good enough tutor for me. He's handy with a sword too. Soon I'll be able to join him on his hunt for those pirates, the Black Dragons."

Kathleen laughed. "Pirates should be shot or hanged for all that money they steal."

"I can't stand those pirates," Richard said. He kissed Kathleen's cheek. "You should get some sleep; you have riding lessons tomorrow." He messed up her hair before leaving.

"That's not funny, Richard." She combed her hair some more before going off to bed. It was very dark that night, and she was asleep in no time.

***

Smith had just tied up a guard to a tree. "Have a nice day, sir." He laughed and walked right into the palace. Smith was sneaking from corridor to corridor, not completely sure how to get to Kathleen's room, and it had been poor planning on his part. Just as he was passing by the prince's room, he stumbled. He heard Richard sit up and cry, "Who's there?"

Smith lay on his stomach in the hall for what seemed like hours before Richard lay back down. The young prince had left his doors opened, and Smith was afraid Richard would see him. Richard sat up again, and Smith froze. He could see him searching for a candle. Smith frantically crawled away from the door, slowly stood up, and walked quickly into the nearest room. Smith looked around him. Posted around the room were wanted posters of various rogues and pirates, including a large one of Smith and the other Black Dragons displayed prominently above a desk. He had walked into the general's room.

He felt a cold chill run up and down his spine. He could see John's face clearly. The general's face was drenched in sweat, and he was shaking as if having a nightmare. Smith inched toward the door. John sat up in bed, breathing heavily. Smith stood still and held his breath. It was obvious that John's eyes had not adjusted to the dark, for he didn't see Smith standing in a corner of his room. John stood and looked around. "Richard? Is that you?"

"Aye, sir," Richard said from the hall. "I heard a noise."

"Boy, go back to bed. You have early lessons tomorrow!" John slammed his door in Richard's face, walked right past Smith, and lay back down.

Smith's heart was racing. John's back was to Smith. Slowly, Smith opened the door, peeked outside, and confirmed that Richard was nowhere to be seen. He began to sweat as he opened the door and left. After he got his breathing under control, Smith made his way through the halls and stairs of the palace. He knew she was in a room high up in one of the towers. He found her room, and while making his way inside, he checked to make sure no one was around. Once inside, he crept over to her bed, where she was sound asleep.

He stood over her bed, reaching his hand out to her. Quickly as he could, he shoved his hand over her mouth and held her down with his other arm. She awoke as soon as he touched her. Kathleen attempted to scream, but Smith had a tight grip over her mouth. Smith jumped on top of her to hold her down. He leaned over and whispered in her ear, "You make one sound, just one little sound, and I'll shoot you. Understand?" Kathleen froze. "Good girl." He yanked her up from her bed. The moment he let go of her, she screamed. While squeezing her arms, he rammed her into a wall, and she started to cry. "Hush," he whispered. "Keep your mouth shut." Smith flung her to the ground, and she stayed there.

He took down her curtains and her sheets; he began tying all the cloth together. He tied one end to her bedpost and tossed the other out the window. By the time he was done with this,

Kathleen was headed for her door. He ran over and wrapped his arms around her waist, yanking her around and forcing her toward the window.

"Get away from me!" she shouted, and he shoved her again.

"It's a long way down, Kathleen. We'd better get started." He pulled her toward the window.

***

Richard was passing by with his little candle when he heard Kathleen crying. When he saw what was going on inside, he knew he had to think quickly. There was a large painting of his grandfather in the hall; above it were two swords he'd used in a battle. Richard took down one of the swords and clenched it tightly. As quickly as he could, he burst through the door and shouted, "Leave her alone!" He held up the sword to Captain Smith. Smith laughed at him and quickly pulled out his own sword, swinging at Richard.

***

Kathleen was knocked over as the swords clanged together. She ducked behind a chair, listening to the continuous sound of their fighting. When she heard Richard cry out, she looked to see that Smith had knocked the sword from Richard's hands, causing him to bleed from his fingers. Smith held his sword in Richard's face.

Kathleen ran, jumped onto Smith's back, and started viciously hitting him on his shoulders. Smith dropped his sword in shock and backed away from Richard. Smith ran backward and rammed Kathleen into the wall; she fell to the ground with a loud gasp. Then Smith went after Richard.

He took Richard by the neck and pulled him to the ground. He punched him, and Richard stopped moving. Kathleen was pulled up by her hair and forced over to the window. Smith wrapped an arm around her waist. "You might want to hold on. You could fall."

Kathleen could see the ground from the top of the tower, and she held on to Smith, burying her face in his shoulder as they scaled down the wall. When they were about halfway down, she could see that Richard had gotten to his feet again and was looking down at them. "Ricky, help!" she called.

Richard started climbing down, a lot faster than Smith was going with Kathleen, and Smith let go. The two of them fell, barely escaping harm. Smith pulled Kathleen away from the castle grounds, where she saw a light gray horse waiting for them. "Okay, Princess, let's go for a ride." He spoke in a joking manner, acting as if the whole thing were a sort of game to him. "Get on," he ordered, forcing Kathleen up onto the horse. They hurried off. Every chance Kathleen got, she punched or kicked at Smith.

"Stop, please!" she pleaded with him.

Suddenly, Richard was beside them on his own horse. He swung his sword at Smith, barely missing.

"You've got a bit of talent with that sword of yours," Smith shouted over at him, while kicking his horse's side to make him run faster.

It was evident that Richard was trying his hardest to stay caught up with Smith. Ahead of them was a fallen tree, and Smith's horse easily jumped it. However, rather than jumping it, Richard's horse stopped suddenly when it came to the tree. Richard tumbled from his horse and hit the ground on the other side of the log just as Smith and Kathleen cleared it. Smith's horse panicked, throwing Kathleen and Smith from his back. The horse reared back when it saw Richard at its feet, and Richard screamed as the horse trampled him.

Ch 6

Smith rushed to get the horse away from Richard. "Hold the horse still," Smith ordered Kathleen, handing her the reins.

Smith lifted the semiconscious Richard and carried him to the side of the woods. "There's a pack on my saddle; bring it here," Smith told Kathleen, and she brought him the sack from the horse's saddle. "Here, tie the horse to the tree." He tossed her some rope from the sack. She did as she was told. Smith pulled out more rope from the sack. "Help me tie up your brother."

"No."

He pulled out his pistol and pointed it at her. "You best do what you're told, Kathleen." She helped him tie Richard up. Smith removed his bandana and handed it to her. "Go to the river and get this wet."

"Aren't you afraid I'll run away?"

"No, sweetheart, I don't think you will." Smith put the pistol to Richard's head. Richard let out a moan, but he did not awaken fully.

Kathleen crossed the road and went to the river, where she wet the bandana and ran back to Smith and her brother. Smith used it to clean out the cuts or scrapes where Richard was bleeding, especially his head. Richard flinched every time Smith touched him. Finally, Smith laid the bandana on Richard's forehead, hoping the cool water would relax him some. Smith pulled a jar of goop from his sack and started rubbing it all over Richard.

"What is that you're putting on his cuts?" asked Kathleen.

"It helps with the pain. A doctor friend of mine gave it to me."

Smith put the jar down and found yet another bottle in the bag. He poured some of its contents into his canteen and shook it up. Surprisingly, Smith was gentle with Richard. "Easy … you're all right. Just relax," Smith told him, helping him drink from the canteen. After a moment or two, Richard seemed to waken completely from his daze.

Realizing who was helping him drink, he kicked at him, but then he cried out in pain. "Release me!" he shouted.

"Here, drink this." Smith put the canteen to his lips, and Richard tried to yank away, crying out from pain again. Smith forced Richard to drink from the canteen. Richard was weak and tired, clearly knowing he was defeated.

"Please don't take my sister from me too!" Richard cried out when Smith started repacking his sack.

Smith had almost forgotten that Richard and Kathleen had lost a brother when they were young. "I promise you no harm will come to your sister." Smith pulled out a small envelope from the sack, the ransom he had nearly forgotten to leave behind because of all the commotion. Smith placed it inside Richard's coat. "Just give this to your father, Richard, and everything will go back to the way it was. No harm is going to come to her." Richard's head bobbed to one side; he was fully unconscious this time.

Kathleen fell to her knees beside her brother. "What was in that water you gave him?"

"It's just medicine to help him sleep through the night. It might be a while before anyone finds him, and he's in a lot of pain." Smith grabbed her by her wrist and yanked her to her feet. "Let's go."

"No." Kathleen tried to yank away from Smith, but he dragged her back to his horse. He forced her up onto the horse.

They rode for about a half hour. Both Smith and Kathleen dismounted the horse, and Smith tied him to a tree. "The horse's owner will be here to pick him up in the morning." Smith turned around and saw Kathleen running off, and he took off after her. He jumped at her, and they both fell to the ground. She wound up on her back, Smith on top of her.

"Get off me! Get off me!" Kathleen was in tears again.

"Sit up!" he screamed, and she listened. "I'm not going to hurt you, I promise. Now, behave yourself." He helped her stand. "Listen, you can either walk, or I'll drag you. The sun will be up in a few hours; we don't have far to go."

"Where are you taking me?" she asked.

He took her by the arm. "Come with me, now," he demanded, and they headed east through the woods. They trudged through the woods for the rest of the night, and come morning, Kathleen was covered in dirt and leaves and had blisters on her ankles.

"I cannot walk any farther, Pirate!" she said as the sun was peeking through the trees. She tried to yank her arm away from him, but she was unsuccessful.

"Relax. We're here." Smith pointed, and she could see a small barn in between some trees.

"This is it? This is where you're dragging me off to?" She tried to pull away again.

"Oh, just for the day," he said as she finally freed her arm from his clutches. "Come nightfall, we'll be off." Immediately, she took off into a sprint. He chased after her, knocking her down into the mud once he caught up. "You keep this up, and I'll have to tie you up until we leave tonight."

"And then what? Where are you taking me tonight?" she cried.

He smiled and said, "Skull Island."

The mere sound of it was frightening.

***

"You mustn't take me to Skull Island, Pirate!" Kathleen shouted at Smith the next morning. "My father has many enemies there."

52

"I know. So unless you want someone to hurt you, you're going to want to stick with me, all right? People won't think twice about taking advantage of you."

When the cockboat reached the docks on Skull Island, he tied the boat up to the dock and pulled Kathleen out of it. He had tied up her wrists and tied her ankles together after her several failed escape attempts. He threw her over his shoulders while she struggled to get away, carrying her toward a large building, Benny's Inn. Kathleen continued kicking and swinging her arms, until finally she struck Smith in the face. He purposely dropped her in the mud. Kathleen could see his face turn red, and he clenched his teeth. Smith dragged her all the way to the inn. As soon as they entered the rambunctious room, it went quiet.

They all knew her as King Harold and Queen Rachel's daughter, and King Harold did not have a good reputation amongst these sorts of people. Even covered in mud and crippled from exhaustion, she was easily recognized.

"Stay close to me, Kathleen." Smith reminded her. "They won't think twice about shooting you down right here." Kathleen did as she was instructed. He dragged her across the room and tossed her into a booth to sit. Smith removed his jacket and put it over her shoulders because all she was wearing was a nightgown.

"Well, well, look who's back." The boy Smith put her beside scooted close to her and put his hands around her waist.

"Don't scare the girl, Mouth," Sea told him.

Kathleen's hands and ankles were still tied; she felt uncomfortable sitting so close to Mouth without being able to protect herself.

Kathleen shook her head, trying to fan away the smell of liquor on him. He gave her a kiss on her cheek and kept his hands on her. Kathleen jolted back in her seat, but he still sat uncomfortably close to her.

"Did you leave the letter?" Sea asked.

"I left it with her brother; he chased after us," Smith explained to them.

While they talked, Kathleen observed these so-called pirates. Mouth was a hormonal boy, from what she could tell. One of them—the one apparently called Ace—seemed odd to her. He was staring at her and Mouth. While most of the others wore red and black, he wore nothing but black. He looked dark and mysterious; he frightened her.

As she was staring, Mouth kissed her neck. She tried to pull away, but he pulled her back toward him. She elbowed his lip, and he took her arms and shoved her to the floor outside the booth. Everyone in the room, excluding Ace and Smith, laughed at her, and she pulled Smith's jacket over her head and cried.

The laughter suddenly stopped; Kathleen peered out from under the jacket to see that Ace had hold of Mouth. Smith hurried between the two of them. Mouth fell to the ground and hurried under the table to hide from Ace, like the coward Kathleen had expected he was.

"Enough!" Smith shouted at him. "I don't know what your problem is, Ace, but I don't want to see you down here again tonight!"

Ace laughed at Smith; he clearly did not respect his captain the way the others on the crew did. He shoved by him and looked down at Kathleen.

"No one's going to hurt her, Ace," Sea said, and Ace then willingly left for his room. Kathleen watched him leave. *Why did he help me?* she wondered. *He seemed so worried about me.*

"You all right, Mouth?" Smith asked as Mouth crawled out from under the table.

"What's wrong with him?" Mouth muttered.

"Perhaps it's best if you stay away from Kathleen." Smith helped Kathleen back into her seat. "I don't want any more trouble from you, Mouth, understand me?"

"She can stay with me," Sea said. "I'll take her to my room."

"All right, but don't scare her any more than she already is."

"You've gone soft," Mouth whispered.

"Hush," Smith ordered him.

Sea held on to Kathleen and dragged her across the bar, stopping at the stairs. "Stay still," she said, taking out her knife to cut the ropes at Kathleen's ankles. "I don't want to have to carry you up those stairs. Walk."

Sea held on to one of Kathleen's arms and led her up two flights of stairs and down a few hallways. She stopped at one of the rooms and opened the door. Kathleen was shoved inside, and she looked around to see that there were two small twin-sized beds, one on each side of the room; a dresser next to the door; and on the far side of the room was a small window. Kathleen smiled. *I can sneak out after she falls asleep.*

Sea somehow sensed Kathleen's thoughts. "Even if you get out of the inn, you'll be gunned down in the streets. No one walks around here alone, sweetie."

Kathleen knew this, but she felt desperate.

"Listen, it's not my job to scare you, Princess. You don't need to worry. Smith won't let anyone lay a hand on you. You'll be back home in a week, tops." Sea pushed Kathleen onto one of the beds and pulled out her blade again to cut the ropes at Kathleen's wrist. "I think you get the idea now. You won't run, will you?"

While Sea cut the ropes, Kathleen noticed a golden bangle around her wrist. It had three gems on it: one red, one green, and another one blue. Sea saw Kathleen eyeing the bangle, and she backed away from Kathleen suddenly. "Smith gave it to me. I didn't steal it, if that's what you were thinking."

"Smith? The captain?"

"Kathleen, he really is a good man. Especially when you compare him to some of the others on our crew."

Do two of the Black Dragons have a love life? If I ever get out of here, I'll be sure to inform Papa of that. Maybe Papa can find a way to use it against Smith. Kathleen sat up on the bed, crossed her legs, and began rubbing her sore ankles. The two of them sat in an awkward silence for some time.

"When are you and the general supposed to marry?" Sea finally asked, as if making conversation to relieve her boredom. Really, she couldn't seem to care less.

"Four weeks from today." Kathleen sipped on the wine that Sea brought over to her.

"Do you want to?"

Kathleen smiled. "Of course. Why wouldn't I? He's an honorable man." Another wave of silence passed over them, and Kathleen knew she hadn't sounded convincing. She looked down at her own golden bangle, identical to the one Sea wore. In Kirkston, the little golden bangle was something a man gave his woman as a way of saying "I love you," and that possibly one day he wished to marry her. It seemed as though both of the girls were on that path, but for two very different reasons. The silence grew more eerie.

"Sea, that older boy, why did he try to help me?"

Sea just shrugged. "It was his idea to bring you here. He probably feels responsible for you now. Trust me, we don't know any more about him than you do. He's not much of a talker."

"Why did you start the Black Dragons?" Kathleen asked her.

Sea tapped her bottle impatiently. "It's a long story."

Kathleen nodded, and they stopped trying to speak with each other. Sea began to drink, sipping from the wine bottle, and the discomfort of the silence was palpable in the air. Kathleen watched as Sea continued to take sips of the heavy wine. As time progressed, Kathleen began to count to herself each time that Sea took a sip. The bottle was soon empty. Kathleen snickered to herself when Sea reached for the second bottle and struggled to keep hold of it. *She's drunk,* Kathleen thought. *Who knows how much she had to drink before I got here?* Kathleen thought that this would be a good opportunity to find out more about the Black Dragons.

"Why did you start the Black Dragons, Sea?" she asked again.

"My parents sort of started it." Sea answered willingly this time, clearly more talkative with alcohol in her system.

Kathleen smiled, glad the silence was over. "What are your parents like?"

"I only know what little I can remember about them." Sea paced. "Stevenson killed them back before he was general."

"They were criminals?"

"They didn't have a choice." Sea's eyes looked like glass; the drunken woman was choking back tears so the princess wouldn't see her cry. "He killed my brothers along with them. My parents were brave for them, but my brothers were so scared. They were so young; they weren't ready to die."

"John wouldn't have killed them unless they were criminals," Kathleen argued, not wanting to imagine her fiancé as a murderous man.

"You didn't know them." Sea struck Kathleen, who immediately backed down. "I was only six. I was scared, and John killed them in front of me."

"I don't believe that." Kathleen crossed her arms. She sighed. "I am sorry, though. I know what it's like to lose a brother."

"Ah yes, James. That was quite a mystery, wasn't it?" Sea leaned against the wall. "Well, I'm sorry about your loss."

"I suppose it's not all awful. I didn't know him well. I was much younger than you when you lost your brothers." Kathleen was eyeing the window again. *I should leave as soon as she's drunk enough. She can't stop me.*

Sea saw her staring at the window. "Kathleen, you don't need to fear for your life. Smith won't let anyone hurt you. You give him hope."

"What do you mean?"

Sea smiled at her. "I don't know why, but he believes in you. He believes that you will change this country for the better."

"He said that?"

Sea looked her in the eye. "Tell me the truth. Do you want to marry John?"

"Yes, I do." Kathleen lay down on her side, facing away from Sea. *Why does she keep bringing that up?*

"Kathleen, you know how you feel. Why don't you stop listening to your father and start listening to yourself? You can keep being Smith's hope, you know? Without you … I don't think he would have any hope for this country. He was hurt greatly because of your father's laws. We all were. Smith needs hope, Kathleen. Try not to take that away from him."

Kathleen sat up. "People don't believe in hope anymore."

"Not all people need hope the way Smith does." Sea sat down beside her. "You give me a little hope too, Your Highness. You can do great things with the crown, if you have the courage to do it." Sea looked at her. "You can keep things from happening, things like what happened to my family. You can change Kirkston, Kathleen. And I pray Smith gets to see it happen. He believes in you." She went over to the other side of the room, got in her bed, and blew out the candle without saying anything more.

Kathleen sat up shortly afterward. "Sea, why does Smith …?" Kathleen knew that Sea was already asleep. *Now's my chance.* Kathleen stood, ready to make a run for it. She knew she couldn't go down through the bar; some of the Black Dragons were probably still down there. Kathleen went over to the window, opened it, and stared out at the streets. She then closed the window and climbed back into bed, unsure why she hadn't left.

***

As the sun shone through the window early in the morning, Kathleen's head was aching. *That wine I had last night was stronger than I thought it would be.* Kathleen sat up and rubbed her temples. *I feel like someone bashed me over the head.* She stood and regained some sort of confidence in her stance. *I shouldn't have had any of that wine Sea gave me. It's making me stumble.* Once she was able to stand up straight, she noticed some clean clothes sitting on the foot of her bed, waiting for her. They were servant clothes.

The clothes waiting for her were disgusting. There was a faded blue shirt and a loose pair of blue pants, as well as a pair of little red moccasins. Although normally she wouldn't be caught dead in such attire, the clothes were better than her muddy nightgown, so she changed. Sea had left her a comb, which Kathleen put to good use. There was also a bowl of water, which she used to clean off any mud left on her face and arms.

Kathleen opened the door to see a young boy in the Black Dragons uniform waiting for her in the hall. "Oh!" he cried when she opened the door. "You surprised me, ma'am."

This boy can't be but five or six. He's adorable! "What's your name?" she asked him.

"They call me Squirt." His cheeks were red when he talked to her, and he wouldn't look her in the eye. Obviously, the boy wasn't around young women and girls too often, with the exception of Sea, who was more of a mother figure to him. "I wanted to talk to you about ... Well, actually, they asked me to watch the door, but I still ..."

Kathleen tried to hold in a laugh while Squirt struggled to get out his words. "Don't be shy. What is it you wanted to say?"

"I ... uh ... I wanted to apologize about the way my brother acted last night. He's not normally like that, really. He had had a bit much to drink—not that he drinks a lot, but ..." Kathleen laughed quietly, and his cheeks grew redder. "Th-they asked me to take you downstairs once you got up."

"Your brother was the one who was rude to me last night?" Kathleen asked, and Squirt nodded. *He seems like such a sweet child; it's hard to believe he was raised by such a rude boy as that Mouth character.* "Well, are you going to take me downstairs?"

"Yes." He walked a short distance ahead of her. As they turned the corner from the staircase into the bar, Kathleen could see the Black Dragons all sitting in the same booth they had been in just the day before. Squirt hurried over to Mouth and crawled into his lap. Mouth wouldn't look at Kathleen.

Ace stared at her. It was as though he had elected himself as her official watch. Smith came over just as Kathleen was sitting down, and he placed a plate of what looked like gray mud in front of her. "Eat up, Your Highness. We have a long day ahead of us."

Eventually, after gazing at it for a good long time, she decided the mudlike food couldn't be as bad as it looked, and she began to eat it. Much to her surprise, it wasn't bad at all. Even in a place like Benny's Inn, she dined like a lady. She sat up straight and ate a small spoonful at a time. Kathleen seemed like a goddess—even in her servant's clothes and even as the hostage of the group—as she looked down at them. She could sense Squirt looking at her, seeming completely awestruck, as though he thought she seemed unreal.

Once she had her fill, the Black Dragons hurried her out of the inn and took her to the docks, where she saw the *Black Dragon* for herself. It was a large red ship with the famous black dragon painted on the sides. Compared to her father's galleons, it was a small ship. However, according to everything she'd ever heard about the ship, it was fast.

When they boarded the ship, Kathleen admired the wooden carvings of the ship itself, and the amazing detail. "Hoist the anchors!" Kathleen heard Smith shout from the wheel.

Kathleen quietly explored the deck of the ship while the crew prepared to set sail. She was distracted with an escape plan when Mouth snuck up on her, scaring her into the side of the mainmast. Knot, the lookout, dumped a bucket of water over the side of the lookout tower. Kathleen was drenched in the dirty water, and the two of them laughed.

"Mouth! Knot! Enough!" Smith said with scorn.

"Sorry, sir," they both said under their breath.

Mouth sighed heavily; Knot climbed the rope ladders back to his post. "Kathleen, about last night—," Mouth began.

"Your brother already apologized for you." Kathleen squeezed out her wet hair.

"I'm not normally like that."

"He said that too." Kathleen crossed her arms in annoyance, not wishing to forgive his rude behavior. "He looks up to you, doesn't he?"

"I'm all he's got." Mouth left.

Squirt arrived on the scene shortly afterward. "Hi." His cheeks were again reddening. "Do you need anything, Kathleen?"

"No, but thank you." Kathleen patted his head and began walking down the main deck. He followed. "Squirt, are your parents still alive?"

"No."

"When did they die?"

Squirt shuffled his feet. "I was little. I don't remember them. Mouth and Sea took good care of me when I was a babe, so did Mr. and Mrs. Keg."

"I'm sorry about all that." Kathleen excused herself; she could see land from where they were. It was Kirkston's shores, and she thought it might be her only chance to escape. She wandered around the deck for a long time, planning out her escape in her head. She quickly climbed up onto the side of the ship and held on to the rope ladders to keep herself from falling. Her nerves froze her.

"Kathleen, are you addled?" Smith cried. She could see him running toward her from the quartering deck. "There are sharks in the waters way out here! You'll never make the swim!" Smith appeared scared for her. "Come on down from there, or you'll fall in and drown!"

She turned to jump, but she felt someone grab her legs. Whoever it was pulled her down back into the ship. His arms were incredibly strong; she was no match against him. She looked to see that it was Ace. "Ah, you bloody pirate, how dare you?" Kathleen tried to pull away from Ace's strong arms.

"Use your deadlights, Kathleen. Ace just saved your life." Smith pointed out toward land. "We're over a mile from land. You wouldn't have made the swim." Smith yanked her out of Ace's arms and held her.

"Smith—" Ace was clearly about to protest the way Smith was holding on to her arms so harshly, but he fell silent.

Smith dragged her below deck and into a dark room; Kathleen could hear the crew laughing at her struggle to get away from Smith. He swung open the iron doors to the jail cell and tossed her inside. She fell over, and he dragged her to the side. He chained her to the wall and stood. "No more surprises like that, Your Majesty."

***

I was afraid Kathleen would die today—luckily Ace scared her. We're keeping her in the cells below deck now. My thoughts kept going back to the prince. I wasn't sure if anyone found him. Luckily, Benny from the inn told us that he had heard that the prince had been found the next morning.

***

It must have been five in the morning when Richard felt someone tapping his cheek. "John?" he said, shaking his head slightly. He'd had an uncomfortable night's sleep. He wouldn't have been able to sleep if it wasn't for the medicine.

"It's Richard!" John shouted. "Your Highness, it's Richard! I've found him!" John turned to Richard. "Are you all right?"

"John, help me," Richard begged. He looked up to see his mother climbing out of a carriage and rushing toward them.

The queen knelt down beside them. "Are you all right, my prince?" She kissed his cheek. John was cutting the ropes, and once he was loose, the queen insisted on removing her son's nightgown to check his bruises.

"Allow me," John said, but Richard cried out in pain when John touched him.

The queen had gentle hands and was able to remove the robe without harming him. "Oh, he's hurt. Do you think his ribs are broken?"

"He's bruised, but I'm not so sure. We need to get him to the palace and have a doctor look at him. Richard, I'm going to have to carry you to the carriage." John attempted to carry Richard without hurting him, but there was no way to do so. "Stop whining, Richard," John whispered to him. He faked a smile and added, "You'll be all right." Richard bit his lip in what was likely an effort to keep from shouting.

Within an hour, Richard was in his bed, with a doctor checking him over. In the room with them were King Harold, Queen Rachel, two servants, and Richard's bride-to-be. "Do you recall Captain Smith giving you any medicine?" the doctor asked him.

"Maybe." Richard could not remember.

"He's a horrible man," the general said. "Why would he do that?"

The doctor laughed. "You're awfully calm, General. You'd think you would be angrier about your future wife running around with all those immature men."

The general clenched his fists. "Excuse me for a moment." He bowed to the royal family and hurried out.

***

John stormed into his own room and stared at the pictures of Smith on his wall. "*Who are you?*" he screamed, tearing one of the pictures off the wall. "I'll find you ... I swear I'll find you." He ripped up the poster, threw it to the ground, and stomped on it. "You're taking away my last chance to rule Kirkston." *Who is this child,* the general thought. *He has it in for me—I know he does!* A knock on the door surprised him. "Come in."

Harold entered John's room, and John was thankful that he didn't appear to notice the torn scraps of paper all over the ground.

"Smith left a note with my son, saying he won't return my daughter unless you are stripped from your title and banned from Kirkston. If not, he'll kill her. I'm going to give you two weeks to find and rescue my daughter. After that, I'll have no choice but to have you banished."

John began to argue. "But, Your Highness, Kirkston is my home."

"I'm sorry, John, but it's my daughter's life or your job." Harold turned to leave. "Really, I am sorry."

"I will find her, Harold. I promise." John waited for Harold to leave before he banged his fists on the table. "I hate those bloody pirates!"

Ch 7

Richard was shaking when he woke up; for the past two days, he had been drifting in and out of sleep. He opened his eyes to see Abigail, his fiancée, sitting in a chair beside him, a small silver tray in her lap. "How long was I out this time?"

"About four hours." Abigail smiled down at him, trying to assure him he would be well soon. Their arranged marriage had been formed before either of them was ever born. They had become friends when they were younger, but neither of them wanted to marry the other. It had become strange when their parents told each of them about the arranged marriage. They could barely stand to be in a room together. Now everything was fake—their smiles, their kisses, and even the light conversation were all an act.

"I brought you some tea and soup." She placed the tray by his bed. He motioned the tray away so she wouldn't put any food in his face.

"Have they found her yet?"

"They saw the ship, but that's all." She placed a hand on his chest.

"I'll kill him." Richard began to sit up. He let out a cry of pain and lay back down.

"Richard, she will be just fine." Abigail kissed him.

No, don't cry in front of her ... Richard felt tears emerging anyway. *No, not in front of her. My sister ... where is she? Is she even alive?*

Abigail met Richard's eyes, which he was sure revealed how hard he was trying to hide the tears from her. "Kathleen will be fine, Richard." She rubbed his shoulder where he had said it was sore.

"You don't know that," Richard said. "Abigail, did you know that I had an older brother?"

"I heard about him once." She stroked his hair in a visible attempt to calm him.

Richard shook his head, disappointed in himself. "I can barely remember him. I do remember him being kind to me. He was killed, and I forgot about him completely. I was six years old when I heard Mama and Papa talking about him. I had forgotten about my own brother; when Mama and Papa started talking about him and I remembered him, I started hating myself for it. If something were to happen to Kathleen, I'd slowly start to forget, the same way I did with James. I'd forget about the way she laughed, her smile, and everything. She'd just be a memory, like James."

"Kathleen will not be forgotten, Richard. Even if something does happen, she won't be forgotten. What happened to James is not your fault; you were so little. But you do remember him, and that's all you can do. I don't think the *Black Dragon* captain will hurt Kathleen. He just wants to get rid of John. I read the letter. Honestly, I think the Black Dragons could be good people."

"They have my sister, and they're threatening her life. That does not make them good people." Richard turned away when she attempted to kiss his cheek.

"Smith could have killed you if he wanted to. Instead, he cleaned away your blood, treated your wounds, gave you water, and fed you medicine. Does he truly sound wicked to you?"

Richard leaned his head back. "I suppose not, but I could never forgive them if they ever harmed Kathleen. I'd kill them."

***

Ace brought down the food for Kathleen. He put it in front of her and relocked the jail cell. But he stayed and watched her.

"What?" she asked, but he did not say anything. "Who are you? Does your crew even know? You're such a strange man, you know?"

Ace looked away from her. "I'm sorry about all this. It'll be over soon."

"I don't understand you." She looked away from him. "You act as if you're the strongest in your crew, but now you seem soft."

"I'm not a cruel man, Kathleen. People just assume that about me—so I let them think it." He sat in the shadows, making him all the more eerie, as though he too were part of the shadows. "They think I'm a brute, but I'm not. I was a child when I ran into the Black Dragons. I was a mute."

"A mute?"

"By choice." He looked down, which made his eyes look even darker than normal. His skin was pale, but there were always dark circles around his eyes, making him look drunk even when he was days sober. "I was afraid of them."

"You? You're stronger than any of them." Kathleen came over to the side of the jail cell and wrapped her hands around the bars, squinting to see him better.

"I suppose it's ridiculous." He stood. "But not entirely. I really am sorry about this, Your Majesty. Hopefully your father realizes we won't be taking you home unless he agrees to our terms."

"What? You won't be taking me home?" Kathleen shook the bars. "I won't live my life in a jail cell on a pirate ship!"

Ace laughed at her. "Calm yourself, Kathleen. All is well. I'll be here, and I won't let anyone harm you. You might even like it here."

"Ha!" Kathleen grinded her teeth at him. "I want to go home—can't you understand that? I want to be with my mama and papa and my brother. I don't want to be on a strange ship with a bunch of young men I hardly know."

"I suppose I can understand that," Ace said. He waited a moment before speaking again. "Listen, Kathleen ... Your Majesty—"

He was cut off when there was shouting above deck. Ace ran above deck to see what was going on.

***

The general's ships were firing on them. Smith drew his sword and immediately took charge.

"Smith, there're too many to fight off," Sea cried out, holding on to him for comfort. The *Black Dragon* shook. One of the general's ships had rammed into the starboard side, and another nudged up against the prow. "Run and get Kathleen. We'll trade her for our release!" Sea shouted.

"Agreed. It's not worth our lives." Smith hurried below deck. He could hear cannons from the general's ships firing.

He saw Kathleen in a jail cell; she was clenching the bars, and her eyes were wide with panic. "What's going on?"

"We're under attack," Smith explained, unchaining Kathleen from the wall. "Stay here for now. I'm going to make a deal with your fiancé, and you'll be on your way, all right?"

Smith ran up the stairs, only to see John shutting the door. He locked it and had his men roll the ship's guns in front. The cannons were far too heavy for Smith to push the door open. In quick haste, he made his way down the flight of stairs, searching for their pickax so he could bust through the door. He struck the door many times, only to realize that he would not get through as long as the cannons were in the way. Through the hole he had created in the door, Smith could see his crew being backed up to the mainmast. John's men strapped them all to the mainmast with rope, chains, or whatever else they could find. Sea was refusing to give in; she was in a tussle with one of John's men on the floor in front of the doorway.

It was quiet. She struck the man in the face repeatedly, until she drew blood. He knocked her away, and the two of them stood. She was patient and waited for the man to strike, and when he did, she stepped out of his way and threw her elbow into his shoulder. "Kick his ass, Sea!" Mouth cheered her on, and a soldier struck him to silence him. The fight continued, but John was growing tedious. Coldly, he lifted his musket as Sea knocked her foe to the floor of the deck. John aimed the musket at her and fired.

Smith's screams echoed below deck. Smith banged on the door, trying his hardest to slide it open, but it was useless.

"What's the matter, Captain?" the general mocked him. "Don't you have something clever to say? You always do. It's not so funny when it's your woman in trouble, is it?"

"Not Sea, please," Smith begged, still leaning on the door in hopes the cannons would slide just enough for him to escape from below deck. "Don't hurt her, please."

Sea was lying motionless on the ground. For all Smith knew, she was already gone.

John motioned to his crewmates; some hurried back onto one of John's ships and started bringing over large barrels. Smith smelled something in the air. "Gunpowder? What are you going to do?" Smith kicked at the door, praying more wood would snap and he could come to his friends.

John shouted to his men, "Kathleen is dead! They have killed Kirkston's heiress!"

"What? Lies!" Smith shouted to John's men. "Come and see for yourselves. She's here and very much alive. Have her and leave my crew alone. A trade, yes? It's a fair trade. Come and take your princess home!"

One of John's men approached the door, but John stopped him. "He deceives you. The second you move those cannons, he'll kill you. Everyone off the ship. Kathleen is dead, so avenge her and stick to my plan!" John's men hurried back to their own ships.

"If you let us go, you can have Kathleen," Smith swore to John, looking him in the eye through the hole in the door. "She's not dead, John. She's right here, honestly! She's in a jail cell."

"I don't care for that arrogant child," John whispered so his crew could not hear. "And as far as they know, I have seen her remains below deck."

"You're mad," Smith said. "What will you accomplish here? You won't be able to get the crown, John."

"You're wrong, Smith. If I were to marry her, I would rule Kirkston by her side. But if something were to happen to her and Richard, there would be no heir. In that case, the crown would fall to the kingdom's general."

"You're going to kill Richard? You're a madman, John. Take Kathleen home with you. Even Harold does not deserve to lose all his children."

"I'm not taking any chances with you this time, Smith." John hurried to his own ship; they were sailing away. Smith could smell smoke. *My friends, when the fire spreads to those barrels, we'll all be dead!* Smith watched Sea force herself to stand, clearly in great pain from her wound. She turned and looked at him. "I love you, Peter."

The fire began to spread.

"I love you too, Courtney." Smith could no longer see her or his crew because of the smoke. He could hear them screaming, all of them trying to get loose from the mainmast.

He knew he had to get off the ship before the fire hit the barrels. Turning around, he could see that the ship was taking on water, and quickly. Smith dove into the water in search of Kathleen. It was dark below deck, and she was difficult to find. *I have to save Kathleen; she's the only innocent life on this ship.*

"John! John!" Kathleen shouted, running past Smith on the stairway.

"Kathleen, stop!" Smith chased her up the stairs.

"John, help! Help! I'm on the ship, John! I'm on the ship! I'm here! I'm here!" She banged on the door. Smith grabbed her. "Let go of me, Pirate! John, save me!"

"He's not here, Kathleen! He's not on the *Black Dragon*; he's on one of your father's galleons!" He dragged her back down the stairs and into the water. The water now reached their chins as they pressed their heads to the ceiling of the lower deck.

Kathleen held on to Smith. "We're sinking! I don't want to die!"

"Relax. I'm going to get you out of here. How long can you hold your breath?"

"Not too long. I'm not a fair swimmer."

"Don't worry, all right?" Smith put his head under and looked around a bit. He came back up again. "Take a deep breath; we're going under." He dragged her under, to the side of the ship, where there was a large hole, probably from a cannon blast. It was just barely big enough for them to crawl through. Kathleen went out first, and Smith noticed she was carrying something with her, but he did not think much of it. Smith crawled through the hole. On his way up, he became dizzy. He had not taken in a good breath of air, and he was unable to make it to the surface.

***

Smith heard a familiar voice shouting. "Wake up, you bloody pirate. Are you all right? Please don't be dead!"

It was Kathleen. He felt that he was lying in sand.

Smith coughed, and his eyes slowly blinked open. When he sat up, he scorned her. "Don't you dare touch me!" He yanked himself away. He looked out into the water, where his ship was in flames. His crewmates, his family, were still on board. Distant screams, followed by gunpowder explosions and the final sound of the ship sinking, filled the air. Smith ran out into the water; Kathleen tried to stop him. "Are you addled? There's no saving your ship and money, Pirate."

"I don't care about the money!" He pulled his arm away from her. "Cannonball, Mouth, Ace … Sea!" he screamed. "They're all out there. Ace! Cannonball! Snake! Snake!" While scanning the water, he kept shouting. "Yin! Yang! Mouth! Squirt!" It was as though he had forgotten Kathleen was watching. "Blade! Knot! Courtney! Courtney! Courtney, answer me!" Trying to see any form of life was useless. The ship was completely underwater now. Before he could embarrass himself in front of Kathleen even further, he ran past her and into the trees. They were on some sort of island. It was covered in all sorts of trees, and he could easily hide in shame from her while he wept.

Within the next few minutes, he heard her shouting: "Hello? Where have you gone, Pirate?" She found him amongst the trees. "I took this before we left. I'm not sure if it means anything to you." Kathleen tossed a small brown bag in front of Smith, and he smiled.

"That was mine when I was young." He looked inside and was relieved. Everything was there: the journal his sisters had given him … and the quilt his mother had knitted. It was wet, so he wrung it out. He touched his sheath and noted that he still had his father's sword as well. The pages of the journal were wet—but at least he had it now. He held a torn, wet piece of paper. It was the drawing that Mr. Katch had done of his family so long ago. He sighed as it dwindled away in his hands. Still he held the journal tightly in his arms. Without even thinking, he stood and hugged Kathleen, thanking her for saving what few things he had left of his childhood.

"Don't touch me, Pirate." She pulled away from him.

"Sorry." He threw the bag over his back. His voice sounded hoarse when he spoke. "We better get going." He snatched the wet quilt and the journal.

"Going? Where?"

"I'm going to take you home." He turned away from her. "I'm retiring from piracy."

"Ah, so you've decided to become a hero rather than a thief?"

"I didn't say that. Now, are you coming or not?" He walked off before giving her a chance to answer, and she followed him.

"It's a two-day hike to the closest point of any civilization, and by that I mean Skull Island. We might be able to build a raft to get there. We'll stay there a night and rent a boat. By the next day, I'll have you home."

Smith suddenly stopped walking. "Why didn't I drown?" he asked, turning around to face her. "I passed out in the middle of the bay. Kathleen, did you save me?"

She nodded.

"Oh, well, thank you." He was sure he sounded as if he'd never thanked anyone before. "I thought you couldn't swim well. How did you manage to save me?"

"It was difficult," she admitted.

"You could have drowned trying to save me. Thank you," he said again.

"And I appreciate your changing your plans and deciding to take me home. I'm no fool; I know you'd be in trouble if we're caught before we get there." She tried to smile at him, but he ignored it.

He's so upset, she thought. *I never thought a man like this pirate could care for his companions like this. He's more upset about losing his crew than the money on board and losing the ship. Even so, he's a pirate. He probably is planning to drown his pain in grog once we get to Benny's Inn.* Kathleen's mind drifted to the night she had spent there with Sea; Sea had called her Smith's hope. *Maybe I can keep giving him hope,* she thought.

***

They walked all day, hardly saying a word to each other. Not a thing they found out in the forests was edible. Eventually, they stopped to rest their legs, and Kathleen rubbed her hungry stomach while Smith made a fire. "Unless you want to walk all night and all day tomorrow, we'll rest here." It didn't take him long to get the fire going, and he hung his mothers quilt over the fire to dry. It was getting cold. A few hours passed, and it grew dark.

Kathleen was shaking, and Smith found it a bit annoying. It got cold in Kirkston at night sometimes. Smith tossed Kathleen the quilt. "Don't get it dirty, all right?" The quilt was dry by now.

"It's beautiful. Who made this?"

"My mother did."

Kathleen asked curiously, "But I thought all the Black Dragons were orphaned?"

"I am an orphan."

"Oh! I-I didn't mean to … I mean, I'm sorry I-I …," she stuttered.

"Hush," he said sternly, lying down next to the fire. "I'll give you a flogging if you keep that up."

"Whip me? You don't have your cat, Captain." Kathleen laughed, and Smith pulled out a whip with nine tails. He did indeed have his cat. She cried out and backed away from the fire.

"At ease, Kathleen." He chuckled. "I'd be a fool to whip the king's daughter."

"Have you ever used it?"

"A quick blow on a couple of them, but not so much. I don't have it in me to make one of my friends kiss the gunner's daughter, but I've threatened them with it before." For a moment, Smith seemed to be enjoying the light conversation, until Kathleen asked him when he'd gone on the account.

"Did you hear me?" she repeated. "I want to know why you went pirate."

"Belay that talk and get some rest," he told her. Not long after Kathleen was asleep, Smith got out his journal and turned to a page that was dry.

> *How I wish I could see Father and Mother again, and my sisters. I've lost everything now. If I don't get Kathleen to the palace before they crown Richard*

*as future king, the general will kill him. Too many
lives have been lost; I have to stop him. Father would
want me to save him, even if he is Harold's son.*

When Smith could no longer write, he cried himself to sleep. He
hadn't done that in a long time. *I have to save Richard. No more
will die. I will not let John take another innocent life!*

***

Richard awoke suddenly. "Kathleen? Where is she?" he asked,
but no one was in the room to answer him. He heard voices
out in the hall. One belonged to his father: "Did you kill
them?"

"Every one of those dirty Black Dragons are at the bottom of
the ocean, Your Highness," the general said.

He did it! John did it; he got rid of the Black Dragons! Richard
smiled.

He heard John say, "I'll tell him, sir."

Tell me what? Richard wondered.

"No, he's my son. I'll speak with him. You'll be rewarded
for this, General. Please rest." A moment later, King Harold
entered the room, closing the doors behind him. "Richard, I have
news."

"I heard John finally got rid of those pirates." Richard smiled
up at his father.

"Richard, something horrible has happened." Harold sat by
his son and took his hand. "It's Kathleen."

"What? What's wrong?"

"The Black Dragons … they've killed her," Harold said.

The prince's cries could be heard throughout the corridors.

Ch 8

"Come on, Kathleen," Smith said. "We're going to be walking for two days, and we don't have any food. It doesn't taste *that* bad."

"Pirate, I swear you better put that thing back in the ground where it belongs!" Kathleen twitched all over when Smith shoved a worm down his throat.

"It's food," he said.

With her thumb and forefinger, Kathleen reluctantly took the worm Smith handed her. "This is absurd." She wiped the mud away from the little worm and then swallowed it. Then she laughed. "That tastes horrible!"

"Then why are you laughing?"

"It felt odd going down my throat," she said.

"When we get to Benny's, we can wash it down with some grog."

"I don't drink grog," Kathleen huffed.

"You are such a poxy, Kathleen," he said.

She stomped her foot in frustration. He just laughed and started singing an old chantey.

"Belay that childish nonsense, Pirate!"

But he kept on singing. Annoying her seemed to be the only thing that could cheer him up at the time. *I do not understand this man. Why does he waste his time taking me home? Not to mention that he's not even going to use me to continue out the ransom. He could make millions of gold pieces and silver shillings!*

Kathleen just followed the pirate blindly, not knowing what dangers lay ahead.

> *It's the second night without my friends. It's hard to believe that I'll never see Courtney again. I'll never kiss her or hold her hand ever again. It just doesn't seem real. It doesn't seem like they're really gone.*

***

Abigail stroked Richard's hair while he lay in his bed, still sore from his fall.

"Can you believe my father?" he said.

"He's just stressed," Abigail said. "He has to worry about these things." Even Abigail thought Harold had been unfeeling. His first concern after losing his daughter was who would take the crown instead. He had sat down and talked long and hard to Richard about the responsibility of holding the crown; it wasn't something Richard wanted to talk about merely a few hours after hearing about the death of his sister. "Are you feeling all right?"

Richard nodded. "All things considered. I never pictured myself on the throne. It's frightening. First Kathleen and now this?"

Abigail gave him a kiss, but he gently shoved her away. "Not now, Abigail." Richard looked away.

Harold entered the room without warning. "Richard, son, how are you feeling?"

"All right," he said.

"I'll be having a tailor come in and fit Abigail for a dress tomorrow," Harold said.

"A dress?"

"You two will have to get married sooner," Harold explained. "Our people demand our heirs to be married before they take the throne."

"But, Papa—"

"Hush." Harold sat by Richard. "Are you sure you're all right? Have you tried standing again?"

"I cannot sit up on my own so don't expect me to stand anytime soon." Richard took Abigail's hand.

"The doctor said that nothing is broken," his father said. You'll be fine, son. We'll wait until you are well, but as soon as you can walk, we'll schedule the wedding." Harold stood. "You are feeling well, yes?"

"Papa, I'm all right." Richard looked his father in the eye. "But are you all right? You'd be quite heartless not to be upset after losing two of your children. How can you go about acting as though it does not trouble you?"

Harold looked away, not looking Richard in the eye. "I have lost my daughter now. Richard, until you have your own children, you cannot understand my hurt. I cannot show my tears outside of my own room."

***

John poured the arsenic into the tea, took a breath, and entered Richard's room. "Your pardons!" He hadn't expected to see both Harold and Abigail in the room with Richard. "I-I brought some tea for Richard." He felt sweat on the back of his neck. Before John could come over to them, they were interrupted by shouting in the hall.

A servant came bursting into the room. "King Harold!" he cried.

"How dare you come in here unannounced!" Harold shouted at the servant boy.

The boy smiled up at him. "I beg your forgiveness, sir, but I have urgent news. It's Kathleen, sir! She's been spotted with Captain Smith on an island just east of here."

"My wife will want to know this!" Harold cried out, clearly overwhelmed. "Send word of an award—fifteen thousand gold pieces for whoever brings me Kathleen, and another nine thousand for whoever brings me Smith." He left the room.

Abigail smiled and gave Richard a kiss. He allowed it this time. She dismissed herself and went to find her family and give them the good news, leaving Richard alone with John. "My sister, thank goodness." Richard smiled at his mentor. "Are you not overjoyed, John?"

"Of course. It is just taking a moment to sink in with me." John looked over at Richard.

"Might I have some of that tea, John?" Richard asked.

Tea? John panicked. "Of course," he said, and purposely stumbled, spilling the poisoned tea all over the floor. "Oh, I'm sorry!" John hurried to clean it up. "I-I have to go." John hurried out of the room.

***

What's wrong with John? Richard wondered when John hurried out of the room. He smiled when he thought of his sister. He felt well. *I should try to walk.* He gently put his legs over the side of the bed. He shouted at the door for a maid to bring him some crutches. He thanked her when she returned and helped him stand. The servant left once he assured her that it was not too painful for him to stand.

I should show John that I can stand now, he thought, and he slowly made his way out of the bedroom and toward John's room. He felt sore when he walked, but he was tired of sitting all day.

"John?" he said, entering the general's room. Inside, papers, wanted posters, and letters were scattered all over his desk. Most of it was about the Black Dragons. *I know they've embarrassed John quite a few times, but I had no idea he'd become so obsessed with them.* He picked up one of the newspapers and read the headline: BLACK DRAGONS: THIEVES OR HEROES? He began to read. *They give away the money they steal?* He was shocked to learn this. Never had Richard been informed of this. His father told him they spent all the money on grog and women.

Another paper was entitled WHO ARE THE BLACK DRAGONS? It discussed them on a personal scale. It indicated that all of them had been orphaned, but no one knew exactly how. In it, there was a rumor that one of the Black Dragons was actually the son of Rob, the former general of Kirkston, and his wife Amy. It said that after John Stevenson was accused of their murder, their son might have joined the Black Dragons. It also said that King Harold had announced John innocent of the crime. *Papa told me that General Rob retired; I didn't know he was murdered.*

He read more and more. *Lies!* he kept telling himself. *These papers must be lies—why would John and Papa keep these from me?*

"Richard!" John had come up behind him.

Richard jumped; John sounded angry. He looked angry. Fear overwhelmed Richard. *Why ... why am I afraid of you all of a sudden?* he thought. He could not speak. *You've been lying to me, John. My whole life you've been lying to me about the Black Dragons.* John came closer, and Richard froze. *What else have you been lying to me about?*

Then John smiled. "Are you all right, Richard? You don't look well."

"I don't feel well." Richard shivered and thought, *I have this terrible sinking feeling, John, a feeling that's not going away. I feel as if my whole life is about to change.*

***

Kathleen had learned from her last trip to Skull Island to stay near Smith. They entered the inn moments after arriving onshore. Smith saw the booth open, as it always was. He went to sit down, and Kathleen sat across from him. They were not there long before Benny came running up to them. "Son!" he cried, hugging Smith. The old man could barely stand. "You're alive! Oh, Peter ... I heard what happened. Are you all right?"

Smith nodded but said nothing.

"We lost a bunch of good kids, Smith. You were all like my own children, especially Sea." Benny had his hands on Smith's shoulders. "Know that you always have a home here, all right, Peter? If you ever need anything—a place to stay or a job—you let me know."

"Thank you, Benny," Smith said quietly.

"You have whatever you want tonight. It's all on the house: food, grog, and water. Whatever you want, it's yours. I only have one room to spare; I kept it open for you. When I heard the rumors that you had survived, I wouldn't rent it out. I had hoped you'd come here." Benny gave Smith a comforting hug.

Smith sat back down with Kathleen, and Benny brought over some heavy grog for Smith and a small glass of wine for Kathleen. As Kathleen sipped on the wine and Smith drank his grog, Benny fixed them a nice dinner. By the time they ate their meal, Smith had gone through two large bottles of grog and was demanding a third.

"You're not really going to give him more, are you?" Kathleen asked Benny with scorn. "He can't even sit up straight."

"Of course I'm not. I'm cutting him off. He's too young to drink like that; he's still just a lad." Benny poured a glass of water and gave it to Smith, who did not even realize he was drinking water instead of grog until the glass was half-empty. "I think you've had enough." Benny helped Smith stand. "Kathleen, help me take him up to the room, all right, sweetheart?"

They walked on either side of him, each gripping one of his arms. Benny opened the door to the room, and they helped Smith sit on one of the little twin beds; Benny put Smith's knapsack by the foot of his bed.

"Thanks, Benny," Smith managed to say after lying down.

Benny nodded. "Kathleen, if he gives you any trouble, you let me know, and I'll see if I can get you a separate room, but for now, this is all I have." Benny left them after making sure Smith was all right.

Smith lay on his back, mumbling and rambling on about Sea and the others. "Oh, Pirate, would you stop that nonsense?" Kathleen said.

"My name's not Pirate," he said.

Kathleen thought for a moment. *Have I been calling him Pirate this whole time?* "I'm sorry, Smith."

"No," Smith said. "Peter, my name's Peter. I'm Peter!" Smith rolled on his side, coughed, and then was out cold.

Peter? What a nice name. Why doesn't he just go by Peter? Isn't that what Benny called him earlier? Feeling daring, Kathleen reached for Smith's brown bag. She wasn't sure what prompted it, but she wanted to know more about Smith. The name Peter kept ringing in her head. She found the journal she had seen Smith with, and she turned to a random page and began to read:

> *Kathleen is so kindhearted. I see her doing much for Kirkston.*

Kathleen smiled, but she saw that the date he wrote this was many, many years before, and it puzzled her. She flipped around some more and continued reading on another page:

> *Papa died last night. Mr. Katch and Mr. Stern dug a grave under the big oak tree by the river. I will start working for Mr. Anderson, the blacksmith. He'll train me like he did Papa. Elizabeth will have to clean houses every day now. I miss my papa very much. I'm afraid of what will happen to us now. I wish my papa was here.*

Kathleen frowned. *That's so strange … This seems familiar somehow.* Kathleen turned to another page.

> *I have no family, just the Black Dragons now. They were so kind to take me in. I miss my parents and my sisters more and more every day. General John Stevenson has gotten away with killing my family; I will not let him do this to anyone else.*

She closed it, not wanting to hear anything bad about John, but then she opened it again. She scanned until she found her name.

> *"I got some fruit from Kathy again today. It'll help feed me and Mama for a while. Princess Kathleen has been so kind to me."* She stopped reading and concentrated. *Smith knew me? How …?* She read page after page for hours, trying to remember. *The stories of his father's and sisters' deaths sounded so familiar, and then she remembered all of it.*

"Peter Barons!" she cried.

Kathleen put the journal back and looked at Smith carefully. From what she could remember, he looked like Peter. Sitting down, she began to shake him awake gently. "What?" he shouted at her.

"You … you're Peter Barons, aren't you?"

Smith was lying on his stomach and did not bother to turn over. "Yes. How did you figure that out?"

She hesitated to answer. "You told me your name was Peter."

Smith seemed embarrassed. "Oh."

"How could I have forgotten about you, Peter?" Kathleen asked.

Smith smiled briefly. Kathleen felt tears roll down her cheeks.

"My name is Smith now, Kathleen," he said to her. "I haven't been called Peter in a long time."

"Look, I know what the general did to you and your family. I know he killed them, and I'm really sorry. I'm sure he was just doing his job, though. I'm sure that you were just a child exaggerating what happened, because what you wrote about the general was—"

He interrupted her. "Wait. What I wrote?" Smith sat up. "What do you mean?"

"I was reading your journal, and you wrote some awful things about John, which I'm sure are exaggerated."

"You read my journal?" Smith took her by the arm. "You went digging through my bag, took it out, and read it?"

Kathleen pushed him down on his back. To keep him there, she put her full weight on her hands, which she placed on top of his chest. Normally Kathleen wouldn't be able to hold Smith down, but he had far too much alcohol in his system to put up much of a fight. Smith kicked his legs around; Kathleen could see him becoming annoyed at how easily she could hold him. He shouted, "Get off me!" And she slapped him.

"You listen to me, Smith! I'm sorry for going through your things. But I think it's time I knew the truth." She pointed a finger in his face. Smith continued to try to break free, but he finally gave up and just let her sit on him.

Smith stayed still, not saying anything at first. "Kathy, the general is not the man you think he is. I'm sorry when I say that neither is your father. They are poor rulers, and they are hurting people. A peasant could get arrested for sticking his tongue out at them, while a man with money in his pockets could kill someone and pay your father or John off to stay out of prison. John shot my father when all he was trying to do was protect my mother from him. John set fire to a blacksmith's shop with my sisters inside—and it killed them. And my mother? I don't know where she is or if she's even alive. John took her away from me." He was no longer on his back. Kathleen had let him go, and they were sitting next to each other. His eyes were like glass.

"I'm not sure who to believe right now, but I can assure you one thing: when I take the throne, things are going to change." Kathleen desperately wanted Smith to keep that hope that Sea had told her about so many nights ago.

Smith was leaning a bit, trying to keep his eyes open. "Kathy, could you call me Peter?"

"I will." Kathleen smiled.

"Kathleen, John wasn't trying to save you—" Smith tried to tell her, but she wouldn't listen.

"Get some rest," she interrupted. "We have a long day ahead of us." Kathleen lay down on the other bed. She had pleasant dreams that night.

Ch 9

Smith and Kathleen were getting closer to her home, deep in the woods east of the palace. "We can get there in another day, Kathy. You're almost home. We'll probably be there by tomorrow if we hurry."

Kathleen clapped her hands together. "I can't wait to see Ricky again, and Mama and Papa." She skipped ahead of him but stopped. "Something wrong?" She turned to see that Smith had stopped walking; she came over to him.

He whispered to her, "We're being followed." Smith could see the terrified look on Kathleen's face when she spotted the five boys hiding amongst the trees. "Bandits," he whispered. "From Skull Island."

The boys came out of hiding, knowing that they had been spotted. The leader of the group was a fat boy who was looking at Kathleen. "Wench, what are you doing running around with a dog like Smith?" The boy was about a year or two younger than Smith, but he definitely did not look it. He was tall and husky, with broad shoulders and a devious look about him. At his side, he a held a stick that he had found on the ground.

"Bilge," Kathleen argued. "Smith's a fine man."

He looked her up and down; she was covered in mud and wore ugly servant's clothes. "Well, you, ma'am, are no lady."

"Leave her alone, Tom," Smith said.

"What's the matter, Smith? Don't want to fight without your little girlfriend to back you up, eh? We heard about Sea and the rest of your crew. You don't have anywhere to run now, Smith." Tom swung the stick at Smith, knocking the air out of him. Smith hurried to get to his feet as the others surrounded him.

Kathleen picked a rock up off the ground and bashed the smallest of the young men in the back of his head, knocking him down. Two of them turned on her. Tom now had Smith pinned to the ground, while another boy kicked him in his side. Tom left Smith and went over to where two of the boys were attempting to get hold of Kathleen. When the boys grabbed her, Tom planted a kiss right on Kathleen, and she started kicking at him. Smith yanked away from the boy holding him down and ran up to Tom. He punched Tom, giving him a bloody nose.

Smith and Kathleen took off running, the boys chasing after them. They came to a ditch that Smith and Kathleen could easily jump across, but when Tom's gang reached it, they gave up and turned around. "They're all so fat; I didn't think they'd be able to make that jump."

"You saved me, Peter. Thank you."

Smith nudged her. "What about you? Who would have known the princess could put up a fight?"

She stuck out her tongue in disgust and said, "That brute Tom put his tongue in my mouth."

"*Nice.*" Smith laughed at her, and they continued on their way, taking a slightly different route to avoid Tom and his gang.

"Where are we going?" Kathleen asked him.

"I want to check on Mrs. Keg while we're so close to town," Smith said. "She lives a few miles south of here."

"Mrs. Keg?"

"She's like our mother," Smith said. "She kept us alive. Her husband died a few years ago; he'd helped raise us. If you don't mind, Kathleen, I just want her to know I'm okay. I'm sure she's heard about … what happened."

They walked mostly in silence for an hour or two before arriving at a small village. Not far from where the Black Dragons' hideout was, Smith pointed at a small house on the corner. He seemed nervous to Kathleen. "You won't tell your papa or anyone about her, will you? I don't want to get her in trouble. She's been a very sad and secluded woman ever since her husband died."

"No, of course not. She hasn't done anything wrong," Kathleen said. She looked at the small house as they entered the little yard. *I'm curious to meet the woman who raised the Black Dragons.*

A small vegetable garden was next to the path that led up to the front door. There was a tree in the yard, and underneath the tree was a grave, which Smith headed over to immediately, Kathleen following. He simply stood there, staring down at the small grave. "It's Mr. Keg," Smith finally said to her.

Kathleen touched his shoulder. "I'm sorry," she said.

"You know, he's the real reason Sea stepped down as captain," Smith said to her.

"What do you mean?"

"He came with us on a pillage when we were about fourteen," he replied. "He was shot by one of John's men, and Sea blamed herself. He was like a father to us. She stepped down as captain, afraid she'd make the same mistake again. I became captain, and she became my first mate. I never was as good as a captain as she was."

"I really am sorry, Smith," she said, and he turned away from her.

"Follow me." He walked up to the front door.

As they passed the vegetable garden, Kathleen couldn't help but notice how poorly tended it was. She gazed down at the dying vegetables. *It's dry ... like it hasn't been watered in days,* she thought. *It doesn't look like Mrs. Keg has been taking care of her garden.*

Kathleen heard Smith cry out, and she turned to see him rushing into the house. "Smith? What's wrong?" She hurried after him. Kathleen swung open the front door to see Smith crouching down next to an unconscious woman. "What happened? Is she okay?"

"She needs a doctor," Smith said calmly, and then he lifted her up into his arms and carried her to the back of the small house and into a bedroom. Kathleen followed.

"Peter?" she heard the woman cry when Smith laid her down in the bed. "You're here?"

"Mrs. Keg, what happened?" Smith covered her with blankets and did whatever else he could to make her comfortable.

Kathleen stood behind Smith, a concerned look on her face. "Is she okay?" Kathleen asked.

"Courtney ...," the woman said, reaching her hand out to Kathleen.

"I'm not Courtney," Kathleen said quickly.

"Can you watch her?" Smith stood, already heading for the door.

"What? Where are you going?" Kathleen started after him.

He abruptly turned, stopping her in the doorway.

"I'm fetching a doctor. You stay here!" He shoved her back into the room. "Don't you dare leave her side until I get back! Please, Kathleen, stay here with her."

Kathleen watched him leave.

"Courtney?" The sickly woman was trying to sit up.

He's so worried about her, Kathleen thought, turning to face Mrs. Keg. She came and sat next to her, encouraging her to sit. Kathleen stayed with her and waited patiently for Smith to return.

***

Kathleen breathed a sigh of relief when Smith returned. Following close behind him was a young doctor, Dr. Conal, a well-known doctor in Kirkston. "My word!" he cried when he saw Kathleen. "Peter, you weren't jesting with me!"

"Scott, please." Smith turned him from Kathleen so he faced Mrs. Keg. "You can help her, can't you?"

"You and Kathleen go on out and wait in the kitchen." Dr. Conal rushed them out of the room.

Kathleen sat with Smith in the little kitchen. She watched him tap his fingers nervously on the table and gaze down at his feet. Kathleen was in awe at the situation. *Dr. Conal,* she thought, *has been at the palace before. He's my doctor, Papa's doctor … and he's a friend of the Black Dragons?* Kathleen glanced back and forth from Smith to the bedroom door. They waited for Dr. Conal to come out of the room, and when he did, Smith jumped up quickly and hurried over to him. Kathleen watched them speak softly for a moment, and Dr. Conal gently placed a hand on Smith's shoulder. *They look scared,* Kathleen thought. Smith hurried back into the bedroom, shutting the door behind him and leaving Kathleen alone in the room with Dr. Conal.

"I thought only peasants befriended Black Dragons. You're my family's doctor. How many times have you helped them? Have you given them private information? Were you their little spy, Scott?"

"How dare you doubt my loyalty?" Dr. Conal approached her. "I've been working for you father since you and your brother were born!"

"If you are so loyal, then why would you help my father's enemies?" Kathleen asked.

"They were children when I met them, Your Majesty." He sat down beside her. "Tell me, if a little girl came knocking on your door in the middle of the night, crying because she feared her friend had caught the fever, and no one else would help them, would you turn her away?"

Kathleen smiled at him. "No, sir. I don't believe I would. I'm just finding it hard to believe you would work so closely with my father and befriend someone who defies us. Do you hate my family?"

"No! Oh no," Dr. Conal said. "Your father is a good king, but even the smartest and wisest of men can be deceived and have his judgment altered because of another man's cruel tricks."

"You're talking about John, aren't you?" she asked.

Dr. Conal looked her in the eye and said, "I mean no disrespect. But I've always had my doubts about him."

Kathleen looked away. "The woman, Mrs. Keg, what's got her?"

"I don't know, Kathleen. It could be anything. There are no signs of any sickness that I know of, but I can see that she is dying. It's in her eyes. I think the news about the Black Dragons broke her heart. Courtney and those boys were all she had left to live for."

It wasn't long before Smith came out of the bedroom. His arms were swinging loosely at his sides, his head down, and his face was full of sorrow. His throat sounded dry and scratchy when he said, "She's passed." Then he leaned against the doorway, still looking down to avoid meeting either of their eyes.

It's not fair, Kathleen thought. *He's already lost so much.* Kathleen gazed out the window as Dr. Conal rose from his seat and headed over to Smith. As Kathleen stared out the window, she started to hear shouting, and then she saw John and several of his men heading down the road in their direction. For a moment, Kathleen smiled—*John's here! He'll take me home!*—but then she turned to look at Smith. *They'll kill him ...*

"Smith!" she cried. "John ... he's coming down the road!"

***

They ran quickly through the trees. Branches hit her face, and briars cut her legs. Even Smith was having a hard time running through the thick trees. Someone had spotted them as they were leaving the house. Kathleen thought about how much it hurt Smith to leave Mrs. Keg's body behind, and it saddened her.

"Stop! Stop now!" Voices were carrying all around them.

Suddenly, a man appeared before them, and as Smith and Kathleen turned to run the other way, several more soldiers appeared around them. John was there with them, clutching his musket in hands. "On the ground, Smith!" he shouted, and when Smith did not move, John thrust his musket into Smith's chest. Kathleen gasped when she saw Smith fall over. "Chain him up!" John ordered, and he turned to Kathleen. He smiled at her. "Thank goodness," he said, embracing her.

"John!" Kathleen pulled away and looked down at Smith. "Don't hurt him!"

John turned to one of the soldiers. "Ride ahead to Caldara and tell King Harold that his daughter is coming home, and that Smith has been captured."

"Aye, sir," the soldier said, and left them.

"Let go of me!" Smith cried, attempting to stand.

"What's this?" John spotted Smith's sword in his belt and reached for it.

"Stop!" Smith shouted, when John took the sword and sheath away. "That was a gift from my father! Give it here! Don't touch it!"

John looked at him with annoyance, his anger toward him growing. Kathleen quickly jumped between them. "John, might I have the sword? And his pack?"

He nodded. "Give the princess his pack," John said, and a man picked the pack up from where Smith had fallen. "Now come with me, my dear. I'm taking you home."

Kathleen smiled happily as John led her to their horses. She glanced back at Smith, and her heart ached to watch him struggle in the soldier's arms. They chained Smith's wrists together and forced him to walk. Kathleen sat on a horse with John, and they began their two-day journey home.

***

Smith was forced to walk the entire way, and there was little hope of escape. There were simply too many men watching his every move. Even so, he still attempted to a few times, none of which ended well. He once managed to untie himself, but he was jumped immediately and beaten. They didn't stop for the night.

Kathleen slept leaning back against John through most of the night.

The general, his men, Princess Kathleen, and even the horses ate without Smith the next morning. He just watched. By the second morning, he was tired, hungry, and thirsty. Luckily, they were close to the palace. Even so, it was midday and the sun was high when Smith's legs finally gave in.

He fell forward on his knees, and the general ordered his men to stop. As Kathleen turned to see why John had dismounted the horse, she got a glimpse of just how cruel he could be. The general had hit Smith and ordered him to stand and press on.

"General! He's hardly eaten a thing in days and you expect him to walk? Give him some water and fruit," Kathleen demanded.

Reluctantly, John gave in to Kathleen's demands and gave Smith an apple and some water. It was enough for Smith to continue. By nightfall, they had reached the palace walls. John dragged Smith inside, holding him by the hair on the back of his head. Kathleen held on to Smith's sword and the little brown pack, hoping she would be able to return it to him one day soon.

"Kathleen!" On his crutches, Richard was the first to greet her. He hugged and kissed her but did not pass up a chance to swear at Smith for a moment. Queen Rachel was there as well, hugging and kissing her daughter.

Before Smith knew what was happening, Kathleen had been directed into another room, and Smith was being marched into the king's courtroom by John and some of his men. King Harold sat on his throne and ignored all of Smith's pleas. "He's lying! He's lying!" Smith cried to the king. "He tried to kill your daughter!" Smith pointed a finger at John. He gazed desperately up at Harold. "He was going to kill Richard!"

"I will hear no more of your lies, pirate!" King Harold shouted at him. "Your crew deserved their fate, and you will be joining them soon." The king stood. "I sentence your hanging for one week from tomorrow."

"Please listen to me!" Smith begged.

"John, take him to the prison chambers and have him whipped. I don't want to see his face for another week." The king came down from his throne. "I want to see my daughter now. Take him away."

"Listen to me!" Smith screamed. "John knew Kathleen was on the ship!"

John struck Smith and took hold of him. "Let's go, Smith." And he dragged him out of the room and down a long hallway, where they went into another room, which had a long staircase. They went down another hallway and stopped at a large door, two guards standing on either side of it. When they entered the prison chambers, an alarming stench took Smith aback for a moment. It was a large room, dark and cold. Along the right wall were individual chambers with iron bars for doors, where the more dangerous prisoners were kept. Some prisoners were chained up to walls, and others were permitted to roam around freely in the giant room.

When the prisoners looked to see who their new guest would be, a murmur went out over the crowd. Even the prisoners had heard, from guards and a few servants, that the Black Dragons had been killed—and that Captain Smith was still alive and running around with the princess. They all recognized the red and black uniform.

The prisoners watched John march Smith to the back of the room to a large door, the torture chamber. John hated Smith more than any other human being, and whatever went on in that room would be John's revenge. It would be revenge for all the public humiliation of not being able to capture a group of children. As soon as the door closed, the prisoners began speaking.

"That was Smith, Captain Smith?" a tall man sitting in a corner far away from the torture room asked the people around him.

"This is awful," one of the women said. "He doesn't deserve to be punished; he's an honorable man. How did this happen?"

A boy no older than Smith addressed the crowd. "A guard told me what happened. John attacked the *Black Dragon*; he shot down Sea and tied the others to the mast. I heard he used gunpowder to blow up the ship."

"The Black Dragons are gone, then?" a saddened voice asked.

"Aye," the boy said.

"But they're just a bunch of kids." A man sitting near the boy sounded horrified. "They were just children. How could Harold let him kill them all?"

Cries ran out from the other side of the door. Smith was pleading with the general to stop harming him.

The tall man stood and screamed, "Stop it, John, please! He's just a boy!"

The whip snapped each time it hit Smith, and each snap was followed by a small cry. The whipping stopped, and there was the sound of the two men tussling around. Then came what sounded like punches and moans. They were in the chamber for a long time. Finally, the door opened, and the prisoners in the cells stuck out their heads to see what the general had done.

Smith had experienced far more than a whipping. The general's knuckles were bloody. Already a black eye was forming on Smith, and his right cheek was swollen. Smith had been stripped down to nothing more than his ripped pants, with no shirt, boots, gloves, bandana, or anything else he had been wearing before the lashing, so he was shivering. It was frightfully cold in the prison cell. Smith was practically lying on the cold ground, holding on to the general's pant leg.

"Let go," the general ordered, kicking him. "Stand up, boy." Smith struggled; he tried and failed even to get to his knees. The general yanked him by both of his arms and pulled him to his feet. After dragging him across the room, John threw him onto a pile of hay that the prisoners used as beds. The general then cuffed Smith's left arm to the wall with a long chain. John knew the prisoners were staring at them; he could see every one of their horrified faces. "Let this be a lesson to all of you," he said, leaving them all in shock.

***

When the doors closed, the prisoners who were not chained up or inside the jail cells all surrounded Smith. "Is he all right?" someone asked.

One woman pushed back the crowd and knelt by his side. "Someone get some water." She tore off a piece of her filthy dress to use as a rag. The tall man brought a bowl of water that was left from what he had been given to drink that day. The woman cleaned Smith's face, and the tall man helped turn him on his side so she could clean his back. Smith was only half-awake, mumbling on and on, and he was not even sure what he was saying. He couldn't even remember where he was. The woman helped him drink some of her water, while the tall man asked her, "You sometimes act as a servant here, don't you? Have you heard of his fate?"

"No, I have not." The woman continued helping him drink. A younger girl started rubbing Smith's feet; they were trying anything to keep him more comfortable. The tall man went around the chambers to see if anyone had water left. The woman touched his swollen face. Smith felt the gentle hands touch his sore cheek, and he started to open his eyes. "Don't worry, Smith. You're safe for now. The general is gone." The woman ran her fingers through his hair and smiled down at him.

Smith gently rubbed his eyes and studied the woman carefully. *I must be seeing things.* He touched her hand. *No, I must be dreaming … or I have surely gone mad.* "Mama?" Smith attempted to sit up, but he could not. "Mama!" He reached his arms out to her.

The woman pulled her hand away. "Excuse me?"

"It's me, it's me, Peter!" Smith took the woman's hand again. "Look at me. Don't you see?"

The woman shook her head. "I don't have any children. I'm sorry, Smith, but I'm not your mother."

"You're her ... I know you're her!" Smith shouted, "Your name's Ellen Barons, and you had a husband and three children! Your husband was William; your daughters were Elizabeth and Anna; and me, your son, I'm Peter. You lived by the river and the big oak tree. You could knit—you knitted me a quilt for my twelfth birthday."

"This is a cruel jest!" she shouted at him. "My son died five years ago. He went over the falls. My son would never go on the account."

The tall man who had been with them most of the time said, "Look at him, Ellen. Do you truly believe this is a jest?"

Ellen stared at him, carefully studying his face. His eyes seemed to make her realize that this truly was her son. "Peter, my baby boy? How can this be?" She helped him sit up, and she cradled him. "I thought you were gone. I thought I'd never see you again." She was in tears.

"I thought the general had killed you," Smith said, while allowing a few tears to escape him.

"I thought you drowned." His mother stroked his hair and wrapped one of her arms around his waist. "I should have known it was you. That is your father's face." She kissed his cheek. Smith hadn't been this happy in a long time. For so long, he'd thought he had lost everything, but here was his mother, sitting right next to him. "I can't believe you went on the account," she said.

"I help people, Mama," he swore to her.

"I know, I know. I know what the Black Dragons do. I am so proud of you." She kissed his cheek again.

I can just picture home. I'll get a job, I'll make money, and I can take care of my mom. Everything will go back to the way it was before the Black Dragons, even if there is no Papa or my sisters. Smith sighed, knowing he was setting himself up for disappointment. *Escape? I'm far too weak even to sit up on my own. A pardon from Harold? Not likely. No, my mother is here with me ... This cannot be the end ... I can't die, not now ...*

Ch 10

A funeral was taking place deep in the woods of Kirkston by the big oak tree. It was the fourth grave to be added. "Good-bye, Sea." Snake looked down at his feet while Ace shoveled the last bit of dirt over the new grave. *Ace was right when he said Smith would want to bury Sea here*, Snake thought. *She's with Smith's family now.*

Ace held on to the bangle that Sea had given him right before she died. She had said, "Give this to Peter."

Snake was reliving the horrid memory in his head. The general had sailed away, and Smith had disappeared in the flames. They knew he was trying to save Kathleen. Sea was dying. *She was dying, and she still tried to help us*, Snake thought. She dragged herself over to them and quickly started cutting the rope that held them to the mast. They had rushed to the cockboats, but someone had filled them with holes. Ace carried Sea; he had taken charge. He ordered everyone to jump. They had held on to wooden pieces of the ship after the explosion to keep themselves afloat. They did not see land for a while, and they were all scared. Ace kept them going. They had to swim a long distance, and Snake wasn't the best swimmer of the group. His head went under, he was cramping, and his legs were too tired to work much longer. *Mouth grabbed on to me*, Snake recalled. *He put his arms around* *me and held on to a board. I could have died. p^*They reached land, and Ace was holding Sea close to him, cradling her. *He wouldn't say it,* Snake thought, *but he knew she was going to die.* Ace had held her so she could have her feet in the water, knowing it would calm her. She took off her bangle and handed it to him, telling him to give it to Peter. Ace and Snake had both kissed her before she finally passed.

After she died, the group was unable to find Smith or Kathleen, and they were mourning over the death of their two fearless leaders. In their place, Ace and Snake were starting to take up the task of groups leaders. It was during their journey from the crash sight to the big oak tree that they had heard Smith and Kathleen were spotted, and they were overjoyed. Unfortunately, they also heard that Smith had been captured. Everyone thought the Black Dragons were dead, and they were trying to keep it that way.

Blade looked up at Snake to see him crying. "Hey, you okay?"

Snake walked off a short distance from the group, wiping away tears. Mouth started to come over, but Ace stopped him and approached Snake himself, putting his hand on his shoulder. "I know you and Sea were close, Snake. You've known her longer than any of us have. I miss her too, but unless we want to lose Smith too, we're going to have to get our heads straight. I promise you I'll do everything it takes to save Smith. We're going to save him."

"How?"

"I have a plan."

"What do you expect to do? We can't just walk up to the palace. Even if they think we're dead, they'll still be expecting a rescue attempt by some members of the poor class." Snake came and sat down by the grave; he was no longer crying. His friends stood around, hopelessly lost in their own thoughts. Ace sat down beside him.

"I know someone who knows the palace inside and out, every hallway, room, and secret passage." Ace smiled, and they all waited for an explanation.

Mouth impatiently questioned, "Who?"

"Me," Ace said.

"What are you talking about?" Cannonball was the first to ask.

"I think it's time to tell the truth, the truth about me." Ace stood and stepped away from the graves, his voice sounding nervous. "I think it's time you all know who I really am." All of them were quiet. They were leaning in, eager to hear the truth from Ace. "My real name is Prince James Lincoln Caldara, King Harold's firstborn son ... and heir to the throne of Kirkston."

They all were stunned silent. Even Mouth was not speaking. Some of them exchanged glances with each other, and suddenly Ace became frightened. *Will they try to turn me in to Harold in exchange for Smith? They are not close to me the way they are with Smith.* It was silent for a bit longer, and then a quiet voice spoke up. Squirt stepped forward and said, "Ace, why have you lied to us for so long?"

Ace sat down on a large stone by a tree. He put his arms out. "Come here, little one." And Squirt came over to him. Ace picked him up and put him on his lap, hugging Squirt to comfort himself. "I was afraid of you, all of you. I was the king's son. I always had a fear of you doing to me exactly what we did to Kathleen."

"But, Ace, it was your idea to kidnap Kathleen," Squirt pointed out, and Ace stroked the little boy's hair.

"I wanted to see my baby sister. I wanted to tell her the truth—her and Richard. I couldn't get to Richard without all of you suspecting something, so I suggested Kathleen. Her marriage to John was coming up, and we wanted John out of the picture. It was a moment I had been waiting for. I was talking to her when John attacked us; I was going to tell her the truth. I didn't stay long enough to, and I was afraid she would hate me for leaving."

"She won't hate you," Squirt said. "I wouldn't hate Mouth." Mouth smiled at his brother.

"Ace, everyone thinks their prince is dead. Why didn't you go back?" Snake asked. "You could have had everything. Instead you stay here with us? Why, my friend?"

"Even when I was young, I knew Kirkston was being ruled harshly, and I was afraid I'd turn out to be just like my father. John was the only one to notice my feelings toward the crown, and he took advantage of it. He and I went riding in the woods by the river. He was going to help me run away, knowing that he would marry my sister and receive the crown. I had no idea that he had decided the plan was too risky to keep me around." Ace could still remember John backing him into a tree with a dagger. "John had planned to kill me, but when the opportunity came, John could not follow through, and he spared me my life."

"John spared you? But why?" Knot asked. "He's never been the sympathetic type."

"I don't know why. I've often pondered it. I was weak in both mind and body when I was young. I suppose John could not bring himself to kill such a ... *pathetic* child. After deciding to let me live, he stripped me of most of my clothes and used his dagger to cut a gash in my leg. John smeared my blood on my clothes and tossed them to the side. He said, 'Don't worry, your papa won't go looking for you,' and then he said, 'Run, boy. Run until your legs are sore because now you're free,' and boy, did I run. I really felt free. For the first time in my life, I was free! I lived on the streets on my own until I found all of you. You were fighting for what I believe in. I didn't want you to know who I was because I was afraid." Ace hugged Squirt tight.

"Afraid?" Snake asked. "Of what?"

"Of all of you. You hated my father, and I was afraid you all might hurt me, or worse, when you found out. Or use me against my father." Ace would not meet any of their eyes. "I wouldn't risk having to go back to Caldara."

"All right, Prince James, it looks like you have a decision," Snake said. "You can go home and live a life of luxury, or you can stay here with us and help us take John down."

Ace laughed. "Trust me, I'd much rather stay here with my *real* family."

Snake stood by Ace. "All right, then, what's the plan?"

***

Kathleen was sitting up in her bed, her nose in Smith's journal. Her eyes were opened wide in surprise. It said that John knew she was on the ship when he sunk it, and that he planned to kill Richard in order to become first in line for the throne. A noise from the hall frightened her, and she quickly shoved Smith's things under her bed. "Kathleen, my dear? It's me, John," the general said, striding into the room.

"John, please tell me you will let Smith go," Kathleen begged him. "He saved my life … twice. He was so kind to me."

"Kathleen, I'm so sorry. Your father determined his punishment; in less than a week, he will be hanged." The general frowned.

"Can't you do something?" she pleaded. "Papa always listens to you."

"I've already tried; its official. He will be dead soon." The general turned to leave.

"*You're lying!*" she screamed, standing up.

"Kathleen, watch your tone," the general said in a shocked voice.

"You knew I was on that ship when you sank it; you were going to kill Richard!" Kathleen screamed. "I will never marry you, and I will have you banished!" She began to walk past him out of her room, but he grabbed her arm.

"Kathleen, I would never harm you." His look seemed innocent.

"Bilge! You think I'm a fool." She slapped him. "I'll have you cleaning the stables by tomorrow!"

"Smith has poisoned your mind. Why would I want to harm you or Richard? Please, Kathleen, you must understand that I would never hurt you. I've treated you with nothing but kindness since you were a little girl. Then Smith comes along and lies to you!" He was visibly flustered. "I love you." He took her in his arms and kissed her. It seemed so sincere. She had missed him, but there was so much doubt in her mind now. John had always been so kind and warmhearted toward her. *Is that all a charade?* she wondered. *Is Smith or John being truthful with me? Did John know I was on that ship?*

"John? Kathleen?" King Harold was in the doorway, a smile on his face. "My, my, you two sure are happy to see each other again. John, if you would come with me ..."

"Of course, sir." John's cheeks were red. "I will see you tomorrow, Kathleen." He kissed her cheek. They left Kathleen behind. She began pacing. She left her room and brought a blanket with her to the kitchen, under which she hid two loaves of breads and a canteen. Then she headed off to the prison chambers, where two guards were surprised to see her.

"Open the doors; I wish to speak with a prisoner," she ordered them.

"Yes, Your Highness, of course." One of the guards let her inside the prison chambers.

"Stay here," Kathleen said. "Do not come in with me."

"But, Lady Kathleen, there are dangerous criminals in here," the second guard warned her.

"Stand by the door and watch me, then. I want to have a private conversation." Kathleen went inside. Most of the prisoners were sleeping, and the others did not notice when she came inside. A tall man stood up and made it known. "Princess Kathleen! What are you doing here?" He politely bowed to her.

"Tell me, who here is in need of food?" she asked.

"Definitely Smith and his mother; the general brought us our food, and he refused Smith any," the tall man said. "His mother has been splitting her food with him these past two days."

"Smith's mother?" She looked over to where the man was pointing and saw Smith and an older woman lying down beside him, sobbing. She was in shock, but she tried not to show it. She was there for a reason. "Very well," she said, pulling out one of the loaves of bread. "Give this loaf to those who need it. I'll give Smith and his mother this one." She handed him the loaf. She looked over to see Smith lying down in the hay. He was in a daze, and he didn't even notice when she came over. The woman next to him was crying.

"He just told her that he is to be hanged in five days." The tall man had followed Kathleen.

"Mrs. Barons?" Kathleen asked. She had never met her personally, so Kathleen wasn't sure if that was she.

"Kathleen?" Smith's mother sat up.

Kathleen came over and knelt by them, while the tall man went to give bread to those who desperately needed it. She broke the bread in half and gave a piece to Mrs. Barons, who ate it quickly. "Peter, are you all right?" Kathleen asked, and he slowly sat up.

"What are you doing here?" He looked so weak, as if he could barely keep himself upright. Mrs. Barons sat near him so he could lean on her. He looked sick and cold; he had dark circles under his eyes. Kathleen almost started crying when she saw her friend this way. It hurt her worse to know that someone she loved had done this to him.

"Here, I brought you food and water." Kathleen had to help him eat the bread and drink from his canteen. "You were right about John." There was sadness in her voice. "I won't let him get away with this. You're going to be okay, Smith." The doors opened, and a new visitor entered the room on crutches. "Richard, what are you doing here?" Kathleen turned back to

Smith for a moment, having Mrs. Barons help her wrap him in the blanket she had used to smuggle in the food. "Stay warm tonight, Peter," she whispered to him, and then she stood to confront her brother. Smith watched them quietly. "What's that you have there, Richard?" Kathleen asked.

He pulled out the newspaper that read BLACK DRAGONS:

THIEVES OR HEROES?

Kathleen stared at the newspaper. "What's all this about? I've never seen that before."

"Papa and John have been hiding things like this from us ever since we were young. They didn't want us to think as the Black Dragons as heroes. I want to hear Smith's side." Richard came over near Smith. "Smith, why did you join the Black Dragons?"

Smith looked up at Richard weakly. "You want to hear my side?" He sighed and said, "John killed my father and my sisters. He arrested my mother when she tried to protect me. I escaped with my life when I fell into the river. I went over the falls; the Black Dragons saved my life."

"You poor man," Richard said.

"Don't you see, Richard?" Kathleen touched her brother's shoulder. "If we let Smith get hanged, we are the real criminals, not him. The Black Dragons did not deserve their fate." Kathleen looked down at Smith. "We're going to save you, Smith. I promise."

They had to leave them. Richard headed to his room, and Kathleen went outside to gather her thoughts. She leaned against the stables, thinking to herself. *What can I do?* Inside the stables, she could hear servants—two young boys—whispering to each other.

"I saw them myself," the first boy whispered. "They're in the woods south of the main town; no doubt they're going to pull something to save Smith."

Kathleen leaned in quietly, listening.

"I don't think so. How could they survive something like that?" the other whispered.

"I don't know how, but they did," the first boy whispered again. "But they're alive, and they're coming. The Black Dragons will save Smith—I know they will. Kirkston can't survive without them."

Kathleen's eyes widened, and she started to run. Before she knew it, she was at Richard's bedroom door.

"Kathleen, what's wrong?" he asked.

"Richard, come with me. There may be a way we can save Smith after all!"

Ch 11

Prince Richard rode on the back of his sister's horse, his arms wrapped tightly around Abigail. "Kathleen, this is not a good idea. You don't know if they're alive or not. You said yourself that you heard it from two young *servants*."

Richard, Abigail, and Kathleen were not permitted outside the palace walls without guards by their sides. It was dark, and they knew they would be in trouble if they were caught.

"But they might be alive, Richard. If they are, then they may need our help." Kathleen was walking next to Richard and Abigail, holding on to her horse's reins. All three wore black robes over their clothes to hide their faces.

"We should go back," Abigail said to them.

"We can't just let Smith die," Richard said to her.

"Right," Kathleen said, agreeing with him. "Richard, which is the closest route through town?"

***

Snake was pacing. Several days had gone by, and they were still unsure of exactly how they planned to rescue Smith.

"I'm worried," Squirt said, sitting down in the dirt and staring at his boots. Mouth looked down, not wanting to meet his younger brother's eyes.

Squirt looked up at him with desperate eyes, waiting for his big brother to say, *It'll be okay, Jacob.* But Mouth wouldn't even look at him.

"Snake?" a voice said from behind the trees.

"Kathleen? What are you doing here?" Snake was the first to approach Kathleen and her entourage. Abigail climbed down from the horse. She and Kathleen helped Richard down, handing him the crutches Kathleen had been carrying.

"We want to help," Abigail said. "We know you must be planning some type of rescue."

"And who the bloody devil are you?" Mouth asked. "Go home before you hurt yourself, wench."

Abigail stomped on his foot and pushed him over backward. Unable to balance with her standing on his foot, he fell down. "My name's Abigail, you poxed pirate." Mouth stood, but she was not done insulting him. "You seem rather dim, even for a pirate."

"Belay that talk, you …" Mouth, surprisingly, seemed at a loss for words after her smirk and her beauty took him aback.

"Hush," Snake said to Mouth. He turned to Kathleen and the others. "Are you really here to help us?"

"Yes," Kathleen said. "Smith's hanging is nearing, so if you're planning a rescue, we're here to help."

Ace got a stick and immediately began drawing a map of the palace in the dirt so they could continue planning.

"How do you know what the inside of the palace looks like?" Kathleen asked him.

Ace placed small rocks in the drawing to resemble the guards. He looked up at Kathleen and Richard and lowered his head. "Before you leave, I need to speak with the two of you. There is … something important I need to tell you two."

Kathleen nodded and then glanced down at the map. "This is wrong. A year ago they tore down this wall and built a new hallway here." Kathleen changed the map a little and reassembled the rocks.

"All right," Ace said. "During big events, like a hanging, guards are well spread out. There are normally about four in the main entrance, and they can signal if anything goes wrong." He placed four rocks at the main doorway.

Kathleen pointed to the east side of the palace. "This is where the hanging is to take place. Father's expecting a large crowd for the hanging of the 'captain of the Black Dragons,' so it will probably spread out all the way here. More guards will be placed here and here for crowd control."

"I'm starting to realize how difficult this is going to be," Snake said. "Shouldn't we get him before the day of the hanging?"

"The door is made from pure steel, and they have guards all over that hall. Smith is chained to a wall. The best time for an escape is when they're moving him from the prison chambers to the site of the hanging, when they're in this main hallway here." Kathleen pointed.

"Won't they have guards in the hallway while they're moving him?" Mouth asked.

"No, just the guards who are moving him," Abigail corrected Mouth. "The guards normally in that hall will be moved outside to keep the crowd under control."

"Still, where can we sneak him to from here?" Ace thought for a moment and then snapped his fingers. "The old passageways!" He added them to the map.

"How do you know about those?" Kathleen asked. "Only the royal family knows about them. They're for emergencies only."

"I'll explain later, Kathleen." Ace added the tunnels to the drawing.

Kathleen suddenly glanced around the group. "Where's Sea?"

It was quiet for a moment. Ace pointed toward the river. "She's by the old oak tree."

Kathleen stood and hurried over. She saw the graves of Smith's family and read their names aloud: "Will Barons, Elizabeth Barons … Anna Barons." Then Kathleen looked at the fourth grave: "Courtney Livingston, 'Our Sea,' a Black Dragon and a Friend." She sighed heavily. She turned around and said, "John killed her, didn't he?"

"He shot her, right in front of Smith. She managed to save all of us; she saved our lives." Snake sounded mortified. "We don't want to lose Smith as well, Kathleen."

"I'm sorry, Snake." Kathleen put a hand on his shoulder. "We'll save him. I promise you."

***

The morning of the hanging, Smith was shivering. "She'll come for me. I know she will. She promised."

"No, boy, she's not coming," the tall man said. "Kathleen has better things to worry about than a mere peasant boy. She doesn't care. She's just like her father."

"No! She's not like Harold. She'll come. She'll save me." Smith was shaking; his mother was crying at his side. He leaned back. *If I weren't so weak,* he thought, *I could maybe escape …*

"I already lost you once. I can't lose you again, Peter," his mother cried against him. "And that girl lied to us. She's not coming."

"She's coming. She promised me." Smith wrapped the blanket tightly around him. Another hour or two passed, and Smith had lost faith in the heiress. The guards would be there soon to escort him to the hanging.

The doors opened, and light shined in at them. "Kathleen?" The tall man looked toward the doorway, and his face saddened.

Mrs. Barons wrapped her arms around Smith as the five guards approached them. "No! Get away from us!" she cried. One man yanked her away, and the others surrounded Smith. They unchained him from the wall and tied his hands together in front of him. They marched him out of the room. Smith turned to get one last look at his mother, but he could not see her. They closed the door before he got the chance.

As they marched, Smith decided to hold his head high. He wasn't going to let the rich, stubborn folks of Kirkston think he regretted anything he had ever done to oppose Harold, other than the one mistake that cost his friends their lives, or so he believed. Smith decided he would not show these people any fear—just pride and absolutely no regrets.

Ch 12

Richard casually made his way down the hall between the royal bedroom and the general's room. It was the morning of Smith's hanging. Around the corner, he could see Ace's dark figure waiting patiently. Like all the Black Dragons that morning, Ace was dressed in a black cloak so he would not be recognized. *My brother,* Richard thought. After Ace told Richard and Kathleen who he really was, Kathleen had been overjoyed, but Richard had merely stood there in disbelief. So many questions had been running through his head the past few days. As Richard passed him in the hall, he slipped Ace some keys and whispered, "Please, don't hurt them. They're family."

"Just make sure you get your father into the right guest room," Ace demanded.

Richard stopped and looked Ace in the eye. "James, before I go, I must ask you why ... why did you leave? I don't understand how you could choose to leave your life here and just run away the way you did. I don't understand."

"Then you will never understand me." Ace squeezed Richard's arm angrily. "I came to realize your father was nothing more than a wolf in sheep's clothing."

"He's your father too, James."

"He's dead to me," Ace exclaimed.

"Then *I* am dead to you."

Ace shoved him back. "Stick to the plan, you spoiled little prince."

Richard leaned on his crutches and asked, "James, will it be strange for you to be in the same room as him?"

"He's not my family anymore, Richard … and do *not* call me James." Ace sensed Richard's discomfort; he knew all Richard wanted was some answers and maybe to get to know his brother. Ace put a hand on Richard's shoulder. "We'll talk more once this is over, I promise. Now go—there's not much time left."

Ace watched Richard struggle to move down the hall with his crutches. Ace headed in the opposite direction, toward the general's bedroom. He put the key Richard had given him in the keyhole and hurried inside.

Ace saw the general sound asleep in his bed. Coming nearer, he could see his face. He placed his pistol against the general's forehead and shoved his hand over the man's mouth. "Hello, General." The general's eyes widened. "Surprised to see me? Get up and keep quiet, or I'll gun you down right here."

The general got out of bed, and Ace held the pistol at his back as they walked down the hall. Ace saw Richard speaking with his father down the hall.

"Hurry, Pa!" Richard said, pointing inside one of the guest rooms. "Mama's hurt," he lied, and his father rushed inside the room.

Harold ran into the guest room, and Ace heard him say, "Richard, son, there's no one in here." And Richard slammed the door shut, holding it closed from the outside. "Richard!" Harold shouted from the other side of the door. "Let me out of here! What's wrong with you? Open this door!"

John was acting nervous; Ace could hear his heavy breathing. "Keep quiet, John," Ace warned him, nudging him with the pistol.

"Aye," John said.

When the two of them approached Richard, the general whispered to him, "Richard, help me."

Instead, the general was visibly shocked to see Richard open the door for Ace. The two went inside, and Richard stayed out in the hall and closed the door.

"Sit down!" Ace ordered, and both the general and King Harold sat down in two chairs that Richard had already prepared for them. Ace tied them to the chairs, their hands behind their backs, with the rope Richard had hidden in the room just the day before.

"What is the meaning of this?" the general asked, and Ace held his pistol to the general's head. Ace kept them quiet, and Richard stood guard outside.

***

With Snake and Abigail at her side, Kathleen stood by a large painting of one of her old ancestors. Snake and Abigail had gunpowder in small bags soaked in various oils.

"Are you sure this will work?" Abigail asked Snake as the two of them left Kathleen standing alone.

"Don't worry. It'll work," Snake said, leading the way.

It wasn't long before they spotted their targets. Five guards surrounded Smith. They were heading down the hallways. Abigail stood in their way, and they stopped out of respect to the future princess. Suddenly, she tossed the little bags of gunpowder and oil, and Snake snuck up from behind and shot the bags with his pistol. They caught fire and the halls quickly filled with a dark and eerie smoke. The men gagged, and Abigail and Snake grabbed on to Smith. Each of them held one of his arms, dragging him up one hallway and down the next so quickly that Smith did not even seem to realize who had him.

One of the guards screamed, "Smith has escaped!" They looked around frantically, but by the time the smoke cleared, Smith was out of sight.

***

Smith had no idea what had happened. All he knew was that a woman and a man with a black cloak were dragging him off. He was weak and could not fight back.

Smith looked up when they stopped, and he saw Kathleen standing by them. She reached out for the painting she was standing by, and it opened out from the wall like a door. "Hurry up," she whispered, and the man in the black cloak dragged Smith inside the small room. The woman stayed outside with Kathleen and closed the door.

The room was extremely small; it was probably meant for only one person to hide out in. Smith couldn't have lain down without bending his legs. There was a rock on the far side of the room, and the ground was a sort of dirt and gravel that hurt to stand on with his bare feet. The room looked almost like a small cave.

Smith's back was to the wall, which was hard and cold against his skin. The hooded man pulled out a knife, and Smith closed his eyes and held his arms over his face, frozen with fear. "Please don't hurt me."

The man took his arm and held it still while he cut the ropes. He threw the knife down and hugged him. "Easy, Peter," the man said. "It's me."

Now Smith could see the man's face, and he was overwhelmed. "I thought you were dead. I thought for sure you died in the explosion or that you drowned."

Snake removed his cloak and put it around Smith to keep him warm. "No, we're alive, my friend." He smiled at Smith. "Get comfortable. We're going to be here a while."

"I don't believe it. You're all alive! Courtney ... I cannot wait to see my Sea. How bad was her bullet wound?" Smith wore such an excited smile, but Snake could not lie to him.

"She didn't make it, Smith." Snake wouldn't look him in the eye. "She's dead."

"She's gone?" Smith felt his whole body shake.

"Smith, I'm so sorry," Snake told him.

Smith felt pain throughout his entire body. He could suddenly feel every sore muscle, feel all his bruises, sense every lash on his back, and he was suddenly aware of his hunger and chills. All the pain he had experienced since arriving at the palace was taunting him. He fell forward, and Snake caught him, bringing him gently to the ground. Snake sat on his knees at Smith's side. Smith cried into Snake's shirt. He could feel Snake wrap his arms around him; he heard Snake say, "I'm sorry, I really am. I knew you two were close."

"I *loved* her." Smith felt Snake grow still when he said this. Snake was such a hateful person at times. He couldn't understand something like love. It took a moment for Smith to calm himself.

"The others? Is everyone okay?" Smith asked.

"Everyone's fine," Snake said. "Mate, mind if I ask you something?"

"Sure."

"How much do you know about where Ace came from? Did he ever tell you?" Snake asked him.

"He never told me much," Smith said. "Why?"

"He finally told us everything." Snake explained, and Smith's interest heightened. "He's Harold's son, James."

"Do you jest?" Smith asked. "No? You don't jest, do you? No wonder he hardly ever spoke." p^The door opened, and Kathleen tossed some things inside quickly, closing the door again. Smith smiled. It was his brown bag and his father's sword.

Snake recognized the bag. "What's in there, anyways?"

"The journal my sisters game me, and some ink. And the blanket my mama made for me." Smith said. "My mama … she's alive, Snake."

"What?"

"She was in prison." Smith smiled. "But she's alive."

Snake smiled at Smith. "I'm happy for you." Snake took Smith's bag and looked inside. "She put some boots and food in here for you two. Your pistol is in here too."

Smith laughed and put the boots on, and the two of them began eating the food. As they ate, Smith removed the cloak because it was getting warm.

Snake stared at the horrid scars. Smith's entire body was bruised. "The general really hurt you. He gave you more than a lashing, didn't he?"

Smith shivered at the memory of it. The general had yanked him from the prison chambers and into a big room; there was another man in there waiting for him. He was a guard. Smith was thrown to the ground, and the general made Smith remove his shirt, boots, and even his bandana. He made Smith stand with his hands on a table, his back facing the general. It started out as just a lashing, but it became much more than that. Smith tried to concentrate on other things, thinking the whipping would end eventually. John whipped him harder; he got violent. Smith could see his own blood on the floor, and he became dizzy. He gashed his teeth to keep from screaming, and tears drizzled down his cheeks and mixed with the blood on his hands.

Each time, the general whipped him harder. Finally, Smith let out a loud scream. The other man in the room looked up for a moment and smiled; the man obviously was not a fan of Smith's work.

Smith explained the entire thing to Snake. Just the memory of the things John had said frightened him.

"I'm sorry, Smith—" Snake started to offer comforting words, but before he could say much, the painting-door swung open. "Kathleen?" Snake looked up. "Are we safe to go?"

"We have a problem." Kathleen sounded scared. "It's Ace! Hurry!"

Ch 13

Ace sat quietly in front of the general and the king. He'd had no idea that the general had untied his hands and was just waiting for the right moment. "Everyone will be looking for you two soon enough," Ace told them and stood to stretch out his legs. As he was standing, John jumped at him. Ace was taken completely by surprise, and he dropped his pistol. John wrestled Ace onto his back and wrapped his hands around Ace's throat. Ace coughed and gagged, but the general refused to let go, even after Ace stopped fighting back. The king sat patiently, probably thinking John had just saved them.

Richard burst into the room with a pistol in his own hands. "Let go!" He aimed the gun at John, who let go of Ace's throat. "Get away from him or I'll kill you."

"Richard, put that gun away!" King Harold demanded.

"Don't talk!" Richard shouted. "John, sit ... now!"

John sat, and Richard tied him up all over again. Richard hurried over to Ace, putting his crutches at his side. He tapped his shoulder, whispering, "Wake up, Ace. Come on. Wake up, please."

"How dare you show sympathy for a pirate!" King Harold shouted at his son. "I'll beat you for this, boy! Get away from that pirate and untie us both."

A man in a black cloak poked his head in the door. "Ace!" the man cried. It was Knot.

"Knot, go get Kathleen and tell her that Ace has been hurt," Richard said, and Knot hurried off.

"Kathleen knows he's here too?" King Harold sounded furious.

Richard ignored him; he stayed next to Ace, trying to wake him. The king watched Richard, worry passing over his face. "Richard, please, tell us what's going on. We'll listen, son."

"Pa, this pirate is James," Richard said. "He's my brother; he's *your* son."

"You lie, Richard! My son?" Harold looked back at Ace. "It can't be. He died years ago. This is James? A pirate? He's alive?" King Harold's expression changed from doubtful to furious. He turned to face the general. "And you've killed him!"

"I didn't know, honest, sir!" John said in a panicked tone.

"James! James! Wake up!"

Richard shook him gently, but he didn't move. Kathleen, Abigail, Smith, and Snake all came rushing inside. "Ace? What happened to him?" Smith ran to his side and cradled him. He held his head up and checked to see if he was all right.

Ace gasped and held on to Smith, blinking his eyes and opening them slowly. "I thought I was going to die." He coughed and breathed heavily.

"You're all right now." Snake assured him. King Harold kept an eye on them. Smith and Snake had left the safety of their hiding spot as soon as they heard that Ace was hurt.

Smith helped Ace to his feet, but he stumbled a bit. "Easy." Smith stood at his side, holding on to his arms while he tried to regain some balance. "Two guards saw us on our way here. We have to go ... now."

"Warn the others," Snake said to Kathleen and Abigail, and the two of them hurried off. Ace put an arm over Snake's shoulder to keep himself upright.

As they started to leave, Harold cried out, "No, wait! James, don't leave."

Ace turned to look at Richard. "You told him?" He struck Richard down, despite his temporary weak state.

Richard looked up at Ace with disbelief, wiping off his bloody lip. "You little spoiled ... worthless cur!"

"Enough, Ace," Smith ordered, helping Richard up. "Finish this dispute later. We have to go." They hurried out, leaving John and Harold behind.

***

The Black Dragons had gone out a secret passageway Ace had told them about, and they were already far enough away from the palace so that no one at the hanging could see them. Kathleen, Abigail, and Richard were saying their good-byes. Kathleen hugged Smith, a little sad that this amazing adventure was ending. "I'll miss you!" she said.

"Same here." Smith laughed. "Thank you so much, Kathy."

"James, stay with us," Richard said to his brother. "Come back with us. Papa will welcome you with open arms. He will."

It was silent for a moment. Ace glared at him. "Don't call me James." He shoved by Richard. "If your father hurts our crew while trying to get to me, we'll know who to blame."

Richard looked away, humiliated. "I'm sorry. I shouldn't have told them."

"Let's go." Ace turned and headed off ahead of the others.

Abigail hugged everyone good-bye, with the exception of Mouth, who hadn't given her the best first impression. "Good luck, Dragons," she told them.

"Good luck to you three as well. You're going to be in a world of trouble for helping us. Thank you for risking so much." Smith smiled at the two girls and then at Richard, who was looking down the road at Ace. "He treats everyone like that; he's not as angry as he seems."

121

Richard shook his head. "He's in trouble now. Pa's going to come after him."

"I wouldn't doubt it," Smith said. "Don't worry. We'll be fine." He hugged his new friends good-bye.

***

The Black Dragons rushed south, not even bothering to go around town. They knew that either way, people would be looking for them by now. Figuring they should find a place to hide until the heat died down, they stumbled into a church, closing the door behind them because they heard footsteps. When they turned and saw that people were in the church, they jumped. There were not many, just the preacher and about nine or so other people. The other church members must have skipped service to go to Smith's hanging. Snake reached for his pistol, but Smith stopped him. "Not here, Snake. Not now."

"Would you like to come and join us?" the preacher asked them.

Nervously, the boys made their way to the front of the church. Squirt seemed more nervous than they were; he had never been to church, even when he was young. He sat with Mouth, clearly not wanting to be anywhere near these people.

Mouth asked them, "Why aren't you at the hanging?"

"I wouldn't want to miss a sermon to go watch a hero die," a woman said.

These people seem so calm having a crew of pirates sitting down with them, and at a church no less, Smith thought.

The preacher began to pray, and the Black Dragons sat down in the pews. Smith felt good about being in a church again. He hadn't been to church since his father died. After becoming a Black Dragon, public appearances were not welcomed. Moments later, they heard horses and voices from outside. "You children better get out of here," the preacher said. "Take the back door. We'll stall for you."

They ran out the back, where trees made good hiding places for them as they continued their way south. They crossed the street once they were far away from the church, heading into the woods. The farther south they traveled into the woods, the louder came the sound of rushing water where the river turned east. Smith smiled because he knew they were almost home.

***

Richard, Kathleen, and Abigail sat quietly, listening to the king shouting. They had been listening to it ever since they'd arrived back at the palace. In the room with them were a few guards, Queen Rachel (the queen was pacing back and forth; Harold had just told her about Ace and how he was her son), and John Stevenson.

Harold shouted, "Because of you three, a dangerous criminal is loose in my kingdom! How dare you help this pirate?"

Kathleen attempted to stand up for Smith. "Smith is more of a privateer."

"He's no hero," John argued.

"Do you have any idea how much they have done for Kirkston?" Kathleen asked.

"They're thieves." Harold turned to look at Richard for a moment. "You helped them tie the general and me up in one of the guest rooms. What were you thinking, Richard?"

Kathleen interrupted. "Papa, listen. Smith saved my life!"

"We'll work this out later." Harold paid no attention to Kathleen. "Right now, the Black Dragons are getting farther from our grasps, and if they get to a ship, we'll never catch them."

Queen Rachel stopped pacing and took her husband's hand. "What about James?"

Harold turned to John. "When you find them, have James brought back safe and unharmed."

"He'll try to run away again. He's not the little boy he once was," John reminded Harold.

"We'll put guards outside his room, locks on his doors, and bars on his windows; we won't allow him outside ever again if we have to," Harold said.

Richard stood. "He'll hate you if you do that to him! He wasn't born for the throne. Just leave him be. Let him stay with the Black Dragons. He's a pirate, not a prince."

"Sit," Harold ordered him in a stern voice. He did as his father ordered. "Follow me, John. We have some criminals to catch." Harold led everyone but Kathleen, Abigail, and Richard out of the room.

Richard stood back up. "We have to talk to Father before they catch up with the Black Dragons."

"About what?" Kathleen asked. "He won't listen to us."

"We'll make him listen! Tell him what you told me. Tell him how John knew you were on the ship when he sunk it, how he planned to kill me."

"He won't believe us," Kathleen said.

"We have to try. Do you want to marry a man like that? Well? Do you want them to kill Smith?" Richard shouted.

"He's right, Kathleen," Abigail said. "If John marries you, he'll become king. It'll destroy this country. You have to at least try to talk to your father."

Kathleen nodded. "All right," she said. "Come on."

As quickly as they could, the three young adults hurried to the stables in hopes of saving the Black Dragons. Richard saw his father standing by the gates. The general and his men were already riding off after Smith and the others.

"Now, Kathleen, you have to talk to him. Make him listen to you," Richard said.

Kathleen gazed over at the gate. Her father was getting up on his horse to lead a second search party. Before he had a chance to turn and leave, she screamed across the yard, "*Stop!*" Her voice screeched, quickly gaining her father's attention.

"Kathleen! Your tone!" he said, but she marched up to him in front of all the soldiers.

"You are going to listen to me!" she screamed up at him. Kathleen could sense her father's embarrassment at her behavior, but she did not back down even after he turned his back to her. "Listen to me, you foolish old man!" There was a shocked look on all the soldiers' faces. Servants from the stables and the gardens were now all looking up at Kathleen and Harold. Not since she was a small child had they seen her throw such a tantrum.

"How dare you behave like this?" King Harold spoke softly, as if hoping to quiet his daughter down. "We will talk later."

"No!" she screamed. "We're going to talk now! Dismount your horse!" She was crying now. "You don't ever listen to me! Listen to me now! Dismount your horse!"

Harold was infuriated. "I do not have time for games, Kathleen!" he yelled at her. "You know better than to act like this."

"Stop it," she said. "Stop talking down to me. Get off your horse and talk to me."

Harold reached down from his horse and pushed her back. "Go inside. We'll talk as soon as I get back, okay?"

"If you leave before you talk to me, I won't forgive you!" Kathleen felt like such a child. She had tears flowing down her cheeks and her fists balled up at her sides.

Harold clearly knew he could no longer control his daughter's fit. Everyone was looking at him with disapproving eyes. He looked his daughter in the eyes, where a terrible sadness was visible. Slowly, he climbed down from his horse. "All right," he said, looking at her with equally sad eyes. "Talk to me, Kathleen. Go on … I'm listening." Kathleen lunged at her father and wrapped her arms around him. Harold was plainly surprised. His cheeks were red from humiliation, but he still smiled down at her. His daughter had not hugged him like this in so long.

Kathleen inhaled deeply. Her father was looking directly at her. For the first time in her life, she knew she had his complete attention.

Ch 14

They were just north of the river. In order to get to their hideout, they would need to cross it and follow it east to the waterfall. Only then would they be safe. The Black Dragons were eager to get home. The past was behind them, so they thought, and they would not have to worry about John.

"We need to hurry!" Smith shouted at his crew. "John and his men could be right behind us." Soon after he said this, shouts started coming from the town. A riot was brewing. Smith urged his group on, knowing that by now someone had told John that they had seen them heading into the wood.

Smith stopped walking when he heard a noise behind them. "Keep quiet," Smith told his teammates, "but keep walking."

A gun went off, and they all shouted out in surprise. Seconds later, John and his men came bursting through the trees. Several of the soldiers ran straight for Ace. Smith drew his sword and hurried to help. "Leave him be!" Smith shouted. Once Ace managed to struggle free, Smith ordered, "Fall back!" He and his group barely escaped deeper into the woods, bullets flying past their heads. "Get out of range! Keep you heads down!"

"Don't shoot! You might hit James!" one of the soldiers shouted, and the shooting ended.

By the time the crew reached the river, they were overcome with exhaustion. "Keep moving!" Smith said, ordering them to swim across. The water was up to their necks, but they did not have time to find a more shallow area. Halfway across the river, Smith glanced back and saw that only John and four other soldiers had managed to follow them through the twists and turns of the thick wood.

"Stop!" John ordered. "Turn back!"

Smith chuckled to himself. Once they crossed the river, there was no chance John could catch up with them. Just as Smith began to feel free again, he heard a loud cry behind him.

"Tommy!" Squirt screamed for his brother.

Smith turned to see John standing by the riverside, clutching Squirt by his hair with one hand and holding a pistol in the other. "Turn back or I'll shoot him!" John shouted.

"You wouldn't!" Smith cried out, and John shot Squirt in his left arm.

Squirt fell to his knees in tears. John still held on to Squirt by his hair. Before hearing any orders from Smith, Mouth hurried back to them.

"Orders?" Cannonball asked.

"Do what you want; I won't decide your fate," Smith said to his crew. He headed back with Mouth. The boys looked at each other for a moment, nodded, and followed Smith back to where John was waiting patiently. John released Squirt, who, still in tears, ran up to Mouth and hid his face in his brother's chest.

"Guns, swords, knives … all of them on the ground," John ordered. They did as they were told. Without any hesitation, John shot off his gun, and they all jumped back in surprise. There was a scream. Smith turned his head to see Ace falling to the ground, clutching his chest. Yang and Blade both ran to Ace's side. John chuckled and turned to his four soldiers. "'Twas an accident, aye?"

"Aye, sir, an accident," one of the soldiers said, a bit of terror in his voice.

John turned back to the Black Dragons, looking down at Ace. "I should have killed you when you were a boy! Harold would so willingly offer his long-lost son the throne. You are no prince. You will not stand between me and my crown." He cocked his gun.

Smith lunged at John, knocking him to the ground and taking his pistol from him. The soldiers raised their guns at Smith, and Smith held the pistol pointed at John's head. "Tell them to put down their arms!"

"Lower your weapons," John said nervously to his men, and they obeyed. As soon as the gun's metal touched John's forehead, he began to shake. "Please ... no!" he begged.

"You give me one reason." Smith sounded furious. "Just one reason ... and I won't pull this trigger." Smith heard voices and glanced up to see King Harold on horseback, along with Kathleen, Richard, Abigail, and several more soldiers approaching. *Did they see John shoot Ace?* Smith wondered hopefully. He looked back at John, his anger growing.

"You killed off my family ..." He looked at his friends for a moment and then back at John. "You killed their families! You killed Snake's parents to take their place in government! You're a liar and a murderer! You don't deserve to live!"

John looked at Snake with shock apparent on his face. "Snake ... Johnny? You? You're Rob and Amy's son?" John shook his head. "The rumors were true, then? You did go on the account?" John stared at him for a moment. "You look just like them." Snake looked away.

Smith struck John with the back of the pistol. "Don't you talk to him, John! Leave him be!"

"Please don't kill me," John begged.

"You're a coward," Smith said.

"Put down the gun, Smith!" King Harold shouted at him as he and his soldiers approached the scene. "John, I'm placing you under arrest!"

"What?" John cried. "Sire ..." He looked at Kathleen. "The girl has poisoned your mind!"

"Speak not of my daughter!" Harold shouted. "Smith, drop that pistol—now! Do not shoot this man!"

Smith looked at the many soldiers behind Harold and then back down at John. *I cannot bring myself to kill,* he thought. *I am no John Stevenson.* "I'm no executioner," Smith said, lowering the gun.

"Toss it here," Harold ordered. The soldiers all had their muskets raised at Smith and the other Black Dragons. Smith clenched his fists and tossed the pistol at King Harold's feet, resentfully admitting defeat.

"You," Harold said, pointing at one of his soldiers, "check my son's wound." The soldier hurried over to Ace.

John rose to his feet and went over to Harold. "Oh, thank you, sire—"

Harold struck John across the face, and he fell at the king's feet. Smith almost laughed to see John on his knees, clutching his bloody nose before a man half his size. "I have spoken with my daughter of your plans, General. She charges you with the cruel plot to murder both her and Richard! Do you deny such charges?"

"The girl lies, sir! She lies!" John cried, still holding a hand over his broken nose.

"And now my son, James! Don't think I did not see you turn your pistol on him! If he dies, your neck will break for it!" Harold turned to the four soldiers who had arrived with John. "And it seems as though you four did little about that!" He turned back to his own men. "One of you chain this man and the Black Dragons as well. John, you can rot in prison with the Black Dragons for all I care. I'm stripping you of your title."

Smith saw John lunge for the pistol he had tossed at Harold's feet. John stood firm as he held the pistol at King Harold. A young soldier honorably threw himself between John and Harold, but John still managed to shoot Harold in his right shoulder. Before John had a chance to fire again, Smith jumped him from behind. During their struggle, John dropped the pistol, and the two of them got dangerously close to the riverside. John lost his footing, and because he had hold of Smith's sleeve, he ended up pulling Smith into the river on top of him. They hit the rocks.

There was a terrible cracking sound, followed by John's scream. John released Smith's shirt, and the current started to carry him away. Smith watched John struggle in the water; it was known that John was a good swimmer, so Smith knew something was wrong for him to be struggling so terribly. *I will not be responsible for the death of this man,* he thought. *No matter what I think of him, I am no murderer.* Smith grabbed John by the collar of his shirt.

"I can't carry you," Smith said, after John's weight dunked him under the water several times. John held on to Smith in his panic, and they both went under.

Smith could hear Kathleen screaming, "Papa! Papa! Do something! Help them!"

He heard Snake shout, "John's going to drown them both!" Then there was a loud splash. Smith's head went above the water for a moment, and he could see Snake swimming toward him. Two of Harold's men jumped in the water after him to help. In John's attempt to get his head above the water, he dragged Smith under again. Smith could no longer reach his feet to the bottom of the river; it was too deep. He opened his eyes and could see bloody water. John was severely injured. "Let go of him, you crazy bastard!" he heard Snake shout as he yanked him away from John.

Smith gasped for air when he finally got his head above the surface. Snake helped him out of the river. Smith looked back to see the two soldiers dragging John out of the river and throwing him to the ground. His right leg was clearly broken, the bone puncturing his skin. He was screaming in agonizing pain.

While the soldiers attempted to help him and chain his wrists, Harold approached Smith. His left hand was clutching his right shoulder, where he had been shot. "You jumped John to save me? Why?" Harold waited for an answer, but Smith merely looked down at his feet. "John could have killed me if you had given him the chance at a second shot." Harold smiled for a moment. "You saved my daughter's life as well, did you not?"

"Aye, sir," Smith said.

"How can I repay you?" Harold asked.

Smith smiled. "You could let us go."

Harold nodded. "I suppose I could do that." He looked at Ace.

"I'm not coming with you," Ace said to him. "I can't."

"Ace is not something to be bargained with," Smith said to Harold.

"Then all of you can go to prison—how's that?" Harold had a smirk on his face.

"All right … I'll go with you," Ace said.

Smith put a hand on Ace's shoulder. "No, Ace, you don't have to do this."

"I'll be fine, Smith." Ace then confronted Harold: "I'll go with you if you let my friends leave in peace."

"That makes me very happy, son. We have so much catching up to do. Smith, can I trust that your frequent pillages will end now?"

Smith chuckled. "No, sir. You'll get a break from us, though, for my ship is at the bottom of the ocean."

Harold shook his head in disbelief. "Even after all that has happened here today, you still insist on a life of piracy?"

"It's all I know, sir." Smith smiled at the king again. "Are you going to keep to your word and let us go free—aye or nay?"

"Aye," Harold said. "Go now and get out of my sight." Harold turned to his men, saying, "Throw the general up on a horse, and we'll take him back to Caldara." He looked down at John. "He'll be spending the night in the prison chambers, where he belongs." He turned to Ace. "It is time, son, that you learned to act as a prince. Take off that foolish bandana and mount one of the horses." Although he sounded cruel when he said this, Harold had a smile on his face. He had clearly missed his son a great deal.

"Ace—" Squirt reached out for him, but Ace ignored him, took the bandana off his head as his father had instructed, and mounted one of the horses.

"I'll be fine, guys," Ace swore.

"Go," Harold said. "Be gone with all of you!"

The Black Dragons departed from Harold's troops, finally heading home to their hideout beneath the waterfall.

***

Queen Rachel blissfully followed closely behind her husband on their way to the guest quarters on the west side of the palace. Her heart had never been merrier than it was that day. The pain of losing her son so many years ago had never truly gone away, but today her pain was finally drifting away from her. The moment word reached her that her son was here in Caldara, she had immediately demanded to see him.

Harold also had a grand smile on his face. When the two of them reached the guest bedroom, there were two guards outside. "Is the prince finished dressing for supper?" Harold asked the guards.

"He should be by now, sire," one of them replied.

Harold took his wife by the hand and led her inside. She passed him in the doorway, letting go of his hand and hurrying into the room. "James?" She looked around for him. "Son? Where are you?"

Harold also glanced around the room. "James!" he shouted, but there was no answer.

"Harry, look!" The queen pointed at the far side of the room, toward the glass doors. They were wide open. She could see that her son had tied sheets to the railing on the balcony. "He climbed down from the balcony!" She hurried over to see if her suspicions were true.

Harold was shouting at the guards who had been in charge of keeping an eye on the rebellious prince. Rachel ignored her husband's tantrum and just stood out on the balcony, looking out at the view with a saddened expression on her face. She took a breath and headed back inside from the balcony, closing the glass doors behind her.

"Don't worry, Rachel, we'll find him," Harold said when he saw the sad look on her face.

"I pray that you do." Rachel left the room, her heart heavy once again.

***

Kathleen, Richard, and Abigail led Mrs. Barons and Ace far from the palace walls. Once they reached the river on the west side of the palace, she stopped and put her feet in the water. She seemed to appreciate everything around her. She sat down by the river and put her hands in the grass. Her eyes were focused up on the clouds for a moment. She had not been outside since she had been arrested so many years ago. "Mrs. Barons, are you ready to go?" Richard asked after a moment of this.

"No," she said, getting to her feet. "There's one place I must go first. There're some old friends I need to see."

Ch 15

Smith tied up the end of Squirt's bandage a bit too tight, causing the child to grunt and make a face at him. "Are you all right, lad?" he asked him.

Squirt did not respond; he just buried his face in Mouth's chest. They were at the hideout south of the waterfall. Mouth sat on a log by the fire with Squirt in his lap. Smith was on his knees in front of them, doctoring Squirt's arm. "I want Tommy to tie it," Squirt told him. "You hurt."

Smith laughed at Squirt and picked him up, sitting down with him in his lap. Mouth gently retied the bandage around Squirt's arm. He had surprisingly gentle hands when it came to taking care of his younger brother. Smith stood, and Squirt climbed back into Mouth's lap.

Mouth looked up at Smith. "Smith, what are we going to do about Ace? He doesn't want to stay with his father."

"I'm not sure, Mouth, but we'll get him out of there, don't worry," Smith assured him.

Yang came over and tapped Smith's shoulder.

"What is it, Yang?"

"Look." He pointed behind them at the hillside path that led to their hideaway, and there stood Kathleen, Richard, Abigail, and Ace ... along with a guest. Smith saw that it was his mother, and he ran up to her. She cried quietly, overwhelmed by the whole ordeal.

Smith looked at Kathleen and said, "Thank you, thank you so much."

Kathleen smiled at him. "I couldn't let your mother stay in prison, could I? No one's coming after her, Smith. There are no records of her arrest, so she is safe from the law. John never filled out any papers."

Smith turned to Ace. "Are you all right?"

Ace smiled. "You really think I was going to stay at Caldara?" he laughed. "Of course not. Kathleen and the others helped me sneak out. It wasn't hard. Harold was convinced I wanted to be there. There definitely were not enough guards around to keep me there. Harold's a fool."

"You knew that you would escape, didn't you?" Smith asked with a smile. The others were running up to them by now, excited to see Ace.

"Yes, I did," Ace said. "Nothing could possibly keep me there."

Squirt had come up to them and wrapped his arms around Ace's legs. "Hey, Squirt," Ace greeted him.

"You scared me," Squirt said. "I thought I'd never see you again."

"I'm here to stay, Squirt. Don't worry." Ace put his hand on Squirt's head.

Smith turned to his mother. "Ma, you'll have to come and stay here with me, then, won't you?"

"Peter, I can't live on a ship." Mrs. Barons kissed her son's cheek. "I'm going to move back home."

"By yourself?" Smith shook his head. "No, no, absolutely not."

"I'm not going to be by myself, Peter," she argued. "Ron and Theresa are building a home next to ours; I went and visited them before coming here. It's been five years since I've seen them. They're looking forward to seeing you again."

"Ron *and* Theresa are moving in next door … together?" Smith asked in a confused voice.

"Yes, Peter." Mrs. Barons smiled. "They are to be married soon."

Smith smiled at that. "Good, good for them. But what of you?"

"Don't worry about me, Peter." Mrs. Barons kissed him on the head.

Squirt turned from Ace to Kathleen. "Hi, Kathleen," he said, his little cheeks red.

Kathleen laughed and gave the little boy a hug. Mouth was coming up behind them along with the others.

Squirt peered up at Mrs. Barons. "Are you Smith's mama?"

"He's so little." Mrs. Barons picked Squirt up and rested him on her hip. Smith introduced his mother to each of his friends, and she held Squirt on her hip the entire time.

"What are you three doing here?" Mouth asked Kathleen.

"They were dropping my mother off," Smith said. "And saving Ace. Be grateful."

"Not exactly, Peter," Kathleen said. "We actually have one other thing for you as well."

"What's that?" he asked.

Abigail stood up straight and proudly said, "*Me.*"

"You?"

"I want to join the crew," she said.

"No," Mouth answered, before Smith had a chance to respond.

Abigail shoved him. "And why not?"

"You wouldn't last a day on a ship," Mouth stated. Abigail leaned in and gave Mouth a kiss on the cheek, and he backed away suddenly. "What was that for?" he asked.

Mouth was then quiet. Abigail turned back around to Smith, a sly grin on her face. "Well, Smith?"

Smith was unsure of this. "Do you know anything about sailing?" he asked her.

"A little. My father was a sailor in his golden years. What I don't know, I can learn," Abigail explained.

Smith looked at Richard. "Are you not to marry her?"

Richard just smiled and said, "No. I told Father I didn't wish to marry Abigail, and that she feels the same. I didn't think he would listen, but he did."

Smith turned back to Abigail. "I'm not so sure ..."

"Come on," Abigail argued. "The only other things I have to go back to are my parents and my little brother, and they're all angry with me about Richard and me canceling the marriage."

"Well, I don't see any harm in it, Abigail," Smith finally said.

"Do I get a nickname?" she asked.

Smith laughed. "That's not really important. We weren't planning on all getting nicknames, Abby."

"I don't want to be the only Black Dragon without a nickname."

Smith laughed again. It seemed as though the ridiculous nicknames had become their true legacy.

"Why don't you just call her 'Spoiled' since she's been living all high and mighty in the palace?" Mouth had found his voice again. Abigail kissed his cheek again, and he turned bright red and began to stammer something unintelligible.

It seems as though Abigail has found the one thing that can silence him! Smith thought. "Welcome to the Black Dragons, Abigail."

"Smith, we don't know anything about this wench," Mouth said. "You're not going to let her on the crew, are you?"

"Yeah, he is, sweetie," Abigail strongly stated.p^"We have to go," Kathleen said. "Wish us luck, Abigail. We must go inform your parents that you have gone on the account." She took her brother's hand and led him up the hillside. He no longer walked with the crutches, but he still had a terrible limp.

Smith glimpsed over at Ace. "Are you going to say good-bye to them, or are you still too stubborn to speak with Richard? He didn't mean to cause trouble with Harold, Ace."

"But he still did." Ace looked away from Smith. "Smith, he's going to come after us now."

"So? We'll manage." Smith put a hand on Ace's shoulder and said, "We always do."

Ace shook Smith's hand away. "Richard made a very foolish mistake, Smith. How can I forgive him for this? He never should have told Harold who I was."

"He's your brother, Ace. He wants an older brother, can't you tell? Every time he looks at you, he seems sad. You left him. Look how happy Mouth makes Squirt; can't you do that for Richard? He thinks you hate him."

***

Ace let out a sigh and headed up the hillside after Kathleen and Richard. They waited for him.

"Is something wrong?" Kathleen asked.

"No, nothing's wrong." He reached out and hugged each of them. "Listen, back when I was young and I was planning on leaving, you two were the only things holding me back. I didn't want you two to grow up and not know me."

"We don't blame you for leaving, Ace," Kathleen said.

Ace turned to Richard. "I'm sorry, Richard. I've been cruel to you. I never gave you a chance." Richard didn't say anything, so Ace continued. "I've missed out on being your brother; we could have been close. There's no reason we can't be now."

Richard leaned his head on Ace's shoulder. "Thank you."

***

Ron and Theresa's wedding was beautiful. It wasn't much, but it still was nice. Sadly, Theresa's parents did not show up at the wedding. Apparently, they did not approve of the relationship. They had a wealthy man willing to take Theresa and bring them out of debt. Theresa was upset at first, but she was quickly over it once she saw Ron. I wound up giving Theresa away at the wedding, and I felt honored. I believe Mouth and Abigail got caught up in it; the two of them actually left holding hands. Squirt announced to everyone that Mouth had given her a golden bangle.

Meanwhile, John is awaiting his sentence in prison. Who knows what Harold will do to the general?

Smith was writing in his journal as the sun was rising. Smith always enjoyed watching sunrises and sunsets, but it was not as satisfying watching them alone as it was watching them with Sea. He looked down at the prow of the ship and smiled. He was by the wheel, and no one else was on the deck but him and the new couple. Abigail leaned out, looking out at the ocean, and Mouth had his hands all over her. It was calm. Smith had ordered them to reef sails, drop anchor, and take a break from all the chaos from the past few weeks. The new ship had been given the name *Black Dragon II*. She was red, just as the one before, and soon they would paint the well-known black dragons on the sides.

Watching Mouth and Abigail made Smith's heart ache. The boys started coming out from below deck; even so, he kept an eye on Mouth and Abigail. Smith reached into his pocket and pulled out Sea's bangle. Ace had given it to him earlier and told him the whole story.

"You really miss her?"

Smith turned to see that Snake had come up behind him. "Yeah," he said. He turned back around and leaned up against the wheel.

Snake wasn't too good at making people feel better. "You look like you could use a good laugh right about now."

"Not now, Snake." Smith tried to look away.

139

"That bad, eh?" Snake leaned up against the wheel by Smith. He rubbed his forehead, and Smith got a glimpse of a horrid scar on his hairline.

"How did that happen?" Smith asked. He hadn't even noticed it before because his hair covered it up.

"I don't even remember. Probably from a street fight when I was a kid." Snake covered the scar with his hair. To Smith, he looked troubled.

"You're afraid John will get the death sentence?" Smith asked.

"It wouldn't matter to me either way." Snake said. He still sounded troubled.

"Don't lie to me, Johnny."

"*Don't* call me Johnny." Snake looked away.

There was a silence for a moment. "John ... Johnny. Snake, were you named after John Stevenson?" Smith asked.

Snake laughed. "Yeah, I was. How else do you think these nicknames really got started?" He leaned back a little. "When I first met up with Sea, I'd lost my parents because of John. I didn't want to be called Johnny; it reminded me too much of him. So it was just 'Snake' and 'Sea' for a long time, and then the twins showed up and we picked on them when they would finish each other's sentences."

"They finished each other's sentences?" Smith laughed along with him.

"Courtney tried to explain the concept of yin and yang to them, and they found it offensive, so we called them that to annoy them," Snake explained. "Then Mouth came along, and we couldn't help but call him 'Mouth,' and then it became a known fact that the Black Dragons all had nicknames."

"Snake, are you going to miss John if Harold has him hanged?" Smith asked, and Snake turned away.

"No."

"Don't lie to me." Smith put a hand on his shoulder. "He was kind to you when you were young, wasn't he?"

"My parents were very neglectful toward me. John was like my father." Snake shook a little. "But I'll be all right Don't worry about me."

"Captain!" Knot was already at the crow's nest this morning. "One of the king's ships has blown off course; it's a huge galley, probably filled with gold pieces! We can catch her if we hurry!"

"Hoist the anchors!" Smith shouted out a large number of orders, and soon they were on their way, catching up to Harold's ship.

"The chase is making full sail, sir!" Knot shouted.

Smith smiled; it was good to be home again.

***

Sometimes I wonder if being a Black Dragon is a gift or a curse. We have so many enemies, but at the same time, we have many friends. I have become the hope that men and women have for this country, just as for so long Kathleen has been my hope. Kirkston has its problems, but it will always be home. The Black Dragons have so much in store for them, and I can't wait to see what is waiting for us beyond the horizon.

PART TWO
Enslaved

Ch 16

It was hard to believe that it had been two years since Abigail had joined their crew. Smith sat with his friend Mouth, who was tapping his foot in the most annoying way possible. Snake, Smith's first mate, stood by them. Only moments ago, the crew had chased down one of the king's ships and had the ship completely in their control. As they were bringing over salts, spices, and gold pieces, Abigail had gone into labor.

The ordeal was exciting to Smith, but Mouth was nervous. When they had gotten married, they had decided to stay with the Black Dragons, mostly for Mouth's younger brother. They didn't want him to have to decide between staying with his crew or staying with his family. Mouth was only nineteen, and already he would have the responsibility of taking care of a young child—but if any of them could do it, he could. He had raised his little brother, after all. Squirt sat by Mouth, offering him some comfort. Squirt was growing up fast, already eight years of age.

After Abigail went into labor, they had ordered the doctors from the king's ship onto the *Black Dragon* and had forced them below deck to take care of her. The doctors had said it was untraditional for the father to be in the room and had shooed all of them out. When Mouth protested, Abigail had shouted at him to, in her own words, to "get his ass out of the bunks," and they had all left. As they sat there waiting, the young crew could hear a few cries from Abigail.

In only a few moments, one of the doctors came above deck. Immediately, they all jumped up from their seats. "Well?" Ace, now twenty-three years of age, was the first to ask, for Mouth was at a loss for words.

"It's a boy. Don't worry, he's perfectly healthy, and your wife is fine as well." The doctor led them below deck. Inside, Abigail was lying down on the bed within the captain's quarters, pillows stuffed behind her so she could sit up after her labor. The other doctor was cleaning off the baby and wrapping him in a little blanket. He handed him off to Abigail, and Mouth hurried over beside her. Mouth took the child from her and displayed him proudly.

"Blade, see to it that the doctors get back to their ship," Smith said, and Blade left with the two doctors.

Squirt crawled up on the bed and looked at his nephew with excited little eyes. "What's his name?"

"Ian," Mouth said.

"That was Papa's name, wasn't it Mouth?" Squirt asked.

"It was." Mouth rocked the child gently when it started to cry.

"Might I see him, Mouth?" Smith reached out his arms, and Mouth ever so carefully put his son into Smith's arms. "Things are about to change, aren't they? Mouth, Abigail, have you two thought about what you're going to do?"

"We're not going anywhere, Smith." Abigail said. "But don't worry—we won't bring Ian on any 'trips.'"

"You brought me on pillages when I was little." Squirt was looking over Smith's shoulders at Ian.

"Aye, but we were less of a problem for Harold back then, and he wasn't always chasing after us like he is now." Mouth rubbed the top of Squirt's head.

Smith handed Ian over to his parents and ordered his crew out of the room so they could be alone with their new child. To

Smith, the birth of Ian was a sign that they weren't just a bunch of children on a ship anymore. It frightened him.

***

It was dark out, and the Black Dragons made their way west, following close by the river. They were going to visit with Smith's mother, Ellen Barons. She treated all of them like her own children. Ellen would clean their clothes, talk to them, and cook them a good meal (it was nice to have something in their stomachs other than hardtack). As they approached the house, they could see the big oak tree by the riverside. They all stopped by the graves under the tree: Will Barons, Elizabeth Barons, Anna Barons, and Courtney "Sea" Livingston. After a while, they headed to the two little houses nearby. They knocked at the first one, but there was no answer.

"Ron and Theresa must be at my mother's," Smith said, leading them past the little vegetable garden to his childhood home.

Smith entered first, and the three people sitting at the little table looked up in surprise. Candles were lit all through the kitchen. It had gotten unexpectedly dark that evening. He could smell food cooking over the fire.

"Peter!" Mrs. Barons stood up excitedly. She kissed Smith's cheek and hugged a couple of them as they came in. Ron and Theresa made room for them to sit. "I wasn't expecting you. Johnny, would you go get a few onions from the garden?"

Snake left quickly, visibly annoyed at Mrs. Barons for calling him Johnny. She always called them by their real names, which occasionally aggravated them, specifically Snake and Ace. Snake hated his name because he was named after John Stevenson, and Ace hated being reminded about his past as Prince James. But she was kind to them, so none of them ever said anything about it. Smith tossed Ron and Theresa a small bag of gold pieces and silver shillings, and he gave his mother one as well.

Abigail sat in a chair, Ian in her arms. He was crying, and she could not manage to get him to quiet down. *Poor Abigail,* Smith thought. *She's sick, and Ian just cries and cries. Mouth is tired too. They've been up every night with Ian.*

Mrs. Barons sat by her. "So this is the little Ian I've heard about." Mrs. Barons took the crying child from Abigail and rocked him until he stopped. "Abigail, you look awful."

Abigail's hair was a mess, her skin was pale, and there were dark circles under her eyes. "You seem to know what you're doing," Abigail said.

"I've raised three of them, Abigail." Mrs. Barons kissed the sleeping baby on the head. "You poor girl, you look like a ghost. You haven't been staying on the ship, have you? You've been resting by the waterfall, right?"

"No," Abigail admitted. She had lost her sea legs since the birth, and she stumbled at the slightest wave. Quite a few times that week, she had gotten nauseous and thrown up off the side of the ship.

"Well, perhaps you and Ian and Tommy should come and stay with me a while?" Mrs. Barons suggested to them. "Well?"

"We need help." Mouth willingly admitted, sitting near them. "We don't know what we're doing. When we were raising Squirt, we had Mr. and Mrs. Keg's help."

Squirt nodded. "Mrs. Keg was like my mama; she was friends with Sea."

"I'll help you with baby Ian." Mrs. Barons rocked Ian back and forth and then handed him over to Abigail. "Abby, you stay here tonight. Tommy, go pack up some clothes for the two of you after dinner and come back in the morning."

Snake came back inside with the onions; Mrs. Barons chopped them up quickly and tossed them in with the soup. After the food was ready, the crew ate with Mrs. Barons and the others. Shortly afterward, Mouth went with the others to gather up some of their things.

"I'll be back tomorrow." Mouth kissed Abigail and Ian before leaving with his crew.

***

It was kind of my mother to offer to let Abigail and Mouth stay with her for the next couple of weeks. She hasn't been feeling well. I've never seen Abigail so lopsided on the ship the way she has been for the past few days. Mouth will join them tomorrow, after he's gathered up some clothes for them to wear. It was nice to have some real food instead of just limes and hardtack. My mother is a good cook. It's too bad none of us can cook.

***

The sun rose high the next morning. Summer was just around the corner. It was sweltering hot, but a cool breeze made the heat bearable. Smith made his way from below deck when he heard Knot shouting from the lookout tower: "Harold's sending a ship down south for trade!"

"Can we catch it?" Smith asked.

Knot looked out over the water. "If we hurry!"

"All right!" Smith screamed, and they were on their way. It wasn't long before they caught up with King Harold's ship. It was a small crew, even smaller than their own. *This should be easy,* Smith thought as they drew alongside the enemy ship. They threw grappling irons onto the enemy vessel. The grappling irons tangled in the rigging, and the crew managed to haul the ships together. The opposing crew quickly accepted that they were outnumbered. It didn't take long before the Black Dragons had the ship under their command and had pillaged it. *It's funny how in all these years we've never had to sink a ship,* Smith thought.

Smith's crew sailed off, leaving Harold's men flustered. "Let's hurry back before Abigail starts to worry." Smith put Snake at the wheel and headed below deck. He went to his cabin. He drew his father's sword and started polishing it. Smith still remembered how excited he was when he first held the sword with the sharp blade and the amazing handle in the figure of a dragon. The blade shined. He saw his reflection in the sword, and his stomach felt twisted. *I never realized how much I look like Pa now.*

He heard cries from above deck, and something in his gut told him to hide his brown knapsack and his father's sword. He lifted up his mattress and tossed everything underneath it. He could not find another sword, so he quickly found an ax and ran up the stairs. The ship shook, and he stumbled for a moment. Someone's firing cannons at us! When he saw who was attacking him, he felt shivers run up and down his back. It wasn't a government ship attacking them; it was the Annihilator, a pirate ship—a real pirate ship. The ship was twice the size of the Black Dragon, with all black sails and a demented crew. The Annihilators flew their rebel flags proudly.

Smith swung the ax he held, hitting one man in the arm. The man fell over, and Smith stole his sword, knife, and flintlock pistol. He stored the knife and pistol in his belt loop and fought with the sword. It was then that Smith realized how many men there were. There had to be six times as many men on their side. They had been attacked by government ships before, but never by pirates. These pirates were ruthless thieves led by the man known as Jackson White.

Five men quickly surrounded Smith; he went for the pistol but was stopped by a large greasy-looking man. He stood his ground, however, and swung his sword at the man who held on to his arm. He had a sudden throbbing pain in the back of his neck, and everything went black.

***

Smith opened his eyes to see that they were aboard the *Annihilator*. "The fleet of Robin Hoods, the Black Dragons—what a treat this is." It was Captain Jackson. Smith felt light-headed. "Take them to their new quarters. We can fetch a good penny for these."

Fetch a good penny? What does he mean? Smith was yanked to his feet. He saw a young boy their age running toward the captain. "They have about a hundred barrels full of gold pieces, silver shillings, and other valuables, sir."

"Good job, Stewart." The captain patted his young ward on his head. The Annihilators had been around for a long time; the ship and her crew had been passed down from its old captain to Jackson White when Smith was just a child. Smith began to wonder if this child Jackson was speaking with would be the next leader of this heartless crew.

They were quickly taken below deck, where they were forced to undress. They were each given a worn-out pair of either brown or black pants to wear, and nothing more. Everyone was shoved into a small storage room. Their iron cells were full of other unlucky prisoners, and there was no room for Smith's crew. Once the doors were closed, Smith quickly counted heads to make sure all of them were alive and well. Everyone was there, safe and unharmed—apart from a few bruises. He looked around at the dark room, but he saw nothing but two stools, an empty barrel, and a hole that probably belonged to a family of rats. The floor was damp, obviously from some sort of leak.

Smith heard Squirt say, "They're going to kill us," and he looked up to see the frightened child burying his face into his brother's side.

"If they were going to kill us, they would have done it already." Mouth put his arms around Squirt and looked back at Smith for some sort of reassurance.

"You'll be all right, Squirt," Smith promised. "We're all here together." Smith felt foolish; he did not even have the chance to help his crew in the battle because he was so quickly knocked out.

The crew got comfortable, figuring they would be there for a while. All of them huddled together because it was dreadfully cold below deck, and the wet floors did nothing to help this. A full day went by, and Smith began to wonder if they were ever going to be set free.

Ch 17

Mrs. Barons could see the worry building up in Abigail. They were in her kitchen, as they had been for the past few days, waiting for Mouth to arrive. All he was supposed to be doing was fetching them some clothes and other belongings they might need. "Abigail, why don't you go check on Ian?" Mrs. Barons was trying to keep Abigail as preoccupied as she could so she would not worry about her husband.

"Where do you think Mouth is?" Abigail leaned back against the table. "It's been three days."

"Don't worry, sweetheart." Mrs. Barons took her hand and offered her a smile. She was just as worried as Abigail; her son was on that ship. "Their ship probably just went off course after a pillage."

The doors opened, and Ron and Theresa entered. "Any news?" Abigail asked.

"Unfortunately, no." Ron sat down at the table. "No one has heard from the Black Dragons in days."

Abigail sat down, flustered. "I'm starting to worry."

***

"I don't feel well." Snake leaned his head on Smith. They were still in the small storage room aboard the *Annihilator*.

"You're probably just hungry," Smith said. The door opened, and it was the young girl whose name they had learned was Gwen. She was about Squirt's age, but she was as tough as a grown man. The girl had been bringing them their food, which was just old hardtack and a couple of limes, which at least they were used to. Today, Smith could see, they would be given bread and a lime to fill them. She tossed each of them their food. Before giving Mouth his, she spit on the bread and ate his lime. On their second day when she'd come to give them food, Mouth had called her something insulting, and she had been cruel to him ever since. Gwen left them after that.

"I wouldn't eat that," Smith said, splitting his slice of bread with Mouth.

A few hours went by, and most of them fell asleep. Mouth was in a corner, and Squirt was lying in his lap, both of them asleep. Yin and Yang were asleep in another corner, curled up together. The others lay spread around the small room, huddling together with one another.

Smith sat up after awakening from a long slumber to find Snake's head resting in his lap. Snake shivered. *Nightmares,* Smith assumed, and he put a hand on his friend's shoulder to comfort him. *The ship seems still.* "Snake, we've stopped." His voice awakened some of the others, and the sudden stillness of the ship eventually awakened everyone.

"Where do you think we are?" Blade asked, stretching out his legs. They could hear footsteps outside the door. Smith felt sick to his stomach when shadows appeared from under the door. A small group of the pirates came into the room, all of them carrying chains. The men ordered all of them to stand. They were then chained together in a line and taken above deck.

"Smith, we're on Kevin's Isle," Ace whispered, after getting his first glance of their new surroundings.

Kevin's Isle was an extremely divided area in Kirkston. The rich and poor classes had social division and discrimination in the main lands of Kirkston, but Kevin's Isle was far worse. Slavery was common on Kevin's Isle. They had few moral values; pirates were even welcomed for trade. They were on the east side of the island at the trading docks, the main town.

Smith and the others were forced into cockboats and brought to land. He could see a crowd gathering in the center of town. A small stage was set up, and a large man stood on top. It was an auction. "Smith, they're going to auction us off." Cannonball grabbed on to Smith's sleeve, fear-stricken.

The Annihilators snickered when Cannonball realized this. The crew was brought to the bottom of the small stage and forced to stand and wait while other men and women were auctioned off into slavery. The man on the stage spoke with one of the Annihilators. The Annihilator came over, unchained Squirt from the group, and dragged him up onto the stage.

When Mouth started to fight back, the Annihilator who had taken Squirt from them hit him in his side with the back of his musket. "Keep quiet," he ordered them. Squirt began to cry while he stood up on the stage. The man auctioning him off struck him to silence him.

Smith could see Mouth shaking, and he put a hand on his shoulder. "They're going to take him away from me." Mouth said. Smith squeezed his shoulder, and the auction began. The bidding started at fifty gold pieces. Once the bidding got higher, it seemed to quiet down. Just as the man on stage started to end the bidding, one last offer was made.

A man shouted above the noise of the crowd, "Ten thousand gold pieces for the entire *Black Dragon* crew!"

One of the Annihilators was quick to argue. "You can't do that."

"Actually, I can." The man boldly made his way up the stage. "Anyone care to outbid me?" There was a murmur, but no more bids were made. "Very well, then," the man in charge of the auction said. "The Black Dragons go to Mr. ..."

"Godart," the man said, shaking hands with the auctioneer. "They're actually going to my employer, Mr. Steven Alvery. He needs workers for his farm." Mr. Godart shoved Squirt back toward the others. Squirt stumbled, and Mr. Godart shrugged his shoulders in disappointment. "He's not a very strong boy. Mr. Alvery might not want him. Perhaps he can stay and be auctioned off, and I'll take the rest of the former pirates with me."

"No!" Mouth shouted at Mr. Godart, but Squirt quickly quieted his older brother and addressed Mr. Godart.

"Your employer would be disappointed with my weak bones, but I assure you I can get as much done as these stubborn mules," Squirt said, and Mr. Godart laughed and patted Squirt on the head.

"All right. Go ahead and chain the boy back up with the others," Godart said.

It seemed to Smith that Squirt had known his smart remark would win Mr. Godart over.

Three men, including Mr. Godart, brought all of them to a carriage, and they climbed in from the back. There was a second carriage, much nicer than the large, cheap one they were riding in. Smith could see a shadow figure sitting in the back of the private carriage from behind the drapes. *Could this be Mr. Alvery?* Smith wondered.

Mr. Godart sat up front and steered while the other two men rode on separate horses alongside the carriage. All three men were well armed. They were heading west, following close behind the private carriage. Smith smiled at Squirt, and the child sat leaning up against his brother, not saying much. It's a miracle that we are together, but why? How did Mr. Godart even know we were the Black Dragons without our uniforms, and why would he want all of us? Why us, why not the other slaves? Smith leaned his back up against the side of the carriage, tired.

They traveled a long distance. Blade looked out the carriage for a moment. "There's nothing out there, Captain. It's almost like a desert. It's just a bunch of empty fields."

"Smith," Snake said when the wagon stopped, "I don't feel well."

"I'm pretty nervous myself," Ace said.

"No, I mean, I really don't …" Snake fell over, onto the floorboard of the wagon; everyone jumped up and made the wagon shake.

Smith hurried to Snake's side. He had chills and was sweating. "He's really sick."

"Get out!" one of the men ordered, coming around back. They all hurried out, except for Smith and Snake. Smith was checking to see if Snake was all right; he looked deathly ill, with dark circles around his eyes. He had the shakes and was coughing. The man pulled out a whip, and Smith quickly got out of the wagon. He turned and looked at Snake and shouted at him to get out. Smith attempted to tell the man that Snake was ill, but before he could, the man cracked his whip inside the wagon at Snake.

"Enough!" a loud voice shouted. "Oswold, put that thing away!" A bearded man had come out of the nicer carriage to greet them. The sight of the man made Smith shiver. He had a messy brown beard and mustache, and he walked with a cane due to a limp. His entire face was disfigured from numerous scars. One of the scars ran from his forehead, through his right eye, and to his chin; his right eye, as far as Smith could tell, seemed to be made of glass. "Is there still one in there?" The man's voice was shrill.

"Aye sir, he's not coming out," Mr. Oswold said.

The strange man leaned on his cane to his right as he walked. His limp was terrible. He looked at the Black Dragons, most of which were trying their hardest not to stare. "Unchain them."

"But Mr. Alvery—"

So this is Mr. Alvery. Smith was standing right next to him, and he froze when the man put a hand on Smith's shoulder for balance. "Hush, Oswold," Mr. Alvery said, and then he turned to address the Black Dragons. "I'll warn you boys now: people here don't take too well to escaped slaves. Don't be fools. Oswold, unchain them all. Take them to their new quarters, bring them something to eat, and let the boys rest for tonight."

"Aye, sir." Mr. Oswold unchained them as Mr. Alvery made his way to the back of the wagon, where he could see Snake lying on the floorboard.

"My word," he muttered. "Come here, child." He helped Snake to the edge of the wagon, and Mr. Oswold quickly unchained him. "Oswold, go fetch a doctor for the boy."

"For your boy?"

"That was an order, Oswold." Mr. Alvery said, helping Snake down out of the wagon. "Now where's that fat man I hired?" The third man came around from the side of the wagon. "Carry him back to the house and put him on the bed in the guest room." The man nodded, lifted Snake up, and carried him away.

Smith wore a serious look of concern, and he took a step away from the group toward where the large man was taking Snake, but Mr. Alvery stopped him. "Your friend will be taken care of ... Smith, is it?"

"Yes."

"Don't worry about your friend. When he's well, I'll send him to work with the rest of you." Mr. Alvery turned around and headed up to the blue house.

Smith and the others were taken to the slave house. It was a long hut-like building. Inside were four mattresses up against the back wall, shoved together in a corner. There were a few chairs around a small table, a small bucket of freshwater to drink, and a small latrine in the far right corner. "You work from morning to night; you will do as Mr. Steven Alvery instructs. He may need one of you in the middle of the night so sleep when you're allowed to turn in. Refer to him as 'sir' or 'master.' Good night." And Mr. Oswold left them, slamming the door on his way out.

"Do you think Snake is all right?" Squirt asked them. He was standing side by side with Mouth; he hadn't drifted far from him since he was almost sold to a separate master. Mouth stood with an arm around Squirt, not saying much. Mouth had said hardly a word since they'd left the *Annihilator*.

"I should have listened to him." Smith sat down on one of the mattresses. "He's been trying to tell me he hasn't been feeling well since this morning."

"What could you have done, anyways?" Ace asked. "It's not your fault."

"I'm scared," Squirt said.

"Don't worry," Smith told him. "We'll play the role of slaves for now, but once Snake is well again, we'll escape."

"But what if we can't escape?" Cannonball said. He leaned up against one of the walls in the cabin. "We'll never see the ocean again."

Ch 18

Mr. Alvery helped Snake crawl into the bed after his other employee left. Snake was sweating and coughing. "Lie down and relax, son," he said, and put a glass of water to Snake's lips. "Here, drink."

He drank the water and lay back down. It wasn't but a few seconds before Snake was asleep.

When he started to come to, he could taste something sour in his mouth. Whatever it was, he spit it out and opened his eyes. Mr. Alvery was helping him sit up, and a doctor was sitting in front of him. The doctor was wet with the medicine that Snake had spit up on him. He was holding a spoon that he had used to feed the medicine to Snake. Mr. Alvery was laughing.

"Well, Mr. Alvery," the doctor said, "just give him a spoonful of this once a day for the next few days, and he'll be fine." The doctor wiped Snake's spit off his face. "But make sure he gets it in his mouth this time."

Mr. Alvery helped Snake lie back down. "Are you feeling all right, lad?"

"Where am I?" Snake's head was throbbing. He was confused. He asked him, "Who are you? Where are my friends?"

"Your friends are in the slave house."

"Slave house?" Snake sat back up. "Why are they in a slave house?"

"Dear boy, do you remember anything that has happened in the past few days?" Mr. Alvery put a hand on Snake's shoulder.

Snake shook his head for a moment. "Yes, now I remember," he said in a low voice.

Somehow, Mr. Alvery must have sensed his sorrow, and he hurried to take Snake's mind off his current situation. "Black Dragons, eh? You're the one they call Snake, Johnny Lee, right?"

"How did you know that?" Snake asked him.

"Everyone knows everything there is to know about the Black Dragons, especially you. Everyone knows about you and your parents now," Mr. Alvery said. "I find it interesting how all you young boys, most of you not a day over twelve, learned how to work a ship in only a few years."

"Master Alvery? How long have I been asleep?" Snake asked.

"You passed out yesterday. It's going to be dark soon." Mr. Alvery must have heard Snake's stomach rumble. "Hungry? I'll have Maria bring you some soup." He shouted for his maid to bring Snake a bowl of soup. A young woman entered the room with a bowl of soup and handed it over to Snake. The young woman left without saying anything. Snake ate the soup. "Lie down, Johnny, and get some rest." Mr. Alvery said.

"Don't call me Joh—"

"Hush," Mr. Alvery interrupted him. "Get some rest."

Snake lay down and was asleep within a few minutes.

***

It was the fourth day the crew had been on Mr. Alvery's land. Snake awoke with a slight smile, feeling miraculously better. Mr. Alvery had been kind to him. He walked with him outside and told him to take it easy that day. Mr. Alvery had Snake pulling seeds from the cotton the others were picking in the fields; he was able to sit at a little table in the shade while the others worked under the incredible heat.

Smith was the first to drop off his basketful of cotton; he looked pleased to find Snake up and well. "I'm glad to see you're feeling better, Snake."

"Mr. Alvery has been kind to me," Snake said.

"Really?" Smith dumped the basket of cotton onto the table. "Well, at least he's kind to you. At least we know he'll treat us well when we're ill."

"Have his men been cruel?" Snake asked him.

"Aye," Smith said. "Mostly just with threats, though. One of them hurt Knot yesterday, bruised his chest. It wasn't anything to worry about, though." Mr. Godart shouted at Smith to hurry back to the fields, and Smith left Snake at the table to deseed the cotton.

As the day dragged on and the sun started to set, Snake was finishing last-minute chores while the others raced to the slave house, but Smith was nowhere to be seen. Snake assumed Mr. Alvery had him working late. Snake was continuing to rake grass seed just outside the barn when he heard Mr. Alvery's voice shouting at someone. His voice sounded harsh, and it frightened Snake for a moment. Smith came running out of the barn. It was dark, and Snake couldn't tell what was wrong. Smith was running so fast that he didn't even notice that he ran right past Snake. He ran with a limp through the fields and tripped. Snake noticed he had to struggle to get up, but when he did, he didn't stop running until he reached the slave house. Snake could see a tall figure—more than likely Ace—help Smith inside.

Mr. Alvery and two of his men came out of the barn. "Johnny, give me that rake, and I'll have one of my men finish that." Snake handed him the rake and asked him what happened to Smith. Mr. Alvery sighed and said, "I don't think your friend is adjusting to his new life too well, Johnny. Go on and get some sleep." Mr. Alvery and his men left him, and Snake hurried to the slave house.

Snake entered their pathetic new home and was terrified to see what had happened to Smith. He was lying on his stomach on one of the mattresses in the room. His back, shoulders, and the backs of his legs were bleeding from what appeared to be a terrible lashing. Smith's face was buried into a pillow. Ace sat by him, dabbing a wet rag on his back. Everyone stood around him. "Smith? What happened?"

"Alvery whipped him and then poured salt water over his wounds," Ace told Snake.

"He didn't do anything wrong!" Squirt exclaimed.

Snake put a hand on Squirt's shoulder and said, "I'm sure Mr. Alvery didn't just whip him without an explanation; he's very kind to me."

"Aye. So while we're working our asses off, you're getting pampered," Blade said, shooting Snake a dirty look.

Ace began to explain what Smith had told them. "Smith was working in the barn, and he backed into Alvery. Alvery got angry, and he had Smith whipped. Then he poured salt water over his cuts so it'd burn."

"Aye," Blade said. "Ace helped him inside, and he passed out the minute he lay down."

Snake refused to believe such a story. He made up excuses for Mr. Alvery, saying that Smith surely overexaggerated.

Squirt argued back and shouted at Snake, "Does it really look like he overexaggerated? Look at him, Snake!" Squirt began to cry.

When the arguing quieted down, everyone thought it best to try to get some sleep. They all crowded together on the four mattresses and were asleep shortly. In the morning, they left the slave house quietly so not to wake Smith so he could rest after such a harsh night. Unfortunately, Mr. Alvery did not approve of his men sleeping in.

When Mr. Alvery found Smith asleep in the slave house the next morning, he had his men beat him until he was up on his feet. From that moment on, Smith became a sort of target for

Mr. Alvery. Smith worked all day like the others, but he woke up earlier and went to bed later, doing several other chores on the farm, whether it was cleaning out the horse stalls, sweeping floors in the house, or picking seeds from cotton. Everyone became angered easily. They all felt horrible for Smith, and they could not take their anger out on Mr. Alvery, so they often ended up taking it out on one another. One thing that angered them was Snake. Alvery treated him well and treated the rest of them like trash.

One night, Snake was given more bread than the others were. Although he did share it with the others, Mouth called him the favorite slave. It was the first time Mouth had truly spoken since they'd arrived on the farm.

Snake sounded offended. "What's your problem?" he asked, waiting for an answer that did not come. Mouth just looked away from him. "That's right, Mouth. Don't talk. You've changed."

Mouth stood and shouted at him, "Yes, I've changed! It's been three weeks since I've seen Abigail or Ian."

"We all want to get out of here," Snake said.

Mouth shoved Snake and shouted at him. "You're not the one with a wife and son back home! I'll never see my son again! I won't hear his first word or see him take his first steps if we don't get out of here. He'll grow up without a father—just like the rest of us!" Mouth shoved Snake again. "It's because of you that we haven't tried to escape yet. If it wasn't for you, I'd be back with Abigail and Ian again." Mouth had hold of Snake by his hair now.

"Let go!" Snake tried to pull away.

Ace hurried between the two of them and made Mouth back away from Snake. "Enough!" Ace screamed.

Mouth shoved Ace, knocking him over backward. Ace angered easily—it was something they all knew about him. It didn't surprise any of them when Ace jumped up and started hitting Mouth. None of them bothered to stop him. They fought amongst each other often, but nothing serious ever happened.

Ace slammed Mouth into the wall, and he fell to the ground. Ace started hitting him repeatedly. Mouth screamed for help. Smith hurried and jumped onto Ace's back, while Yin and Yang held him by his arms.

"What's wrong with you?" Smith struck Ace and hurried to Mouth's side.

Ace's heart sank. Mouth was leaning up against the wall with his hands over his head, as though he thought Ace would come back and hurt him. Ace could hear Smith say to Mouth, "Calm down, Tommy. We won't let him hurt you again. We won't let him touch you." And Ace felt sick to his stomach.

"Mouth, I'm sorry." Ace felt uncomfortable. Everyone was looking at him with a horrified face, especially Mouth. Squirt darted across the room and crawled into Mouth's arms. "Tommy ..." Ace knelt down beside his friend, and Squirt snatched Ace by the arm and bit him. "Ah!" Ace yanked away, "He bit me!"

Mouth laughed. "I'm all right." He wiped blood from his lip.

"I could have really hurt you," Ace said. "I'm sorry."

"Aye," Mouth said. "I know." He stood and went to sit on one of the mattresses. Squirt sat with him.

They all stood around awkwardly. Squirt had begun to cry. "I want to go home," he said. "You're all mean here."

Ace came over and knelt back down beside him. He kissed Squirt on the head. "I'm sorry, lad. I didn't mean to scare you."

Smith looked over at Snake. "How are you felling?"

"Better," he said.

"Good. Because we're getting out of here tomorrow night."

Ch 19

Late one night, Smith and his crew rushed down the path that led to the main town. They had forgotten how far the town was from Alvery's farm. A few hours after they left the slave house, they found themselves wandering around in utter darkness. The path split into two different directions, and no one was sure which path would take them back to the main town.

"Knot, you're good with direction," Smith said. "Which path?"

"Sorry, Captain, but I'm at a loss," Knot said. "But we'd better decide soon; the sun will be up in a few hours, and Alvery's men will realize we're gone."

"Both paths have got to lead somewhere so let's just pick one," Smith said, starting down the path to their right. His crew followed him. They traveled along the path for another hour before Squirt began to complain of tired legs.

"I think we took the wrong path," Mouth said, while allowing his younger brother to climb onto his back. "It didn't take this long to get to the farm from the main town."

"He's right," Yang said. "We should head back."

"No," Smith said and pointed east. "The sun's coming up. Alvery's men will be headed this way looking for us. If we turn back, we'll run into them." He encouraged them to press on.

As the sun rose higher in the sky, it grew scorching hot. It was around noon when they saw men on horseback coming at them from behind. There were about twenty men, all armed and led by Mr. Godart.

Smith pointed south. "Head for the woods!" They ran, but they were no match for men on horseback. The men surrounded them before any of them reached the woods.

"Stop!" Godart's voice carried around them. "You boys are in more trouble than you could possibly imagine!"

***

After they were marched back to Alvery's farm that day, Smith and the others were told to stand outside the slave house. Smith stood nervously by the door while more than twenty of Alvery's men kept a close eye on all of them. Smith could see Mr. Godart speaking with Mr. Alvery by the house, and then Alvery headed inside. When Godart came back down to the slave house, Smith was not sure of what to expect.

Godart grabbed Squirt and threw him to the ground. "Leave him alone!" Mouth started toward him, but some of Alvery's men shot their guns off at his feet, and Mouth retreated.

Godart took his whip and began lashing Squirt. As Squirt screamed out in pain, the others looked at one another helplessly, unable to run to his aid in fear of being shot at. The young child squirmed on the ground while Godart whipped him and kicked him in his side.

"Tommy!" Squirt cried out for help. Mouth fell to his knees and screamed, clearly feeling useless.

Smith watched Squirt curl up in a ball on the ground as Godart repeatedly whipped him. From the corner of his eyes, he saw Mouth jump to his feet and lunge at Godart. Smith expected Mouth to jump at Godart, and he feared that his dear friend would be gunned down for it. To Smith's surprise, Mouth got down on his hands and knees in front of him.

"Please!" Mouth begged. "Don't hurt him anymore!" He reached for Squirt and held his brother in his arms. "I will *never* try to escape again; I don't know what we were thinking. Please don't hurt him."

Smith was wide-eyed. Never had he seen Mouth so vulnerable. "Well, this one's learned his lesson." Godart chuckled and turned to face the rest of the Black Dragons. "Have you boys learned from this incident, or do I have to shoot the little runt to get it through to you?"

"No!" Smith jumped when Godart cocked his pistol. "We're not going anywhere."

"Good," Godart said. "Get inside the slave house. You boys will be up working again tomorrow morning."

Mouth carried Squirt into the slave house, his head down and full of shame. The others headed inside after them. Mouth found himself a corner to sit in, and he held Squirt in his arms. Squirt sat in his lap with his little arms wrapped around Mouth's neck. He was in tears. Smith watched them for a moment before coming over. He knelt down next to them and put a hang on Squirt's shoulder. "Don't touch him!" Mouth shouted at Smith.

Smith looked Mouth in the eyes. "I only want to see if he's okay." Smith could see that Squirt was asleep.

"Squirt?" Mouth shook him gently. "Jacob! Jacob, wake up!"

"Easy," Smith said. "He's all right. We walked all night and all day ... and Godart really hurt him. But he's all right; he's just tired."

Mouth looked up at all of his friends. "What?" he snarled. "I know I looked pathetic, okay?"

"No," Yin said. "You weren't pathetic. He's your baby brother."

"I'm not going to try to run away again," Mouth said. "Squirt and I are staying here."

"What?" Smith asked. "What about Abigail and Ian?"

Mouth's eyes were watering. "They'll be okay. I just can't let them hurt Squirt again."

"You can't just stay here," Smith said.

"Yes, I can!" Mouth shouted. "Not again. I won't do anything to make them hurt Squirt again."

Squirt wiggled in Mouth's arms. "My back hurts!" he cried. Squirt opened his eyes and hugged Mouth tightly. "Where's Sea? I want Courtney!"

"It's okay. They're not going to hurt you again, okay?" Mouth kissed him on his head.

"Courtney!" Squirt cried out. "I want Courtney!"

Mouth carried Squirt over to the mattresses. Smith followed them, and he and the others tried to get some sleep before Alvery's men woke them the next morning. They all lay there in silence, listening to Squirt cry himself to sleep.

Ch 20

"I'm so worried," Abigail said, taking yet another drink. By now, the poor girl was extremely drunk.

"I know, sweetheart." Mrs. Barons was sitting with Abigail at Benny's Inn on Skull Island, having a few sips of wine. She was nervous being on Skull Island. The men there were drunks, criminals, or both, but Benny had invited them; he'd had one of his busboys bring them the invite. Mrs. Barons thought it would be a good idea. Abigail needed to get out of the house, and she figured a few drinks would do her good. "I miss my baby," Mrs. Barons said. "We'll find them."

"Hush," Abigail snapped. "It's been almost a month."

"My baby." Mrs. Barons looked down. "I haven't seen Peter in so long. I'm so worried about all of them."

"Listen." Benny leaned over from the other side of the bar next to them. "There's a reason I asked you ladies to come here. I think I might be able to help you find them."

"What?" Abigail jumped in her seat. "How?"

"About a week ago, I was on a ship passing by a bunch of those small islands down south when I saw a young boy marooned on one. I saved him, brought him back here, and have been letting him stay here at the inn in exchange for work." Benny pointed to the back of the bar at a boy Abigail's age. "The poor lad says he was marooned by his crew, the Annihilators."

"Benny, you took in an Annihilator?" Abigail gasped, knowing the cruel reputation the Annihilators had earned for themselves.

"An ex-Annihilator. He's just a kid, and he was scared, all right? The boy was unconscious on an island when I found him. His captain left him with an empty pistol. But take a good look at him." Benny was still whispering. "Look at what he's wearing."

Abigail and Mrs. Barons looked. It took them a minute to realize what Benny was talking about. When she saw that the boy was wearing her husband's shirt, Abigail flew into a rage. "How did he come across that?" she demanded to know.

"About a month ago, right around the time the Black Dragons went missing, he claims his crew attacked another pirate ship and the captain gave it to him," Benny said. "If anyone knows what happened to our boys he'll know."

Mrs. Barons stood. "I'll beat that child!"

Benny stopped them. "Be easy on him, girls. He's just a boy."

Abigail led Mrs. Barons over to the increasingly drunk young man. She seized him by the collar and yanked him to his feet. He almost laughed at her. "You look so cute trying to act all tough, sweetheart," he told Abigail. He tried to kiss her, but she wouldn't allow it. Then he turned from Abigail to Mrs. Barons and looked straight down her dress without even the least bit of concern about whether she caught him.

Mrs. Barons quickly covered herself; she got the notion that he normally wouldn't act this way. He seemed like an innocent young man who was attempting to drown his sorrows in grog and women.

"What do you know abut the Black Dragons?" Abigail shouted.

"Nothing." He had a sudden annoyed look on his face.

"Don't lie to me." Abigail sounded threatening. "That's my husband's shirt you're wearing."

He huffed. "I'm leaving." He attempted to leave, so Mrs. Barons pulled out a knife that Abigail had told her she should take to Skull Island with her. "You're insane," the boy said, visibly surprised at her. Mrs. Barons and Abigail led him out onto the beach far from the docks where the rocks were.

"What do you know about the Black Dragons?" Abigail asked again.

"Nothing I can remember." He then smiled at her and touched her cheek. "But there might be a way you can jog my memory." He reached for her and forced a kiss on her.

"You filthy child!" Mrs. Barons took him by his hair and yanked him away from Abigail. She marched him toward the ocean, where a large round rock was, and threw him up against it.

His chest was up against the stone, and Mrs. Barons leaned up against his back. She took his wrist and held it on top of the stone, palm up, and jabbed the knife into his palm. He screamed, and she dug the knife deeper into his hand. He screamed louder. "I'll tell you!" he cried. "I'll tell you what you want to know."

She stopped pushing the knife deeper into his hand. "Where are they?" her voice sounded wicked.

"My crew … we-we ambushed them almost a month ago. We sold them off as slaves." He tried to struggle free, and Mrs. Barons pushed the knife deeper into his hand. "Stop it!" he shouted at her, dropping to his knees. "Stop it, please!"

She was using the full weight of her body to keep him still. Her chest was positioned behind his head, keeping his face against the large stone. His free arm was tensed up at his side. "Where are they now?" He didn't answer right away, so she took hold of him by his hair again, still gripping the knife that was piercing his hand, and rammed his face hard into the stone, causing his lips and gums to bleed. "Where are they?" she shouted at him.

"We sold them, just north of here. Kevin's Isle!" he cried.

"And their ship?" She twisted the knife in his hand, and he screamed again.

"It's with my crew," he said quickly. "Our ship makes birth at the tip of the peninsula." He was in tears. They quickly learned that this pirate was, surprisingly, a Christian man. He started murmuring prayers for help from God, evidently thinking that Mrs. Barons was going to kill him.

Mrs. Barons was saddened to hear these pleas coming from his lips, but she refused to allow herself to back down. "You are going to help us steal back the *Black Dragon*."

"What? How are three people supposed to sail a ship?" he asked. "Two women such as yourselves probably haven't ever even been on a ship."

Once again, Mrs. Barons dug the knife deeper into his palm, and he cried out, "I'll help you; I'll do whatever you say!"

She yanked the knife out of his hand quickly, only causing it to slice even more skin. She then shoved him to the ground, and he fell into the shallow water, gripping his bloody hand.

Abigail, who had just sat by and watched the scene unfold, was smiling. She was actually a little proud of Mrs. Barons. "I can't believe you did that."

"Neither do I." She tossed the knife onto the beach and got down beside the boy. "Here, honey, let me help you." She put her arms around the boy's waist and helped him stand. "What's your name, boy?"

"Stewart." He spit blood into the sand and continued to put pressure on his hand.

"Well, don't worry Stewart. I won't do anything like that again." She walked him inside and bought him a drink. She even cleaned his hand and bandaged it up for him.

Abigail shook her head, disappointed. "You can't stand to be cruel, can you?"

"I don't like to be," Mrs. Barons said. "But my son was on that ship. One of these days, Abigail, you'll know what it's like. Ian will be in trouble one day, even if it's something little like falling and scraping his knee or getting a cold, and you'll know what I'm feeling."

"I know how you feel," Abigail insisted. "My husband is out there."

"That's different," Mrs. Barons argued. "He's your husband; inside, you know that he is a man and can take care of himself."

"Smith is just as much a man as my husband is," she said. "If not more," she quietly added.

"Not to me. Peter is my baby boy. It doesn't matter how old they get, Abigail. Ian will always be your baby, and you'll always feel like he needs you." She realized that Stewart was listening in on them, which she couldn't blame him for, seeing that they were making him sit with them, but it still annoyed her, and she openly slapped him.

"I thought you said you were being nice now!" he shouted, rubbing his cheek.

"I am *trying* to be nice," she said.

"If you're trying to be nice, can I not go with you, then?" He attempted to leave, but Mrs. Barons stopped him.

"I'm not *that* nice. Sit!" She shoved him back in his seat.

"Please! My crew will kill me if they see me again," Stewart begged her.

Again, Mrs. Barons struck him. "Listen to me, boy! I know nothing about sailing, and Abigail can't sail a ship on her own, so you're coming with us."

Stewart nodded and sat quietly.

***

This is what I get, Stewart thought. *I sell men off as slaves ... and now I am one!* Stewart sat quietly on the little couch in Mrs. Barons's home. His hands were tied behind his back. He had tried to run off once at the inn, so he was tied up. He had tried to run again when they reached the house, so they tied his ankles together. "Don't worry; we'll watch Ian for you. I have a friend who I'm sure will willingly nurse for you while you're gone," the woman he now knew was Theresa said to Mrs. Barons and Abigail.

Ron was sitting near Stewart, keeping a close eye on him. He laughed and said, "I can't believe a sweet woman like Mrs. Barons stabbed you with a knife."

"All right, Stewart, ready to go?" Mrs. Barons came over, and Stewart started shaking a bit. "Don't try to run away, and I won't hurt you, son." She untied his ankles and helped him stand, refusing to untie his hands.

"I should go with you," Ron said.

"No," Mrs. Barons said, when a worried look passed over Theresa's face. "You need to stay here with your wife."

Ron nodded in agreement. "All right," he said. "Just be careful."

Mrs. Barons and Abigail said their farewells, and Stewart went with them on their journey south.

It took them a few days to find their way to the tip of the peninsula; it would have taken longer if it weren't for Stewart, who knew his way around the southlands.

When they arrived, the three of them stayed hidden in the woods, looking down at the camp on the beach, planning their next course of action. The *Black Dragon* sat out in the water near the *Annihilator*. Stewart was trying to escape again. Mrs. Barons sat on him to keep him still. Finally, he shouted, "Captain Jackson! Thieves! Thieves!" and Abigail struck him.

"They marooned you on an island," Mrs. Barons whispered. "Don't you want to help us and get them back for what they did to you?"

"If they see me, they'll kill my sister," he finally said. He began to cry quietly. "Please don't make me do this."

"Why didn't you tell us?" Mrs. Barons asked him, helping him stand.

"Why? You shout at me, drag me down the beach, stab me with a knife, and demand I help you steal a ship from my old crew. How was I to know you would even care?" Stewart was still crying, not concerned with his dignity. "When I last saw her, she was so scared ... and they took her away from me."

"We'll help you get her back," Mrs. Barons told him.

"No we won't!" Abigail argued. "Ellen, these people aren't like us. They're real pirates—they'll kill us if they catch us."

Mrs. Barons looked down, eyeing the men at camp. "Is that her?" She pointed at a young girl sitting nervously by one of the campfires.

Stewart nodded. "That's her." All the men were drunk, most of them half-asleep on the ground around her. It seemed no one was watching the ship or the girl.

"Abigail, you and Stewart sneak onto the ship. The girl and I will steal a cockboat and head out to the *Black Dragon*. Keep quiet."

Before anyone could say anything to that, Mrs. Barons was heading down toward camp.

***

"Let me go!" the young girl shouted, and Mrs. Barons clasped her hand over her mouth.

"Listen," Mrs. Barons whispered to her as they reached the beach, "your brother is alive. You have to trust me, sweetheart." Mrs. Barons let her go. "My name's Ellen Barons."

"I'm Gwenhwyfar," she said, "but everyone calls me Gwen."

Mrs. Barons climbed into the cockboat, and Gwen followed. "Your brother was saved by a friend of mine," Mrs. Barons told Gwen.

"What about Alex?" she asked.

"I'm sorry, who?" Mrs. Barons rowed the boat toward the *Black Dragon*; the girl was leaning in, listening to every word Mrs. Barons said. The sun would be coming up soon, and she knew they only had about another hour of nightfall to cover up their escape. "Your brother never mentioned anyone else."

"Then Alex is dead?" Gwen looked away. "He was a friend of ours; he was marooned with Stewart."

"I'm sorry," Mrs. Barons said. They reached the side of the ship, and by the time they were on deck, Stewart and Abigail had most everything ready to go. Mrs. Barons smiled at Stewart and Gwen when they embraced each other, proud to be a part of that. "My word!" she cried when she saw all the barrels full of gold pieces and silver shillings. "Think of all the good we could do with this!"

"The Annihilators have been using it to store money from pillages," Gwen explained. Stewart had his arms wrapped around his little sister; his hands had been untied so he could help.

She doesn't look much older than Squirt, Mrs. Barons thought.

"We're ready to go. We need to hurry." Abigail broke them up, and they soon had the ship moving. They could hear the Annihilators screaming from the shore as they drifted away. By now, the sun was rising high, and the *Black Dragon* was on her way to Kevin's Isle.

Ch 21

Snake sat on Mr. Alvery's porch, washing clothes in a small barrel. Mr. Alvery sat in his rocking chair, chatting with Snake while he did the laundry. "You know, Johnny, you remind me of myself when I was your age," he said, rocking in his chair, his nose in what seemed to be a good book.

"How so, sir?"

He leaned in and said quietly, "You could always tell when I was up to something." He then laughed and leaned back in his chair. "You boys aren't planning on running off again, are you?"

"No, sir." Snake laughed and carried on with his chores. All Snake's chores were simple and consisted of sitting on Alvery's porch, doing something with his hands, while the old man sat in his rocking chair and all the others worked out in the fields. Although he'd never admit it to the others, Snake enjoyed the company. It appeared as though Alvery also enjoyed Snake's presence each day out on the porch. He would sometimes have his house slave, Maria, bring Snake tea whenever Alvery requested some. Snake never spoke with the others about how well Alvery treated him, in fear that it would cause hatred between them. While his friends broke their backs each day, Snake was beginning to build a close relationship with the slave master. Even though he preferred his working conditions to those his friends were put through, he could not help but feel guilt each time he sat by Mr. Alvery on the porch, wishing that he were actually out in the fields.

The sun began to set, so Mr. Alvery told Snake to head back to the cabins. The crewmates sat around for a while, waiting for Smith because he had been kept out late that night. When he finally came in, he sat down in a corner for a bit. He was fiddling with something, and Mouth pointed it out. "That's Sea's bangle!" They all looked over excitedly.

"I was sure those bloody pirates took it when they made us change, seeing that you always carry it around on your person," Ace said, watching as Smith held up the bangle.

All of them still wore the same clothes the Annihilators had given them to wear. "I would never part with this." Smith smiled.

"Those bangles are expensive. I know you didn't talk your way into keeping it. How did you hide it?" Cannonball asked.

"I took it out of my pocket and put it in a barrel of hay while we were changing," he explained. "When they started taking us to the storage room, I took it and put it back in my pocket."

"I miss her." Squirt began to pout. "I hate it here."

"We're going to try to get out of here again," Smith said.

"No," Mouth said quickly. "I don't want to risk getting Squirt hurt again."

"You can't make him stay here." Smith stood. "He's scared. He's still a babe. He'll die if you make him stay here."

"Godart almost killed him last time!" Mouth cried. "Enough. I don't want to talk about this!"

"Stop fighting!" Squirt screamed, "I want to go home! I want Courtney!"

"Well, she's not here!" Mouth snapped at Squirt. "She's dead and buried! Shut your trap and stop whining about it!"

Squirt retreated, slowly backing away from Mouth. "I hate you!" he cried. Everyone was quiet. Squirt ran to Smith and wrapped his arms around his leg. "Take me home!" he begged him. "I want to go home! Please, Peter." He started crying.

Mouth hurried over. "It's okay. Don't cry," he said, but Squirt yanked away from him. Mouth stood next to them awkwardly, while Squirt cried into Smith's leg, clearly not want to be near Mouth, who now retreated into a corner, ashamed at how cruel he had just been to his little brother. The others slowly began turning in for the night.

As Smith held on to Squirt while he cried, he looked over at Mouth. *He doesn't hate you, Tommy,* Smith tried to tell Mouth with his eyes. *He's just scared. We all are.*

p^

Ch 22

When Smith and the others were told to turn in almost two hours before the sun set, Smith got a terrible feeling in his stomach. Snake had been instructed to report to Mr. Alvery. The others sat around in the slave house, anxiously awaiting his return. When he arrived, Smith was standing in the doorway. "Where have you been?" Snake had a disturbed looked on his face, and he did not answer Smith. He just sat down on one of the mattresses. "You all right?" Smith asked, and the others crowded around.

"I'm fine," he said.

"What did Alvery say to you?" Blade asked.

Snake spoke slowly, still sounding baffled. "Alvery wants to adopt me." The room was silent. All of them stared up at Snake, waiting for him to say more, but he did not utter another word.

Finally, Smith spoke: "You told him no, right?"

"I didn't say anything." Snake leaned against the doorway. "Just that I'd think about it."

"Think about it?" Mouth roared. He stood and approached Snake angrily. "What's there to think about?"

"Yeah," Yang added, his brother nodding along with him as he spoke. "We're not staying here. We'll escape and go home."

"But what if we can't escape?" Snake said. "What if we stay trapped here?"

"We won't," Smith said.

"But what if we do?" Snake argued. "Alvery is an old man. If I were to let him adopt me, I'd inherit everything when he dies because he has no other kin, or so he's told me. And if I inherit everything, that would include the farm."

Smith shook his head. "And the people who work it. I see what you're trying to do here. You'd inherit us and you could set us free."

Knot stood and confronted Snake, shouting in his face, "So you just expect us to wait around for some old man to die while you live it up in Alvery's care?"

"No, but if we can't escape, this may be our only option for freedom," Snake said.

"Who says we have to wait? If Snake were to let Alvery adopt him ... and *something* were to happen to him ..." Ace was speaking with a grin on his face. "Like if a gun were to go off or a horse were to run him over ... some sort of *accident* ..."

"No!" Snake said. "You're not a killer any more than the rest of us, Ace."

"We know what this is really about." Mouth began to scorn him: "You actually *want* this man as a father, don't you?"

"I don't, no!" Snake argued with him.

"Enough!" Smith shouted. "Snake, think about it. Think hard. You're my friend. It's unlikely you'll get another opportunity to be a free man. We already tried to escape once, and they almost killed Squirt because of it. We'll talk more about this later. For now, everyone get some sleep."

They all crammed together on the mattresses in an attempt to get some sleep that night.

***

The next night, Smith was in the barn working late. He was raking up hay, and Mr. Alvery and his men were outside the barn. Mr. Alvery came inside. "Tomorrow I want you up early to paint the barn, but I still expect you to pick your share of cotton."

"I can't do both. I'd have to stay up all night to get that done," Smith complained.

"I didn't ask how long it would take you, now did I?" Mr. Alvery was breathing down his neck.

Smith didn't turn around to face him. "Are you trying to kill me? Why do you hate me so much? I've done nothing to you, and you treat me like dirt! I bend over backward to please you, and you only hate me more!" Smith turned around quickly, and the rake knocked Mr. Alvery in the face. In his surprise, Alvery stumbled back and tripped, landing in a pile of hay.

"My leg! My leg!" he cried, and his men hurried into the barn. Mr. Alvery had twisted his bad leg in the fall.

Smith, realizing how much trouble he was in, screamed, "I'm sorry, sir!"

They helped him stand; Smith could see how angry Alvery was. "You clumsy cretin!" he shouted at Smith. "Give that boy ten lashes!"

"Ten?" Smith backed away. "It was an accident!" He turned to run, but Mr. Oswold and Mr. Godart grabbed on to him.

The men forced him on his knees and held on to his arms. They held him down while he tried to struggle away. "No! Stop!" Smith still tried to pull away.

The third man reached for a whip that hung from a hook on a wall. With each whip, Smith fell forward some, and Mr. Oswold and Mr. Godart sat him up for the third man to whip him again. "Stop! Please stop!" Smith cried.

In the middle of his lashing, Smith gathered up enough strength to yank away. He stood up and turned around. Mr. Oswold and Mr. Godart held on to him again, and the man whipped him across his face and chest. It surprised the man, and he dropped the whip. Smith fell over.

"Ah!" Smith screamed, holding his hand over his face. Blood oozed between his fingers.

"You fool!" Smith heard Alvery yell at the man who had whipped him in the face. "If he has to have his eye removed, the money for a doctor is coming out of your salary! I won't waste my money on my field slaves!" Smith shivered when Mr. Alvery seized him by the hair on the back of his neck and forced him to look at him. He took Smith's face in his hands to examine his wound. "You're lucky—it didn't get his eye."

Smith looked Alvery in the eyes for a moment and froze. Mr. Alvery's face seemed familiar all of a sudden. For a moment, Smith was able to look past his disfigured face, his eerie scars, ridiculous facial hair, and crippled body. He recognized him and was ashamed he hadn't seen it before. *It's him* ... Smith began to quiver when he realized it.

"John Stevenson?" he said.

Ch 23

Smith went to swing at John, but Godart and Oswold grabbed him and threw him to the ground. He was far too weak to get up again on his own. The third man backed away, shocked. "You're John Stevenson?" he cried out. "Why didn't any of you tell me?"

Smith looked up at him. He felt foolish for not realizing it before then. Smith looked at his glass eye, his hairy face, and crippled body. "What happened to you?" Smith asked.

"It's your fault, you know." The old general came close to him, backing Smith up to the wall of the barn. "After you broke my leg when we fell into the river, you crippled me! When you and your friends turned me in to Harold, he had me beaten! I lost an eye from a lashing. They scheduled my hanging, and while I was in prison, Kathleen came and visited me. She hit me and shouted at me, saying I was getting what I deserved. Prisoners beat me as some sort of revenge! I got away by snatching Kathleen and holding on to her until the guards showed and I could steal a key from them." He walked slowly around Smith, staring him down. "I changed my name and made a few wise investments. I hired my old friends, Oswold and Godart, and then I hired that fat Anderson, that woman Maria, and a few others."

"Anderson?" Smith looked up at him. "The old blacksmith?"

"He went out of business." John touched the back of Smith's neck, causing his shoulder to tense up. "So now a once-powerful general is hiding from the law, and the boy who caused it is begging at his feet."

"Why did you buy us? Is this your revenge, Stevenson?" Smith asked.

He laughed. "Of course." John squeezed the back of Smith's neck. "I don't want your friends finding out about me." He waved his men over to them. "Whip him."

Smith tried to get to his feet and run, but Oswold and Godart grasped on to him and turned him around. John handed Anderson the whip, but he threw it to the ground. "Listen, Stevenson—," Anderson began, but John stopped him.

"You'll be living on the streets again if you don't whip this boy, Anderson!" John shouted at him, and Mr. Anderson picked the whip back up willingly. He started whipping Smith. "Harder!" John shouted repeatedly. Smith began to scream, and Mr. Anderson started to slow down. "Why are you stopping? *Kill him!*" John shouted.

"Mr. Anderson, stop!" Smith shouted, and Anderson lowered his whip.

He looked at Smith and threw the whip to the ground. Mr. Oswold and Mr. Godart let go of Smith, and he fell down. Anderson stared at Smith. "William? William's son?" he said, and Smith managed to smile at him.

"John, this is mad. You let these boys go," Anderson said.

"I do not take orders from you!" John stepped by him, toward Smith, and Anderson shoved John away.

Anderson hurried over to Smith and helped him sit. He whispered, "You're him, aren't you? Will's son?" Smith nodded. Mr. Anderson looked up at John. "I'm going to tell the other boys about this, John—especially your little friend Johnny."

"Tie that fat man down!" John ordered. Oswold and Godart ran at Anderson. He was a very strong man, but he wasn't fast.

The men eventually had him down, and they tied up his arms and legs. "Whip him!" John ordered.

"No!" Smith shouted. "Don't hurt him!"

They whipped Anderson, and John knocked him in the back of the head with his cane, causing him to pass out. John's men dragged Anderson outside. When Smith tried to follow, he fell at the doors of the barn. He could not walk; he could barely stand. Smith saw Maria, the housemaid, hurrying out of the house when they raised their voices. Smith watched them throw his old friend into the back of a carriage. John told Maria to take him and dump him in the ocean before he awakened. When the carriage rode off, John turned to face Smith. "Bring him over here," he said.

John's men dragged him across the yard, cutting up his feet as they dragged him against the ground. They threw him down in front of John, waiting patiently for their next orders. "What are you going to do John, kill me? My friends will notice if I go missing."

"As far as they know, I sold you," John said. He ordered his men to tie Smith's hands together. "Tie up his ankles too," he added.

While they were doing this, Smith asked, "What is to become of my friends, then?"

"I can't hide forever. I'm going to take your friend Ace back to his father in exchange for my pardon."

"You can't do that!" Smith cried. "He'll kill himself."

"So?" John laughed.

"John, please …," Smith began, but John ordered his men to drag him to the road. They stood in the middle of the road while Mr. Godart fetched John a horse and some rope. When he came back, John ordered them to tie the rope from Smith's ankles to the horse's saddle.

"Good-bye, Smith," John said. He lit a match. The poor horse reared back when its tail caught fire. It took off running. The horse ran a long way, with Smith dragging behind it. It ran and ran, and it didn't seem like it was going to stop. Smith struggled, trying to get away. *I'm going to die!*

***

Snake and the others were in the fields. They hadn't seen Smith all day, and they were beginning to worry. "Maybe you should go talk with Alvery, Snake," Ace suggested. "I haven't seen him all day either."

Snake took Ace's advice and was permitted by Godart to go inside to visit with his master. When Snake went inside, Maria told him to go to the kitchen, where he found him sitting at the table. John Stevenson was rubbing his sore leg that he had twisted the night before. He had been off it all day.

"Mr. Alvery? Are you all right?"

John smiled at him and invited Snake to sit. "Quite all right, Johnny. Your friend Smith knocked me over with a rake last night."

Snake could not deny the bruise on John's cheekbone from where Smith had clearly hit him, but Snake found it hard to believe that Smith would hit an old man with a rake. "I'm sure it was a mistake," Snake said, vouching for Smith.

"Maybe so, but after that I sold him to—"

"You sold him?" Snake interrupted him. He stood.

"Do you blame me?" John asked. "I've had nothing but trouble from Smith since the day I bought him." John seemed to sense that Snake was becoming upset with him, which was the last thing he would want. "Listen, boy, Smith attacked me in the barn and tossed my cane so I couldn't stand. If it wasn't for Oswold and Godart, he would have killed me."

"I don't believe that." Snake turned to leave.

"Son, wait!"

"I'm not your son," Snake said sternly. He stood still for a moment, and a frightening thought crossed his mind: *I'll never see Smith again.*

"Johnny, how about you and I go down to the docks one day? We could go sailing. You'd like that, right?"

"Now you're trying to bribe me?" Snake shouted at him, turning back around.

"Johnny, I didn't realize how close you were to him." John motioned for Snake to come back and sit with him. "I'll find the man I sold him to, all right?"

"You would do that?" Snake asked in a surprised tone.

"I'll get him back for you," John lied easily, as one could assume that Smith was already dead. "I'll have my men go out and look for him. You don't need to worry. I'll get him back. Go on back outside."

Snake thanked him before leaving.

Ch 24

When Smith opened his eyes, a sudden sharp pain shot through his body. He was covered from head to toe in his own blood. From the corner of his eye, he could see the horse drinking from a small pond. The rope had torn so he could no longer be dragged by it. *I'm so thirsty*, he thought, edging closer to the pond and frightening the young stallion. It jumped and took off running; Smith could see where the flame had scalded its tail. His hands were still tied and so were his ankles.

Smith managed to drag himself through the dirt toward the little pond. His arms and back ached when he did this. Finally, he was close enough to the pond to glimpse at his reflection in the water. His own face disgusted him; blood and dirt were trapped in his sores. He reached his hands toward the water.

A loud screech made him jump, and he looked up to see that a large black bird had landed on a branch of the small tree by the pond. "I'm not dead, you bloody bird!" he cried up at it. His chest hurt from the shouting. He lay still a bit longer, and the bird flew down and landed by his hands, which were stretched out in front of him. The crow started pecking at his hand, and he shooed it away, but it came back and pecked at his hand again. He didn't have the energy to shoo it away again. He was in tears, and he began to breathe heavily. "Please … someone help me!"

***

Smith was awake, but he kept his eyes closed. He felt better and began to wonder if he was dead. When he moved, he could feel that he was covered in bandages; one bandage was wrapped around his entire left arm and side, and one was around his right hand, where the bird had been pecking at him. Another was strapped around his entire right leg, and one last bandage was wrapped around his forehead. As far as he could tell, he was in a bed, with blankets wrapped around him tightly to keep him comfortable.

He smelled food; the smell forced his eyes opened. A young woman in her early twenties sat on a stool beside the little bed, stroking his hair. The room was empty apart from the bed in the back of the room and a window above him. The young woman wore an expensive green dress, a matching green bonnet, and lots of diamond jewelry. She wet a rag and dabbed it on his face. "He's waking up!" she shouted toward the door on the far side of the room. He heard footsteps.

"Where am I?" he asked her.

"Don't worry, you're safe." She leaned over and kissed him, and even his lips had sores on them. His eyes widened in embarrassment.

"No fair! Susan got to kiss him first!" a much younger girl shouted from the doorway, and Smith grew even more embarrassed. The young girl came into the room, followed by an even younger girl. The girl who had shouted looked about fifteen or so; she was wearing a large blue dress similar to that of the older girl, but no bonnet. The other girl who had followed behind her wasn't but a year younger. She wore a red dress that looked almost exactly like her sister's blue dress.

The two younger girls stood at his feet, staring at him and talking amongst themselves about him. The girl in red smiled at him. "I want to kiss him too!"

"You're not of marriage age," the girl in blue said. "You shouldn't be kissing men."

"You're not of marriage age either!" she squeaked.

"I will be in four days, thank you very much."

"Hush up, girls. Leave the man alone," the oldest of the three girls said.

"Excuse me, but ... who are you?" Smith asked, not sitting up at all.

The oldest girl put a hand on his chest. "I'm Susan. These are my little sisters. This is Hannah." She pointed at the girl in blue. "And this is my youngest sister, Anna." She pointed at the girl in red.

Smith smiled at Anna. "Anna? My little sister's name was Anna."

A man came into the room; he was dressed in a blue linen suit, as was the young boy standing behind him. "Ah, the boy is awake," he said, sounding pleased.

"He's not dead, then?" the little boy asked and trotted into the room. Susan slapped him for his comment. The little boy, being only about seven, started to pout, seeming embarrassed that his sister had struck him. Susan, attempting to make peace with him, put a hand on his shoulder and smiled. "This is my little brother, Jimmy. And that is my older brother Maxi."

Maxi shrugged when she said his name. "I'll go tell Mama that he's up."

A few minutes later, another woman came into the room. She did not look very old, but Smith could tell that she was the mother of this wholesome group. The woman was wearing the same green dress and bonnet as Susan. "My heavens, is the boy all right?" She came over by Smith.

"He'll live, Mama," Maxi said.

Despite all the people staring at him, Smith was able to fall asleep before he even had any of the food they'd made for him. The next time he woke up, it was late in the day, and the only one in the room with him was Maxi. He was sitting on the stool by his bed, reading a book. "Looks like you're feeling better." Maxi put down the book and helped him sit up. "We had a doctor look

at you while you were asleep; he said you'd be fine. He rewrapped
your bandages and gave you medicine."

"Thank you, Maxi."

He laughed. "You could just call me Max. Maxi is what my
mother calls me."

The young boy, Jimmy, came darting into the room. "Is he
dead?"

"Jim!" Maxi shouted at his brother. "Don't talk like that. The
man is fine."

Jimmy stared up at Smith. "He looks like our Papa, doesn't
he, Maxi?" Maxi just shrugged. Jimmy leaned against the bed
and asked, "What happened to you?"

"Jimmy, leave him alone," Maxi told him. Then he said to
Smith, "If Jim is bothering you, let me know."

"He's quite all right," Smith said.

"Are you hungry?" Maxi asked him as his two youngest sisters,
Hannah and Anna, entered the room.

"I wouldn't want to impose."

"It's all right." Maxi put a hand out to him. "Can you stand
up? I'll help you downstairs to the dining room so we can eat.
The servants should have dinner ready by now."

"Servants? Are you slave owners?" Smith asked nervously.

"No, not at all," Maxi assured him. "Are you hungry or
not?"

"Yes."

Smith stood, holding on to Maxi so he could stay up. "Sit
down!" Maxi shouted and tossed the blankets over him. Anna
and Hannah giggled. "Girls, look away." He sounded angry
with them. "Sorry about that. I forgot the doctor took off your
clothes."

"Oh!" Smith covered himself up so Anna and Hannah could
not see; he hadn't realized that they had removed his pants.

"Jimmy, go get a pair of my old trousers for the man," Maxi
said, and the boy ran out of the room. He came back in a few
minutes with a decent pair of pants. Maxi looked at his sisters,

who were still just standing and smiling. "Girls, leave so I can help the man."

The two of them scurried out of the room, and Maxi helped Smith into the pants. Smith leaned on Maxi, who helped him out of the room and down a small flight of stairs; they apparently had put him in the attic. They walked down the hall on the second floor, and Smith observed the paintings on the wall. *A family portrait ... I always wanted one of my family.* It was an old painting, he knew, because Jimmy was still a babe, and Susan still looked like a young girl. He looked at the man in the painting. *I have yet to meet the father,* he thought. They went down another flight of stairs to the main floor.

Maxi helped Smith sit at the table. The table was large, and maids set down several bowls and plates. The women serving the family all seemed kind. The mother came into the room. "Why is he out of bed? Why did you bring him down here, Maxi?"

"He was hungry, Mama," Maxi explained.

"He's hardly eaten a thing in almost four days," the mother said, and Smith shifted in his seat. "You should have just brought the food to him instead of making him walk down here!"

"Ma'am? Four days?" Smith sounded shocked. "I've been asleep for four days?"

"In and out," Maxi said. "You've only been awake for a few minutes at a time. You haven't eaten much, just some fruit and bread."

"No wonder I'm hungry," Smith said. He could recall being awakened a few times and eating, but it was difficult to recall anything that had happened to him since he had been on the farm. *My friends must be so worried. They have no idea where I am.*

"Well, don't worry," the mother said. "Susan's in the kitchen helping Jenny finish supper."

"I'm sorry, ma'am, who's Jenny?" Smith asked.

"She's one of our servants," she said. "We have nine." The mother went to the kitchen and returned with a bowl of soup, which she put in front of him. "Here, go ahead and eat this."

"Thank you, Mrs. ..." Smith thought for a second, unsure of her name.

"Mrs. Cook," she told him. "Jane Cook."

"Thank you, Mrs. Cook." Smith ate the soup while the servants finished putting out supper. Smith wasn't much of the mannerly type. After all, he had grown up on a pirate ship. When everyone started eating, he asked, "Are we not waiting on Mr. Cook?" There was a sudden silence, and Smith wished he hadn't asked.

"There is no Mr. Cook," Mrs. Cook said. "He died six years ago."

"Oh." Smith noticed everyone stopped eating, with the exception of Jimmy, who didn't seem to mind. "I didn't mean to upset any of you."

"It's okay," Jimmy said, biting into some bread.

It was silent for a while until Maxi spoke: "Jenny, do we still have those crutches in the closet in the main hall?"

"Yes, Master Cook. Would you like me to fetch them?" the servant asked. He nodded, and she hurried to bring Smith the crutches. She leaned them against a wall for him.

Now that the silence was broken, Jimmy began asking Smith many questions. Before he had a chance to answer one, he was on to the next question. "What's your name? Where are you from? Why were you out in the middle of nowhere?"

"Jimmy, I told you to stop asking the man so many questions," Maxi said.

Jimmy stuck out his tongue at Maxi. "I just want to know his name."

"Jim!" Mrs. Cook shouted. "Don't stick out your tongue."

"Where are you from?" Jimmy asked. "Do you have a family? How did you get hurt?"

"Jim!" Maxi slapped him on the back of the head. "Stop asking him all those questions. It's obvious he doesn't want to answer them."

"I think we have a right to know his name," Susan muttered.

"Don't backtalk me," Maxi said scornfully to his sister. Everyone seemed to listen to what Maxi had to say, even Mrs. Cook, Smith noticed. It seemed to Smith that Maxi had become the head of the household.

They won't trust me forever. If I tell them I'm Smith, they might report me to King Harold, but if I tell them I'm Peter Barons, and then they find out I'm Smith, then my mother could get in trouble. He knew he should give them a name or they would not trust him. "It's all right, Maxi. My name's Will, William Barons."

Ch 25

Mr. Anderson was struggling in the cold water. Maria had shoved him into a cockboat when he was still unconscious, and then she took him out into the harbor and dumped him there. His hands and ankles were still tied, and he struggled to keep his head above the water. Maria was long gone by now. He finally came across a sand dune, which saved his life. He was able to untie himself and take a short rest before making the long swim to shore.

As he swam, he cursed himself. *Will's son. It was William's son—and I helped hurt him! I have to do something. I have to make this right. What did they do to Peter after Maria took me away?* When he got to the port, he went into town, heading straight toward the bar to drown his sorrows after the thought that Peter was dead because of him crossed his mind.

He found the bar and headed inside. He figured using John's tab for grog would be a small revenge. *Everyone here still thinks I work for "Alvery."* Once he was inside, he sat at the bar and started drinking. He heard some ruckus coming from the back of the room, and he turned to see what it was. Two women were dressed in men's clothing, in black and red colors. Who else could they be but Black Dragons? Mr. Anderson had a terrible feeling in his stomach. There were rumors that a woman had joined the Black Dragons, and he was sure her name was Abigail. Abigail was defiantly the younger of the two. The other woman seemed oddly familiar to Mr. Anderson, but he couldn't put his finger on it. He didn't want to bother them, for many reasons.

If those women find out what I did to their captain, they'll try to kill me. Mr. Anderson sat at the bar, sipping on his grog and trying to remain unnoticed.

The oldest woman had a man by the collar of his shirt, and she was holding him a foot off the ground. He was shaking and begging to be let go. "Well? Where are they?" the woman screamed in his face.

"I-I ...," he mumbled.

Mr. Anderson recognized the man; he was the auctioneer that sold them the Black Dragons. The younger woman slammed his back into a wall. "*Speak up!*" she ordered.

The poor man spoke quietly. Anderson could see that he definitely was the one who had been in charge at the auction. "I don't know. Almost everyone in town was at that auction." The woman let go of him, and he fell to the ground, whimpering in the corner.

She stood in the middle of the bar and shouted, "Everyone, listen here!" A few people turned and looked at her, but eventually they went back to what they were doing. From pure frustration, she pulled out a pistol and shot it at the ceiling. "On the floor, everyone!" she screamed, and everyone, including Anderson, dropped to the floor. "Who bought the Black Dragons ... about a month ago?"

"They were sold to Mr. Alvery's men. They probably took them to his farm," one man said; he was hiding behind some stools.

"Where's his farm?" the woman asked.

Anderson took a breath and stood. "I know," he said. "I can show you."

The younger woman marched right up to Mr. Anderson. "Let's go," she said, and Anderson followed, as did the older woman.

The two women met up with a young man and a younger girl. "Another hostage?" The boy sounded as if he was joking, so Anderson didn't get concerned.

"He's going to help us find the boys," the older woman explained. She smiled at Mr. Anderson. "Are you all right, Mr. Anderson?" she asked. "You're soaking wet."

"Who are you?" Mr. Anderson asked. "My word, Mrs. Barons?" he cried out when he recognized her. He hugged her. "Oh, Ellen—I've done something so terrible!"

He explained everything. He told them how his blacksmithing shop went out of business and he came to Kevin's Isle looking for work. He was hired by a crippled man called Mr. Alvery. He told her of the pain the Black Dragons had suffered, especially poor Smith. Then he told them how Smith found out that Alvery was really Stevenson and had been beaten. He told them that when he refused to harm Smith any longer, he had been hit over the head, and it was the last he saw of Smith.

By the time he was done, Mrs. Barons had started to cry. "My Peter! My Peter is hurt … or worse. John Stevenson wishes him dead; we have to find him."

"And Mouth! What has become of him?" Abigail cried.

"Oh, don't cry!" Stewart tried to comfort them.

"We'll save them," Anderson assured her.

Mrs. Barons smiled. "All right. We'll find them, and we'll save them. I'll kill John if I have to."

***

Smith woke up suddenly in the middle of the night. *That noise. Where's it coming from?* He sat up in the little bed. He heard crying. He struggled to stand up and get the crutches from beside the bed. He slowly hobbled down the small flight of stairs and looked down the hall; the crying was louder. Smith went down the hall. Even though it hurt even with the crutches, he could at least keep himself from falling. "Hello? Is anyone there?"

He opened a door slightly, peering inside to see Jimmy crying. "Jim!" Smith moved over to the bed. "What's wrong, lad?"

"Nothing." Jim buried his face in his pillow when Smith sat down on the bed.

"Are you all right?" Smith couldn't possibly imagine what would make such a happy child cry. He started wondering if it had anything to do with the conversation at dinner. "Is this about your papa, Jim?" He put the crutches down on the floor.

"Go away," Jim said. "I'm not crying."

Smith made Jimmy roll over on his back by tickling him. "Those look like tears to me."

"Men don't cry." The child crossed his arms and began to pout.

"I cry," Smith willingly admitted.

Jimmy shrugged. "You're a strange man. I don't even think Will is your real name."

"I was named after my father." Smith figured this was only half a lie.

"Maxi was named after his papa."

Smith looked at the little boy, slightly disturbed. "Don't you mean 'our papa,' Jim? He's your papa too."

"I don't know," Jimmy said. "I never knew him. He died when I was only a year old."

"Is that why you were crying?" Smith asked him.

"I wasn't crying!" Jimmy shouted.

Smith rolled his eyes and corrected himself. "Is that why you were upset, Jimmy?"

"I guess so," Jimmy muttered. "I just never had a papa. It's not fair that Maxi and Susan and Hannah and Anna remember him and I don't! I want to remember him, but I can't. I only know what I see in paintings. I don't remember Papa, just what Mama and my sisters and my brother tells me. I don't even know exactly what happened the day he died!"

Smith looked at the sad little boy, not sure what to say to him. *Will Ian be like this? Will he cry at night because he doesn't have a father? Now I see what Mouth was talking about.* "Jimmy, how is it that your father died?"

"I only know what Maxi has told me. Mama doesn't like to talk about him. It makes her cry, and I don't like to make her cry. My papa was a sailor, did you know that? He built and sold ships all around Kirkston. Maxi took over Papa's business—did you know that?" Jimmy sounded as if he was enjoying talking to Smith.

"No, I didn't know that," Smith said.

"He was attacked by pirates," Jimmy continued. "They keelhauled him." Then he whispered, "Do you know what that is?"

Smith nodded. It was a terrible way to die. It's when they threw a man into the water and drag him under the ship from one side to another. The victim of keelhauling would normally drown. If he didn't die from drowning, he would die from being cut up by the barnacles that grew beneath a ship.

"Papa didn't drown from it. He was hurt bad, though, and he died the next day. It's because of bloody pirates that I don't have a pa. I hate pirates." Jimmy crossed his arms.

"I'm sorry about your father," Smith said.

"I hate pirates."

"What about the Black Dragons?" Smith couldn't help but ask.

"Who?" he asked. "Oh, Maxi's told me about them. They're pirates, right?"

"I wouldn't call them real pirates, but I guess they are," Smith said. "I mean, they steal to help people."

"They're still pirates, and I hate pirates," Jimmy huffed. "The Black Dragons are stupid to give away all the money they steal. What's the point of that? No matter how much money they steal, no matter how many people they save, there will still be poverty no matter where they go."

"True," Smith said. "But don't you think it's worth a shot, to try to help a poor-class citizen?"

"I guess so," Jimmy agreed. "King Harold doesn't do much to help them, though."

I love this kid, Smith thought.

Jimmy seemed to be observing him, recalling the rags he had been wearing when they had found him. "I'm sorry you don't have any money." Jimmy suddenly jumped up and headed to his dresser drawer. He pulled out a sock and brought it over to his bed. He turned the sock over and dumped out a few gold pieces and silver shillings. "Take my money. You need it more than I do."

"Jimmy, no," Smith said.

"You need it; you should take it." Jimmy shoved the coins toward him.

"There are people out there who need money far more than I do, people who are dying. There are people who only make one gold piece a week to feed their entire families. There are children who will never know their parents, like you, but unlike you, it could be prevented if someone would just reach out and help them." Smith felt saddened. "This right here"—he pointed at the money—"would have been enough to feed my entire family for a month when I was young."

Jimmy laughed. "This couldn't feed our chickens." Then he apparently realized that Smith wasn't joking. "I'm sorry, Will. I guess you're not used to three-course meals like me."

"No, I'm not." Smith picked the boy up and put him on his lap. "The world is not as kind to everyone the way it is to your family."

"I'm sorry, Will."

Smith rubbed the child's head. "You're a good boy, Jimmy. I'm sure your father would be very proud of you." Smith could tell Jimmy was holding in tears, and so he hugged him. "You know, Jimmy, it's okay to cry."

***

Smith woke up the next morning when he heard shouting; he was still in Jimmy's room. Jimmy wasn't next to him, so he figured the child had already gotten up and gone downstairs.

"Hey, Will!" Jimmy peeked inside the room. "Breakfast is ready."

"I'll be there in a minute, Jim," Smith told him, and the boy ran off. "He's in a better mood," Smith said aloud. He looked for the crutches he had left somewhere on the floor.

"Will?" Maxi came inside the room. He helped Smith up and handed him the crutches. "I wanted to thank you."

"For what?"

"I heard you and Jimmy talking last night," Maxi said. "Oh, and there's an idiot downstairs trying to buy some eggs from us. Don't mind him. He's just our neighbor, Mr. Watson."

"Is that the shouting I heard earlier?" Smith asked.

"Mr. Watson's quite a character, Will. He shouts when he speaks," Maxi explained. "I don't think it wise to point it out, though. He's not a real kind man." Maxi led him downstairs, and Smith could hear this Mr. Watson person.

"Who's your friend there, Maxi!" the man screamed, and Smith was taken aback for a moment.

"This is William," Maxi said.

"It's nice to meet you, sir." Smith put his hand out to shake.

"Speak up, boy!" Mr. Watson shouted, refusing to shake his hand. "Keep out of trouble, peasant! You don't belong here!"

Thankfully, the insane man left after purchasing eggs from them. "What's wrong with him?" Smith asked once he was gone.

"We think he may be a bit deaf," Maxi explained. "I'm sorry about him." Maxi led Smith to the table.

They all ate together. Smith had eaten more in the past two days than he had the entire time he had been with John Stevenson. Despite the wonderful food, he decided he had to leave soon. Ace was in danger. *Ace will be forced back to the palace, Snake will be adopted, and the others will surely be killed.* Smith was in bad shape, but he had to find his friends before they were hurt.

***

Late one night, Smith tried to leave without telling the Cook family, but Maxi saw him sneaking out. He took Smith's crutches from him.

"I need those," Smith said.

"If you still need these, then you don't need to leave," Maxi told him. They were outside by the front door.

Smith shook his head, annoyed. "Fine, I don't need them." Smith took no more than five or six painful steps before he fell to his knees.

"Will!" Maxi rushed over to him. "You mustn't leave. You're hurt!" He went to help him up.

"Get off me!" Smith said angrily. "I don't need your help!" Smith attempted to stand up, but he fell over. He tried a second time and fell, but he succeeded his third time. But standing was so painful that Smith couldn't bear it. Maxi watched him as he walked slowly. Smith hated being cruel to Maxi—he was a kind man—but he knew he had to do something before one of his friends was hurt. Smith fell again by the gate. Maxi hurried over to him, and Smith screamed, "I can get up by myself!"

Maxi just laughed. "You're really stubborn, aren't you?" He bent down beside him. "Oh no! Will, your feet are bleeding again!"

Smith looked down at his feet; he had reopened the sores on his ankles from when Stevenson's men had dragged him. "Ah!" Smith moaned. "It really hurts!"

Before Smith had a chance to push him away, Maxi scooped Smith up in his arms and carried him as he would a small child.

"Put me down, Maxi," Smith demanded, attempting to kick his legs. "You're freakishly strong!"

"Stop it, William. You're hurt, and all I want to do it help, understand me, lad?" Maxi shouted at him.

He would have to wait until he was better. Maxi would be keeping a close eye on him now, and Smith knew that. Maxi carried him inside and set him down on the couch in their den.

"Don't go anywhere," Maxi told him, leaving for a moment. He came back a few minutes later with a bucket of water, some rags, and bandages. He put the bucket on the floor in front of Smith and told him to put his feet in it. Smith did as he was told. The cold water felt good on his blistered feet. Maxi lifted one of Smith's feet and dabbed the sores with the rag. It stung, but Smith let him do it. Afterward, he dried his foot with the second rag and wrapped a bandage around it. Then he did the same thing with his other foot. "I'm not sure if I want to know how you were hurt like this, Will. But something tells me it was no accident."

Smith looked away from him. "That's nothing you need to be concerned with."

"Will, I have nothing but concern for you," Maxi said. "Tell me the truth. Are you some type of escaped criminal?"

"That would be the least of my worries." Smith quickly looked away.

"Were you a slave?"

"Yes," Smith said. "About a month ago, my friends and I were forced into slavery."

"I'm sorry," Maxi said. "You don't have to explain anything to me; I just want to help you."

"Thank you, Maxi." Smith smiled, knowing he could trust this man. For the first time in the last month, Smith felt safe.

Ch 26

"Thank you for helping me so late, Johnny," John said in his kind *Mr. Alvery* tone. He even patted Snake on the back and smiled.

"It's no trouble at all, sir." Snake yawned. It was the third night in a row his master had kept him up late.

"I'll be right back. I need to check with Mr. Godart about something." John left Snake to his work. He waited outside the room patiently.

About an hour later, John glanced inside the room. Snake had fallen asleep at the desk. "It's about time," he muttered. He went out on the porch, where Mr. Godart and Mr. Oswold were waiting for him. "Are all those boys asleep?"

"I just checked, and they're asleep," Mr. Oswold said. "But I must ask—why did you want Johnny inside?"

"If one of the others woke up and saw us, we could just get rid of them the way we did with Smith ... but not Johnny." John was whispering in order to avoid waking Snake. I want all of them clueless about who I really am as long as possible. Do you two remember what to do?"

"Why are we going to do this tonight, John?" Mr. Godart asked.

"They'll suspect something if he goes missing the same day you leave for the capital. They're not fools, Godart. We want them to think he ran off. We'll keep him hidden for a few days in the barn."

They went to the slave house; John held a candle so his men could see what they were doing. Godart went inside and tapped on Ace's shoulder. "Wake up, boy. Mr. Alvery needs you."

***

"Yes, sir," Ace said quickly. By now, he had figured out that Mr. Godart was always itching to hit him or one of the others. The two of them left the slave house and met up with Mr. Oswold and John, who Ace still believed to be Mr. Alvery. Even so, he sensed that something was amiss. "What's going on?" He kept his distance from all of them. Mr. Oswold had a sack with him. When Oswold approached Ace with it, he knew something bad was about to happen.

On impulse, Ace turned to run. He ran right into Mr. Godart, and his comrade threw the brown sack over Ace's head, pressing his hand firmly where his mouth was. Ace was kicking and trying to move his arms, but Mr. Oswold held them to his side. Mr. Godart grabbed his legs, and they carried him off. Ace couldn't scream with Oswold clamping his hand over his mouth, and he obviously couldn't see where they were headed.

When he was thrown to the ground, he yanked the sack off himself to see that they were in the back of the barn, along with six more of John's men. Two of John's men jumped him and held him down. Maria, who had been waiting for them in the barn, brought forth cuffs and chains. The men cuffed Ace's hands together, and his ankles as well. They wrapped him in chains and locked them tight. His heart was racing. "Why are you doing this to me?"

When Mr. Oswold and Mr. Godart were able to let go of Ace, they were out of breath. Ace was a strong young man.

"Here he is!" John mocked him. "The great Prince James Lincoln Caldara, heir to the throne of Kirkston!"

Ace's eyes widened. "How did you know that?"

"You, it was always you." John's fists were clenched. "You've been in my way since the beginning." John struck him. Ace looked at him in disgust. John continued his rant, saying, "If I hadn't broken out of prison, I would be dead because of you and your friends. Because of you, I must hide my face in shame!"

"What are you going to do to me?" Despite his grim situation, Ace still had a smirk look on his face that seemed to challenge John.

"I'm sending you home, boy, back to your father at Caldara Palace, to win my pardon!" John said.

"No, you can't send me back there!" Ace shouted. "I don't understand what I ever did to you. Why do you hate me and my friends?"

"It's me, boy, General John Stevenson."

***

"Peter! Peter, where are you?" Mrs. Barons screamed as they walked down the dreadfully humid terrain.

"I don't see him anywhere." Mr. Anderson sat down on the dirt road they had been following. "This is all my fault, that poor boy. I hurt him. I was hoping he'd escaped and we'd find him along the road … if he's still at the farm … Who knows what John might have done to him?"

Abigail tried to comfort him. "No, don't blame yourself. I'm sure he's fine. He's probably still at the farm."

"He was half-dead when I was there. I can only imagine how bad off he is now." Mr. Anderson buried his face in his hands, and he could hear Mr. Barons crying. He looked up to see that his words had frightened her. "Ellen, I'm so sorry."

"We should hurry to the farm and try to find him," Stewart suggested. "If he's not there, we should free the Black Dragons, and then we'll have more people to look for him."

"Are we almost there?" Gwen asked for the tenth time that morning.

"We're almost there, lass," Mr. Anderson said.

Soon they were walking again. They had been walking for almost a day, and it was getting tiring. "I'm thirsty!" Gwen cried. "I'm tired of walking. Can we stop?"

Stewart bent down, and Gwen jumped on his back so he could carry her. They continued for a long distance, until they came to a small pond. Gwen jumped off Stewart's back and ran to the water. When she bent down to drink, her knee hit something. "What's this?" she asked, picking it up. "It's a bangle! A gold bangle!"

Immediately, Mrs. Barons snatched it from her. "It's Courtney's bangle!"

"How do you know that?" Abigail asked her. "It's not exactly a rare find. There're hundreds of those bangles in Kirkston." She held up her own wrist. "See, Tommy gave me one just like it."

"Look here! Peter had it engraved on the inside." Mrs. Barons pointed to where it read *I love you, Courtney. Peter.* It was a sign to Mrs. Barons that her son was near. "Let's hurry!" she demanded, turning around. "He must be near."

Abigail stopped her. "Was that where he was going to or where he was coming from?" Abigail asked, and Mrs. Barons stomped her feet in annoyance. "I think it's best we go to the farm first," Abigail said.

"I suppose you're right." She put the bangle in her pocket for safekeeping. "Don't worry, Courtney. I promise I'll get this back to Peter."

***

"Let go of me!" Ace kicked and screamed. "I won't go back to the palace! I refuse!" The chains rubbed up against his skin, slicing his wrists and ankles.

"Stay still!" John and his men were about to stuff Ace into a cupboard in the barn. They had emptied everything out of it and taken out the shelves. It was taking a long time to get Ace inside, even with him chained up.

"Tie something over his mouth!" John shouted. Mr. Oswold handed him some rope. They forced Ace to bite down on it, and he tied it tightly over Ace's mouth. They threw him inside the cupboard and locked it tight. Then they pitched the cupboard to the ground, with the door on bottom so Ace couldn't manage to open it. They could hear him kicking from inside the cupboard.

"If one of them comes in here, they'll hear him," Mr. Godart said.

"He'll tire out eventually, but until then the barn is off limits," John said.

"But what will we tell them? They'll suspect something," Mr. Godart pointed out.

"You're right. We'll have to come up with something. I have an idea. Put the cupboard in one of the horse stalls. Tell them one of the horses gave birth, and we don't want them disturbing it, so they're not allowed in."

"Shall I go buy a colt in order to fool them?" Mr. Oswold asked. "That Erikson fellow's horse just gave birth awhile back; he'll probably sell it cheap. As long as we keep them away from the horse long enough, they'll believe it was born today."

"Good idea, Oswold," John said. "Go to town now."

The next morning, John announced to the Black Dragons that one of their horses gave birth the night before, and that they were not permitted near the barn.

"Where's Ace?" Snake asked after this announcement.

"Ran off last night. Mr. Oswold is out looking for him before he gets himself killed." John turned and left.

"Ran off? He ditched us!" Cannonball clenched his fists. "I don't believe it!"

"Why would Ace run away and not take us with him?" Squirt asked.

"Maybe he went looking for Smith!" Snake said excitedly.

"Yeah, it's not like your buddy Alvery is looking for him," Mouth agreed. "I'm sure that's where he is."

Squirt kicked his feet around in the dirt and nervously asked, "Then why didn't he say something?"

***

"Strange, isn't it?" Mouth said later that night, as they were heading to bed in the slave house. "Isn't it odd that the day Ace goes missing, we're not permitted inside the barn?"

"There's something going on here, and I don't like it," Blade said. "There's something in that barn. I say we go see if there really is a colt in there or not."

"We'll be lashed if we're caught," Squirt told them.

"Then only one of us should go," Mouth said. "I'll go see what's going on in there."

"No, Mouth," Snake said. "I should. Mr. Alvery won't whip me. Or at least I don't think he will."

"You don't know for sure. I'll be fine." Mouth stood up. "I have quiet footsteps."

"What if you're caught?" Snake asked.

"Then I'll get a lashing for disobeying him. How bad could it be?" Mouth was already at the door.

"A lot worse than you're letting on," Squirt argued. "Don't go, please?"

"I'll just go check and see if there *is* a colt in there … and see what he's hiding. Even if there is one, I know there's something else going on!" Mouth was already heading toward the barn.

"Careful, Mouth!" Squirt called after him.

It was late now. Mouth walked carefully and quietly toward the barn. He was hopeful that he wouldn't run into Mr. Alvery. When he reached the barn, he wasn't sure if he wanted to go inside. After a moment of debating with himself, he opened the large doors and headed in. To his surprise, there was a colt inside the barn. "Well, what do you know! The ruddy old cripple wasn't lying." Mouth looked at all the other horses carefully. Mr. Alvery had about six other horses apart from the young colt. Then he saw lots of junk lying out on the floor, junk that was once inside the cupboard. "Where's the cupboard?" he asked himself aloud.

He looked around in the stalls, eyeing all the horses. Something was wrong here. Inside one of the stalls, he saw the cupboard lying down with holes drilled in the back. *Perhaps so something inside could breathe?* Suddenly he felt a presence, and a man put his hands on Mouth's shoulders and spun him around.

"What are you doing here?" Mr. Oswold asked, throwing him to the ground. Mr. Godart and John were there as well.

"You're in trouble, boy!" John shouted. "I'll teach you to disobey me!"

***

Smith was in a panic. He was crawling around on the floors of the attic, muttering, "Where is it? Where is it?"

"Will? Are you all right?" It was Maxi and his mother.

"I've lost it!" Smith cried.

"What? What have you lost?" Mrs. Cook was clearly surprised to see Smith so upset.

"The bangle! Courtney's bangle!" Smith had remembered leaving his bangle in his old pants, and when he went to check the pockets, they were empty.

"Courtney?" Maxi smiled. "I didn't think a boy like you would have a woman to go after, Will." He sounded as if he was just joking with him, but Smith was not in the mood.

"Relax, boy. We would be glad to give you money to buy her a new one," Mrs. Cook said. "It wouldn't be a problem."

"No, no. You don't understand. Courtney is dead." Smith continued searching desperately on the floor.

"Will, you probably just dropped it by the pond where Maxi found you," the woman said. "We'll take you there in the morning, sweetheart, I promise."

Smith thanked her, realizing how foolish he must look. She left the room, and the two young men were alone.

Maxi came and sat by Smith on the bed. "Courtney? Who is she, an old girlfriend?"

"Aye." Smith's voice sounded horse. "She passed away about three years ago."

"What happened?" Maxi asked him.

"John Stevenson killed her."

"Say no more." Maxi put a hand on Smith's shoulder. "He was one of the worst generals this country has ever seen. All he did was keep the poor poor and make the rich richer."

"You're not like most rich folks around here," Smith said. "Why is that?"

"My father grew up on the streets; he was born into a poor family. He won my mother over and took over my grandfather's business on my mother's side. My grandfather had no son, just my mother. My father made sure we weren't spoiled growing up, well, with the exception of Anna and Hannah a little. Susan was his little girl, but she never was interested in feminine things when she was younger, so when Hannah came along, Father spoiled her rotten, and then you have Anna, who became jealous of Hannah easily, seeing that she was just a year younger." Maxi laughed. "They're good girls, though. Tell me, Will, what was your father like?"

"He was childlike. I always loved how, despite his age, he always had time to act like a child. On my birthdays, he would always give me something my mother disapproved of, and they would argue about it, but he would always win. Except for once, when he caught a snake in the garden and gave it to me as a pet. My mother tossed it out the window, and it slithered away." Smith laughed at the mere memory of it. "He was a good man."

"He sounds like a good man. He sounds like he's a lot like you," Maxi told him. "Childish."

Smith shook his head. "You're hilarious."

"Come on, Will, it's time for supper." Maxi helped Smith down to the dinner table.

After they had settled and begun eating, Mrs. Cook said to Smith, "Will, Hannah tells me you have a little sister named Anna?"

"*Had* a little sister named Anna."

"Will, I'm sorry ..."

"I actually had two sisters," he said. "They both died when I was twelve. Anna was five, and my older sister, Elizabeth, was fifteen. They died around the same time as my father."

"Elizabeth died at marriage age! She didn't even get a chance to marry!" Hannah sighed. "That's horrible!"

"Well, his sister Anna died before she even reached marriage age. She was a babe," Anna pointed out.

"What happened to them?" Jimmy asked, and Maxi kicked him under the table, whispering for him not to upset their guest.

"It's all right. I don't mind," Smith said. "My father died on my twelfth birthday. General John Stevenson shot him. We couldn't afford the taxes, and my father said he was going to file a complaint to King Harold, and John became angry and almost hurt my mother. My father fought back, and that was when John shot him. He died ... and I had to take over at work as apprentice blacksmith. One day John and his men set fire to the blacksmith's shop with my sisters inside ... and they died. It's just me and my mother now, but I don't even know where she is." When Smith was done, the room seemed quiet.

"We're so sorry, William," Susan said. "Is there anything we can do to help?"

"You've all done so much for me," Smith said. "And all I've done is lie to you."

"What do you mean, Will?" Maxi asked. There was a knock on the door, and he went to answer it. The others stared at Smith, waiting for him to continue.

Before he could, Maxi came storming into the room, Mr. Watson right behind him. "I told you that peasant boy was no good!" he screamed. "He's a priate!" Mr. Watson was waving a wanted poster that he had probably gotten one day when he went to town.

Smith could see their angry faces. All of them jumped right out of their chairs, and Smith was overcome with shock and fear.

"Grab him, Maxi!"

Ch 27

Mouth was curled up on the floor. *Thirty-five lashes! The man is mad,* Mouth thought. *Surely he knows that this could kill me.* "Mr. Alvery, please stop!"

"Go back to the slave house." John yanked Mouth to his feet. "You will never disobey one of my orders again, no matter how small."

"Yes, sir." Mouth left the barn, but he could not walk far. He fell in the fields; thankfully, Knot and Blade saw him and carried him back to the slave house. They laid him down on one of the mattress. Snake cleaned his wounds while Mouth lay on his stomach, his face buried in a pillow. "He tried to kill me," Mouth swore under his breath.

"This was no lashing!" Snake cried. "He *was* trying to kill you."

Knot asked, "Was there even a colt in there?"

"There was," Mouth said.

"So he wasn't lying …" Snake sighed. "That means Ace really did abandon us."

"No, he was lying." Mouth looked up. His eyes were bloodshot, and tears were streaming down his cheeks.

"But you said there was a colt in there." Like everyone else, Yin was visibly confused.

"There was … but there wasn't a mother." Mouth moaned; he ached all over. "All of Alvery's horses are male. He went out and bought a baby horse as an excuse to keep us out of the barn."

"But why?" Squirt asked, but his brother had already passed out.

"He's unconscious," Snake said, touching Mouth on his head.

"He's lost a lot of blood. Maybe we should put bandages on him? We could use some of the sheets." Yang said this as he was already ripping a sheet.

"Do you think he'll be okay?" Squirt asked, sitting beside Mouth.

"Don't worry, Squirt. He'll be fine," Snake promised.

Squirt held Mouth's hand tightly. "I want to go home."

Snake touched Mouth's head gently again. *How can any man do this to another human being?* "Tommy, can you hear me?" Snake asked him. Then he said to the others, "I'm worried. Mouth is badly hurt."

"He'll die if he works tomorrow," Squirt said. "Mr. Alvery will make him work tomorrow, and it'll kill him." Squirt was crying. "I want to go home!"

"I know," Snake said. "I want to go home too. We need to find out what Alvery's hiding."

***

John sat on his front porch the next morning, looking out into the fields. "I don't see Johnny or that cretin they call Mouth," he said to Mr. Godart. The two of them went to the slave house, where Snake was sitting next to Mouth, placing a wet rag on his head. Mouth was unconscious still, and Snake was making sure none of John's men came near him. "Johnny, what are you still doing in here?"

"Taking care of Mouth; you really hurt him," Snake said bluntly. The two of them came over, and Snake threw himself over Mouth. "Don't you dare come near him!"

"Johnny—"

"Don't call me Johnny!" Snake shouted. "You can't do this. You could have killed him! You can't treat us like this!"

"Us? I've treated you like my own son," John said.

"I am not your son, and I never will be." Snake cradled Mouth.

"Johnny, please let me make this up to you," John said.

"Me? It's my friends you have been cruel to!"

"Then I will make it up to them." John turned to Mr. Godart. "Take the boy back to the house and put him to bed. Have Maria fix him something good to eat." John looked at Snake and said, "You get back to the fields."

"If you hurt him—"

"I'm not going to hurt him, Johnny," John said. "I promise you this."

Mr. Godart woke up Mouth and helped him to the house. As Snake started to leave, John stopped him. "I put up posters and had Mr. Oswold warn everyone in town about your friend Smith. Everyone in town is looking for him and the man I sold him to."

"Thank you, Mr. Alvery," Snake said, heading out of the slave house. John Stevenson went back up to the house. He spotted Mr. Godart coming down the stairs after putting Mouth in a guest room.

"That boy Johnny has a hold on you." Mr. Godart laughed at him. "He can get you to do just about anything, can't he?"

John just shook his head and told Mr. Godart to get back to work. He looked out into the fields and was pleased to see that Snake was telling the others that their *kind* master was looking for Smith.

***

Mrs. Barons, Mr. Anderson, Abigail, Stewart, and Gwen were hopelessly lost, unsure if they were heading in the right direction.

They had gone to sleep one night and had awakened confused as to which way they had come from and which way they were going. The road looked the same both ways for miles. They decided on a direction and pressed on; it was late at night when they ran into a small wood.

"We already went by these woods," Stewart said. "We've been going in the wrong direction all day!"

"Look." Mrs. Barons pointed to the sky above the trees. "Smoke. And smoke means fireplaces, and fireplaces mean people. Let's go see if we can't find someone to help us." They headed off into the woods, where they found a small group of houses, maybe three or four large homes. Their attention was drawn to an old man running across the road to another house, waving a wanted poster around. He was screaming so loud that they couldn't quite make out what he was saying. The ridiculous man ran shouting into the neighbors' house.

***

Smith was inside that house, and he was in a panic. Smith had just about been ready to tell the Cook family the truth. He was going to explain it to them in a way that wouldn't make them angry, but Mr. Watson gave it to them straight and they had panicked. Pirates killed their father, so when they found out Smith was a pirate, they all became furious.

Someone shouted, "Grab him, Maxi!" Maxi had jumped up quickly and snatched Smith's arm. He yanked him from his seat and threw him to the floor. Then he jumped on him and forced him to his knees. Mr. Watson grabbed on to him too, by his right arm and the back off his neck. Maxi had hold of his left arm and his hair. It wasn't hard to take Smith down in his present condition.

Hannah and Anna fled from their seats, and Susan jumped up after them. Jimmy just looked at him with hurtful eyes, which Smith found far worse than Maxi's tight grip. Before Smith could comprehend what had just happened, Susan had already fetched a musket and given it to her mother. Mrs. Cook held the gun right at Smith's chest. "Please wait!" Smith cried out. "You don't understand!" Smith closed his eyes.

"We'll take this boy to Caldara," Mrs. Cook said. "Harold will have you hung for your crimes!"

Smith heard a gun go off, but it sure didn't sound like a musket. *Am I dead?* He opened his eyes to see that Mrs. Cook had dropped the musket; her dress was covered in blood.

"Mama!" Jimmy jumped down from his seat.

Smith was so confused that he couldn't move. Maxi and Mr. Watson let go of him, and Mr. Watson ran out the door.

"Mama!" Maxi hurried next to his mother, just as terrified as the little seven-year-old. Susan was clearly upset as well.

Mrs. Cook was on the ground, clenching her side and crying out for help. "What happened?"

Smith hurried to help, but Maxi shoved him away. "Don't you touch her, pirate!"

"Peter!" Mrs. Barons was in the doorway, along with Abigail, Mr. Anderson, and two people he didn't know. Abigail was the one holding a pistol.

"Mama! Abigail!" Smith hurried over to them. "Mrs. Cook is hurt!"

"You're worried about her when she was just about to kill you?" Abigail asked.

Abigail and Mrs. Barons knelt next to Smith and the others, checking to see if Mrs. Cook was all right. "Get out!" Maxi swung at Abigail. She clasped his arm before he could hit her, bending his elbow until he cried out for her to let go.

When she did, he went to swing at Smith. "Enough, boy!" Mrs. Barons swiped Abigail's pistol and pointed it right at him. "Stand up!" she shouted, and he did as he was told. "Stand over there. We're going to help." Maxi stood in a corner; his sisters all hurried over to him. They were crying, and little Jimmy just stood there taking it all in.

Abigail held the pistol now, and Mrs. Barons checked Mrs. Cook over. Immediately, Mrs. Barons pointed at one of the servants who had hurried into the room after the gunshot, telling her to go fetch a doctor. She pointed at Susan. "You, go get a bucket of water." Then she pointed at Anna. "You, go find a rag." Then she pointed at Hannah. "You, fetch me a knife." Mrs. Barons rolled Mrs. Cook over and said, "Bring her to a bed." Maxi picked up his mother and carried her back to her bedroom, placing her on the bed. "Someone go get some bandages."

Mrs. Barons removed her large dress and much of her clothing underneath so she could find where the bullet had gotten her in the side. Mrs. Barons carefully removed the bullet with the knife, cleaned her wound, and bandaged it. The entire time Stewart, who Smith still didn't know, was praying under his breath.

Mrs. Barons tried to assure everyone that Mrs. Cook would be okay, but no one calmed down until the doctor arrived and said the same thing. Before he left, the doctor told them that she just needed to rest for a few days. Mrs. Barons had told the doctor that the gunshot had been accidental. Once the doctor was gone, things started to quiet down. Mrs. Barons and Abigail were hugging and kissing Smith, excited to see him again. Mr. Anderson begged for Smith's forgiveness, which Smith immediately accepted.

"Who are they?" Smith asked, pointing to Stewart and Gwen. "Do I know you?" he asked Stewart, not realizing he was the same boy he had seen on the *Annihilator* almost two months before.

"They helped us find you. We'll explain everything later," his mother told him.

"I'm in your debt." Smith thanked them. He shook Stewart's hand. "What the bloody devil happened to your hand, lad?"

"Can we explain that later too?" Stewart smiled at Mrs. Barons, whom he had become fond of after she'd rescued his sister.

After a long silence, Maxi pulled Smith aside, saying, "I heard your mother call you Peter. Who are you really?"

Smith admitted the truth to Maxi. He told him, "My real name is Peter Barons. My *father* was Will Barons. After the death of my father and my sisters, and the false arrest of my mother, I joined the Black Dragons and took the name Smith. I *am* a pirate, and I'm sorry I didn't say something earlier. I knew what pirates did to your family, and I was afraid of how you would react."

Mrs. Cook sat up in her bed and called Smith over. "I thought the Black Dragons' little crime sprees were much farther south of here."

"Yes, Peter, what happened?" Mrs. Barons asked, taking her son's hand. "We know the Annihilators got to you."

"How did you know that?" Smith asked. "Never mind." He went on to explain what had happened to them in the past several weeks.

"How could he torture you like that?" Mrs. Barons cried, kissing her son on his cheek when he finished explaining how he came to be at the Cook household.

"I want to help, Smith," Jimmy said, hugging Smith around his legs. "We can save your friends."

"Yes," Maxi agreed. "Don't worry, Peter. We're going to help you."

***

Ace was in the barn. He was alone and frightened. John Stevenson sometimes would come to visit him, giving him food late at night. It didn't matter to him; he wanted to be with his friends, not trapped in a cupboard lying on the ground. The chains rubbed up against him, and his arms and sides were blistered from them. He heard a knocking on the cupboard and prepared himself to be rolled over. He was, and the cupboard doors opened. John Stevenson had food for him. Mr. Oswold stood by him in case Ace managed to hurt John.

"Time for dinner," John told him. "Have you been crying, lad?"

"Please let me go, John," Ace begged, after John removed the rope covering his mouth. "I won't tell anyone. Please. I won't tell Snake about this—just please let me go. Don't take me back to my father."

"Enough, James." John made him eat some bread. When he was done, John and Mr. Oswold forced him back into the cupboard. Ace was weak; he wished John Stevenson fed him more.

He started crying and shivering. The thought of being forced back to Caldara frightened him more than anything else did. Hours passed. He started to hear voices, the cupboard was rolled over, and the doors swung open. "Ace!"

Ch 28

When the doors opened on the cupboard, Ace sat up quickly. Snake untied the rope from around his mouth, and Ace told them everything he knew—as well as what John and his men had done to him. Most of them found it hard to believe that Mr. Alvery was John Stevenson. He had been completely unrecognizable because of his scarred face and facial hair, but his cruel behavior was all too familiar.

"We have to get out of here," Ace said. "Smith could be dead."

"We're slaves," Mouth said. "If Stevenson sends word that we've escaped, we'll be killed or recaptured before we even reach the ocean. Just like last time. He'll hurt Squirt again!" Mouth tried to shake the thought from his mind.

"He's going to take me back to my father," Ace said.

"Then you have to run," Snake said.

"I can't leave all of you here," Ace argued.

"Can you leave Smith? He's probably out dying somewhere!" Snake couldn't bear the thought. "You have to try to find him and go for help."

"Who's going to want to help the Black Dragons?" Yang asked.

"There's got to be somebody out there who still has faith in us," Snake said to him. "What else can we do? We have to go on pretending that we think Stevenson is really Mr. Alvery, and that we have no idea what's going on, just until we get backup."

Hanging on a post in the barn were the keys to the locks Ace wore, and they released him. When he stood up, he almost fell down. Because he had been lying on his side for almost three days, it took him a minute to get his balance back. "Split up and find what you can for Ace," Snake said, and they all ran around quietly throughout the farm, searching for food and supplies for Ace.

Snake fetched a horse from the barn and strapped everything onto its saddle. Ace jumped on the horse.

"We should go with him!" Squirt cried. "I want to go with him!"

"No," Mouth said, "it's too dangerous. Ace can travel faster on his own anyways."

"Don't worry, lad," Ace said to Squirt. "I'll find Smith, and we'll get help."

"Hurry," Snake said, and Ace rode away, quickly heading east on the road. The others went to the slave house, hoping to get some rest before Stevenson's men come to wake them that morning.

Mouth laughed at the thought of Stevenson's face when he went into the barn. They made it look as though Ace had escaped. They had turned the cupboard back over to where the doors were on the bottom and then broken a hole in the back to make it appear as though Ace had kicked a hole through it. Then they kicked up the dirt everywhere to make it seem as though there was a struggle in getting the chains off.

***

Ace crawled under a tree in the woods in hopes of avoiding the rain. All day it had been unbelievably humid. He had ridden for hours under the hot sun, and his horse had thrown him. Two days went by, and he managed to find some woods for some shade. Now it was storming, and he was using the trees as a sort of shelter. He was hungry, and he started pulling bark from the tree to eat. He was also dehydrated. He dug a small hole in the ground and mucky water built up. Despite its horrid taste, he drank it. A little while later, his stomach started to ache, and he lay down on his side. He closed his eyes, feeling weak. The last thing he remembered was a man standing over him. The man put a coat around him.

When Ace opened his eyes, he saw a young woman sitting on a stool beside his bed. "Hello, Ace," she said, touching his hand. "Don't worry; you're just a bit sickly. You'll be fine."

Ace sat up and coughed. "How do you know my name?"

"Your friends told me." She tried to get him to lie down.

"Who are you?"

"My name's Susan." She smiled, which made Ace smile for a moment as well.

"Wait." He threw his legs over the side of the bed. "Friends? My friends are back at the farm."

"No, no, you must rest. Don't get up." She urged him to sit down again, but he shoved her.

"Leave her be!" An older man came running into the room. It was Maxi. He knocked Ace back onto the bed. "Don't hurt her, peasant."

Ace was not going to put up with this man shoving him around like a sickly child. "I'm leaving." Just as he was heading to the door, another woman came running into the room, but this time it was someone he recognized.

"James!" she cried out, hugging him. "James, sweetheart, are you all right?" The woman was hard to recognize at first in the Black Dragon uniform.

"Mrs. Barons?" He smiled, surprised to see her. He hadn't ever been so pleased to see her before. "What are you doing here?"

"I could ask you the same thing." She let go of him and started checking him over as a mother would her child. "My poor boy, what happened to you?" she cried when she saw his back where he had been whipped. "Why aren't you on the farm?"

"I ran away to find Smith. Stevenson was going to bring me back to the palace." His voice sounded shrill at the mention of his father.

"Don't worry. You're safe here," Mrs. Barons assured him.

"How did you know about the farm?" Ace asked her.

Before she could answer, Susan came over to them and said, "He needs bed rest."

"He needs something to eat," Mrs. Barons said. "You look as if you haven't eaten in days."

"Just some bark from a tree," Ace admitted to her.

"That's what made you so sick, fool." Maxi pushed past them and left the room.

"Come on down to the kitchen and we'll get you some food," Mrs. Barons said.

"Aye, we'll have our maids fix you something." Susan led the way.

When they were in the kitchen, Ace was excited to see two more familiar faces at the table. "Smith … Abigail?" He stood in the doorway of the kitchen, and Abigail hurried over to him. Smith struggled to stand, but Hannah and Anna helped him.

Abigail hugged him and kissed his cheek. "Tell me, what has become of my husband? Is he safe? What about the others?"

"They're all safe for now, Abigail," he assured her. Ace looked at Smith, horrified at his appearance. "I thought Stevenson might have killed you."

"Almost," Smith jested. Smith had Sea's golden bangle in his hands. He had been fiddling with it while Ace was upstairs. When Mrs. Barons had given Smith the bangle and told him she found it by the pond, he had been overcome with joy.

Smith went on to explain to Ace what had happened to him, and Ace was quickly full of rage toward John. As they were sitting down for supper, they began to discuss their next course of action. On most days, as pointed out by Ace, only two or three of John's men stayed on the farm to keep the Black Dragons in check. That was not too many people to fight through to save their friends. They decided to attack the farm.

***

"I will kill whoever is responsible for this!" John banged his fist on his desk.

Maria placed some tea in front of him and sat down in the chair with him. "John, he ran. I'm not sure how he managed to kick open that cupboard, but he did. The Black Dragons obviously didn't know he was there. They aren't acting any differently at all."

"I suppose threatening to send him home to his father was the one thing that could get him to abandon his friends. I scared him." John sighed heavily and then sipped on his tea for a minute. He put down his cup and leaned back in his chair, thinking intently.

Maria leaned in and gave John a kiss. "So now what, John?"

"Ace is out there somewhere. We have to act. If word gets back to Harold where I am, or even if Ace gets help, we're in danger. We have to leave."

"Should I pack, señor?" she asked him.

He nodded. "Pack lightly, my dear, and don't let the Black Dragons know what we're up to. I have a plan. Tomorrow ends the era of the Black Dragons." He smiled, pleased with the plan he had going on in his head.

"What are you planning?" she asked curiously, getting to her feet.

John stood next to her and tapped her cheek. "Maria, my dear, you ask far too many questions." He kissed her and sent her on her way.

Ch 29

John and ten of his hired men stood outside the slave house early one morning. Near them was a wagon, loaded with supplies. "Go on. Go get them," John said to Oswold.

"Yes, sir." Oswold headed inside the slave house shouting, "Get up, boys! Wake up!" One by one, the Black Dragons piled out of the small building.

"Line up, boys," John said.

"What's going on, Mr. Alvery?" Snake asked, pretending not to know John's true identity.

"We're moving. I bought some new property on the mainland," John lied. "Chain the boys up," he ordered.

"Why do you have to chain us up?" Mouth questioned him.

John chuckled. "Two of your friends have already run away, and I'm not taking any chances. Johnny, come with Maria and me in the carriage. It's a long ride to the docks, and I need someone to talk to."

Mouth rolled his eyes when Snake headed toward the carriage. The others were chained up in a line as the carriage rode off with John, Snake, Maria, and two of John's men. The other men stood with the Black Dragons. "Aren't we going?" Yin asked when they followed the carriage after being chained together. All of John's men held up their muskets.

"You boys aren't going anywhere," one of the men said. When he raised his musket, the crew attempted to run, but it was an inconceivable effort with them all chained together and eight other men holding them at gunpoint. John's men simply grabbed on to one or two of them, keeping the entire group detained. The man fired his gun, shooting Yin in the head. Yin fell, lying there on the ground completely motionless. "Ha! Got 'im right in the eye!" The man sounded proud of himself.

"Mathew!" Yang cried out, dropping down on his knees next to his brother. "Wake up! Wake up!" Yang shook him. The man raised his gun at Yang. "No! No … please!" He looked away.

Cannonball snatched the end of the musket. The man pulled back and kicked Cannonball over. When he fell, he pulled Knot down beside him, for they were chained next to each other. Another gun suddenly went off, and they all frantically looked around to see which of their friends had been shot next, but it was one of John's men who went down. The man who had shot Yin dropped dead to the ground. "Drop your gun!" Ace was riding up on horseback, a musket in his hands. Behind him were several others on horseback, each carrying a musket in his hands or on his back. Ace jumped off his horse, his gun pointed at another of John's men. The Cook family, Smith, Mrs. Barons, and Abigail surrounded them. The men dropped their guns. Ace ordered them to sit in a row and give up the keys to his friends' chains. He unchained Yin first.

Mrs. Barons hurried to his side. "Sweetheart, can you hear me?" she said softly. She removed the bandana from her head and pressed it against the left side of his face to stop the bleeding.

Yang hurried beside them after Ace unchained him. "Wake up! Wake up! Don't die, please don't die!" He took his brother's hand. Yin opened his right eye and squeezed Yang's hand. "Stay awake," Yang said. "Please don't die."

"Enough!" Mrs. Barons popped Yang in the jaw. "You're scaring him." Smith had come over to them.

He knelt down by them. When Yin saw him, he managed a smile. "Captain? You're alive?"

"Aye." Smith smiled back at him.

"You'll be okay," Mrs. Barons said. "We'll get you to a doctor, and everything will be okay."

Smith looked up from Yin to see everyone's concerned faces staring back at them. Cannonball had a hand on Yang's shoulder. Mouth had his arms around Abigail, and Squirt held on to Mouth's leg. Smith stood up quickly. "Where's Snake?"

"John!" Blade shouted. "John took him!"

Smith threw himself up on a horse. "Peter, what are you doing?" Mrs. Barons cried.

"I'm going after Snake." Smith rode off down the road, heading after John.

***

Godart wrestled with Snake in the back of the carriage. When Snake heard the gunshots, he had realized what was going on. John and Maria sat in the back of the carriage as well, trying to get Snake to sit still. "Johnny, enough!" John screamed at him. "Calm down."

Godart managed to tie Snake's hands behind his back. "You're going to kill them!" Snake screamed at John. "I hate you! Stop the carriage! Let me go!" Snake kicked John's bad leg.

John screamed out in pain, "You child!" He snatched Snake by his hair and forced him to the floor of the carriage. "I've been nothing but kind to you! Godart, keep the boy still."

"Why aren't you going to kill me? Why just my friends?" Snake exclaimed, while Godart forced him to sit beside him.

"You know who I am, don't you?" John asked, and Snake nodded.

"Yeah, I know," Snake said. "I know, *General.* So what is it? Why me? Why don't you kill me too?"

"I made a promise to your parents, boy, that I'd take care of you," John said. "They were my friends, so I intend to keep that promise."

"When did you make such a promise?" Snake snapped. "Before or after you planned to kill them?"

The carriage abruptly stopped. "Oswold!" John shouted. "Why'd you stop the carriage?"

The carriage door swung open, and Smith stood there with a pistol in his hands. "Hey, John, remember me?"

"Smith!" John raved. "You're alive."

Snake smiled. *Thank goodness,* he thought, when he saw Smith alive and well.

"Come on, Snake. It's about time we went home," Smith said and ordered Godart to cut the ropes around Snake's wrists. Snake climbed out of the carriage. "I'd get out of here, John," Smith warned him, "My friend Maxi already warned the authorities that you were here, so I'd start running instead of trying to follow us!"

"You cretin!" John shouted.

Smith chuckled and closed the carriage door. He and Snake climbed onto the horse Smith had used to chase them down, and the two of them rode back to the farm.

Ch 30

It was nice to be able to stand out in the open; the people on Kevin's Isle didn't mind pirates so much because they traded with them even more than they did with King Harold himself. They were standing by the docks, and the *Black Dragon* was in the water. Mrs. Barons and the others had sailed to Kevin's Isle on the ship. Yin was up and walking. They had had a doctor look at him and remove the bullet. He was wrapped in bandages. The doctor had told them that Yin might lose his eye. Smith planned to have Dr. Conal look at him once they got home.

The Cooks were currently saying good-bye to them. Smith was smiling when he looked at Anna, Knot, Hannah, and Blade. Knot and Anna had been shy around each other at first, while Blade and Hannah had held hands, kissed, and were leaning up against each other when they spoke. The four of them were saying good-bye. Anna and Hannah had written down their address so the boys could write to them, and Blade and Knot had given them the address at Benny's Inn. Smith was just glad that the overly flirtatious girls had moved on from him.

Mr. Anderson would be coming back to Kirkston with them; he was planning to start up his business again. While they were saying their farewells, Squirt ran right up to the docks and jumped into the water. He belonged in the water.

"Come by and visit again, Smith." Maxi shook Smith's hand.

"Aye, you too," Smith said. "Feel free to come visit at Benny's some time, but don't let your sisters wear any pearls down there—they're bound to get stolen."

Maxi laughed. "We sure would stick out down there, now wouldn't we?"

"You'll come back soon, won't you, Smith?" Jimmy asked, and Smith picked him up and hugged him.

"Of course, Jim," Smith promised, and put him back down. "Behave yourself, all right?" Jimmy nodded, and they all said their final good-byes.

The looks on all their faces when they climbed aboard the *Black Dragon* clearly excited Mrs. Barons; the entire deck was covered in gold pieces. "Where did all this come from?" Smith asked.

"We stole it from the Annihilators," Stewart told him.

"Aren't you an Annihilator?" Smith still hadn't gotten a straight answer from Stewart or Gwen or even his mother about what happened; all he knew was that his mother had stabbed him with a knife, which he honestly didn't believe.

"Not anymore, I'm not," Stewart said.

"Well, then, I welcome you and your sister aboard our crew, Stewart," Smith said to him. "Do you know much about sailing?"

"I grew up on the *Annihilator,* but honestly my little sister knows more than I do. I was just cabin boy; I helped the cook in the galley all day."

Smith smiled. "You cook?"

"Stewie is a great cook," Gwen interrupted.

Smith nodded and asked, "How old are you, pip-squeak?"

"I'm not a pip-squeak." She crossed her arms in annoyance. "I'm eight."

"You're about Squirt's age," Smith said.

"Isn't that cute?" Mouth said. "Pip-squeak and Squirt." The girl stuck her tongue out at Mouth.

Smith just shook his head and said, "Welcome aboard, you two."

Smith headed below deck to the captain's quarters. He saw his bag sitting on his desk. His mother had obviously found it and set it out for him. He picked up his father's sword and held it in his hands. As he was sitting down on the bed, he started taking things out of the bag. He wrapped the blanket around him and placed the journal his sisters had given him in his lap. He looked down at the journal, and a smile crossed over his face. "I can write again."

***

"Captain, we're ready to sail!" It was Gwen, already calling him captain. "We need you on deck!"

He came above deck; he could see that everyone was ready. Mouth and Abigail were distracted with each other, which Smith knew he should let go this time because they hadn't see each other in so long. "All hands on deck! Raise the anchor! Handsomely now—let's get this ship moving!" he shouted, and they all ran to their posts. Soon the *Black Dragon* was on her way.

They sailed off into the open ocean. Smith looked over and could see Squirt at the prow, staring at the sunset. Squirt always loved this time of day when they were out at sea. Smith saw Gwen approach him, and Squirt's cheek turned a bright pink. *Poor Squirt,* Smith thought, when he saw how shy the boy looked. Smith opened his journal, which he had brought with him to the wheel. Before he started to write, he glanced at Mouth and Abigail.

Snake came up to Smith, and the two of them looked over the rest of the crew as they always did. Smith turned the wheel and fell down when he did so. "Sea legs ... I need to get my sea legs back!"

Snake laughed at him and helped him up. "Don't worry Smith; you're not the only one. I've fallen a few times today myself."

Snake chuckled and headed to the main deck, passing Ace on his way down. "Hey, Smith," Ace said.

"Something wrong, Ace?" Smith asked him.

"No."

"Don't lie to me." Smith stared him down. "Something's bothering you."

"I killed someone today," Ace told him.

"Aye … I thought that might be what was wrong," Smith said. He looked down at the main deck and all his friends. "You saved their lives."

"But I might have been able to do that without killing that man," Ace said. "I saw Yin lying there, and I thought he was dead. I was so angry that I just shot him."

"I'm sorry, mate," Smith said.

"We've been the Black Dragons for years now, and none of us have ever had to kill on a pillage. We never wanted to be like the Annihilators; we wanted to help people. We wanted to be heroes. Now I've *killed* someone, Smith." Ace leaned against the side of the ship.

"You'll be all right, Ace," Smith said to him. "I don't think you ever meant to kill him. You were just trying to save Yin, and you did."

Ace nodded. "Aye," he said and went back to the main deck.

***

A few days passed, and soon the *Black Dragon* was back in familiar waters. They dropped off Mr. Anderson and headed to their secret hideaway south of the waterfall. They made bay and left their hideout. Together they all headed west, following the river upstream toward Mrs. Barons's home. Smith had Snake fetch Dr.

Conal on their way and meet them at the house to examine Yin's wound. Inside, Ron and Theresa were waiting for them.

"Peter!" Theresa shouted when they arrived. She jumped out of her seat and hugged him and kissed his cheek. She hugged the others and demanded to know everything that had happened to them.

Mouth interrupted the storytelling quickly. "Where is he?"

"Calm yourself, Mouth," Theresa told him. She headed to the back of the house, returning with Ian. He was crying softly. "We've grown attached to your baby boy."

Mouth took Ian from her and rocked him, and he stopped crying. Mouth felt himself starting to cry. He was incredibly relieved to be here with his son again. He bounced Ian, and the baby giggled. "Oh!" Mouth said. "Has he done that before?"

"No," Theresa said, and Mouth smiled.

"I made him laugh." Mouth held his son close to him; Abigail leaned up against Mouth and watched her son.

Dr. Conal had arrived and was looking over Yin. "Do you think you can save his eye?" Smith asked.

"I think so." He smiled. "Yin's going to be all right. It barely missed his eye. It cracked part of his skull here, though." The doctor pointed to where Yin was beginning to bruise severely. "If you're careful, it'll heal."

"Good," Smith said. "Rest up, Yin."

For now, all was quiet and good in their world. However, there were still troubles awaiting them. John Stevenson was still out there looking for revenge, still wanting Snake as his son; King Harold was after Ace; and the people of Kirkston still needed them. John had managed to elude the authorities on Kevin's Isle, and he was on the run again.

The baby's eyes narrowed, and soon he was fast asleep in his father's arms. It was quiet. Theresa was smiling, but she broke the silence, making sure everyone was listening. "I have some news."

"What's that?" Smith asked.

She sat down on the little couch in the den and took her husband's hand. "Ronald, everybody, I'm pregnant."

Ron stared. He was obviously happy but surprised "You're pregnant?"

"Yes." Theresa had an excited look on her face, and everyone congratulated her and Ron. She rubbed her stomach.

Nothing ever seemed to stay the same for them. Something was always changing.

The day went by quickly, and not wanting to overstay their welcome, the Black Dragons finally headed home. Aboard the ship at last, the *Black Dragon* sailed off. The crewmates had no destination. They were just sailing to sail. Mouth was sitting on the main deck, rocking his son to sleep. Abigail sat next to him. Smith was watching them from the wheel. He smiled. For such a young baby, Ian rarely cried anymore.

***

After the incident on Kevin's Isle with John, my crew seems so different somehow. When Ian was first born, it seemed to hit all of us that we aren't children anymore, but now that doesn't seem so frightening.

***

A week passed, and even with two new hands on deck—Stewart and Gwenhwyfar—things seemed to return to normal. As always, though, Smith was writing in his journal:

Blade and Knot got letters from Hannah and Anna yesterday when we visited Skull Island. Stewart and Gwen are adjusting to life on our ship. We don't know much about the two of them, but they seem like good people. I know Squirt thinks so; Gwen gave him a kiss yesterday.

Good news for Mr. Anderson: his blacksmith shop is up and running again. I wish him the best of luck. More good news: Ron and Theresa's baby is due in a few months. The doctor says Theresa is doing fine.

I can't believe all the things that have happened to us these past few months, or even these past few years. It's hard to believe how suddenly our lives can change. But for now, we are heading up north because Benny has some grog and some rooms waiting for us at the inn.

Smith put down his journal and took the wheel. His crew was ready to go. Soon they had the ship moving, heading north to Benny's Inn. The sun was setting, and there was a cool breeze that evening. Summer was ending, and they would be able to leave behind their unpleasant memories of their summer at John's farm. For now, the young crew pressed on, eager for whatever life would throw at them next.

Characters

Peter "Smith" Barons—After the deaths of his father and sisters, and the unlawful arrest of his mother, he strives to make a change in his country, Kirkston. He joins the Black Dragons and later becomes captain of the crew.

William Barons—Smith's father. He's a blacksmith who worked in Mr. Anderson's blacksmithing shop. He is killed on his son's twelfth birthday by General John Stevenson.

Ellen Barons—Smith's mother and William Baron's wife. She's a mother of three and the strong hand in the Barons family. Ellen is wrongfully arrested by the general and separated from her son.

Elizabeth Barons—Smith's older sister of fifteen, the marriage age in Kirkston.

Anna Barons—Smith's little sister, who is only five years old.

Mr. Anderson—William's employer, and later Smith's. He's a blacksmith who befriends the Barons family.

John Stevenson—The harsh general of Kirkston who kills off Smith's family. John is the Black Dragons' biggest enemy.

Ron and Theresa—Smith's childhood friends

King Harold and Queen Rachel—The rulers of Kirkston. John Stevenson easily manipulates the king into doing his deeds.

Prince Richard—The prince of Kirkston

Princess Kathleen—The princess of Kirkston and heir to the throne after the death of her brother Prince James. Kathleen is engaged to John Stevenson as part of an old tradition.

Sea—Original captain of the Black Dragons. She and Smith look out for the crew together. She's a strong leader and a motherly figure to all the Black Dragons.

Snake—Second member to join the Black Dragons. Before they were even known as the Black Dragons, he and Sea robbed carriages. He's best friends with Sea and Smith. His father was once the general of Kirkston, before he was killed by John Stevenson.

Yin and Yang—The third and fourth members of the crew, they're twin brothers. Yin is the smaller and weaker of the two and is often intimidated by his brother, but even so, the two of them are close.

Mouth and Squirt—Members five and six of the Black Dragons. Mouth finds it hard to trust people after some of his closest friends betrayed him when he was young. Squirt was just a baby when he joined the crew, and someone is always needing to take care of him; he's almost twelve years younger than his brother.

Cannonball—Seventh member of the Black Dragons. He's the only member not born in Kirkston—he's an Irishman. He earned his nickname because he knew a lot about weaponry on ships. He lost his father and older brother, Thomas, in a shipwreck when he was younger.

Blade and Knot—Eighth and ninth members of the Black Dragons. They were best friends when they were younger, and they stuck together after their parents' deaths. Knot is a year younger than the others and is small for his age.

Ace—Tenth member of the Black Dragons. Not much is known about him, and no one really want to ask. He's a mystery even to the ones he's closest to.

Mr. and Mrs. Keg—A couple who raised the *Black Dragon* crew and prepared them for their life at sea.

Rob and Amy—Snake's parents. Rob was once the general of Kirkston, until John Stevenson murdered him and his wife.

Benny—Owns Benny's Inn on Skull Island and often lets the Black Dragons stay there and eat free of charge

Abigail—Engaged to Prince Richard under an arranged marriage, but soon she starts to become interested in one of the Black Dragons.

Tom—Leader of a rival gang on Skull Island

Dr. Conal—Physician friend of the Black Dragons

Ian—Mouth and Abigail's son, he's named after Mouth's father.

Captain Jackson—Captain of the Annihilators

Stewart and Gwenhwyfar (Gwen)—Two children on the *Annihilator*. Stewart later befriends Mrs. Barons and Abigail and helps save the Black Dragons. Gwenhwyfar is his littler sister, and she's about Squirt's age.

Mr. Steven Alvery—A cruel slave owner who wishes to adopt Snake as his son. Mr. Alvery has a bitter hatred toward Smith.

Mr. Godart and Mr. Oswold—Two of the men who work for Mr. Alvery.

Maria—Mr. Alvery's housemaid and girlfriend

Susan Cook—One of the Cook children, in her early twenties. She took care of Smith while he was out cold for a few days.

Hannah Cook—She's fifteen, almost. She's also one of the Cook children. She and her little sister are flirty toward Smith, but she later falls for Blade.

Anna Cook—She's fourteen. She's one of the Cook children; she and her older sister Hannah are flirty toward Smith, but she later chases after Knot.

Maxi Cook Junior—He's the oldest of the Cook children. He became the father figure of the house after the death of his father.

Jimmy Cook—Youngest of the Cook children. Jimmy's seven years old and is always getting into trouble; he doesn't remember his father, which affects him greatly.

Jane Cook—The mother of the Cook children

Jenny—One of the Cook's nine servants

Mr. Watson—The Cook's annoying neighbor

Pirate 2

Everything seems to be going great for Smith and his crew, but an accident during a horrible storm causes a serious injury for their lookout, Knot. Things only get more terrifying when Ace's father kidnaps him and forces him into complete isolation. Even worse, someone is poisoning the captive prince, and the Black Dragons must team up with a face from Ace's mysterious past to save his life!

About the Author

Stephanie Lauren is a student at Whitewater High School. She is seventeen years old and has been writing for most of her young life. Lauren lives in the small town of Brooks, Georgia, with her mother and two brothers.

LaVergne, TN USA
19 February 2010
173625LV00002B/2/P